the Lilies

the Lilies

Quinn Diacon-Furtado

HARPER TEEN
An Imprint of HarperCollinsPublishers

HarperTeen is an imprint of HarperCollins Publishers.

The Lilies

Library of Congress Control Number: 2023943362
ISBN 978-0-06-331819-9

Typography by Julia Feingold
24 25 26 27 28 LBC 5 4 3 2 1

First Edition

As long as women are using class or race power to dominate other women, feminist sisterhood cannot be fully realized.

—bell hooks,
Feminism Is for Everybody: Passionate Politics

This book is dedicated to everybody

Prologue

CAN YOU KEEP A SECRET? Most Archwell girls can. Particularly the ones who call themselves the Lilies.

They say they chose this name out of love, just as I chose mine. They pretend it is some kind of tribute. But I know the difference between chosen and stolen. I hear the truth of what they did every time they utter my name in the dark: Lillian . . . Lillian.

They took my name and buried the secret of me. Then they kept it underground with whispered threats, hushed confessions, and empty vows of sisterhood.

This is how the Lilies Society came to be, and this is how it continues—in an infinite loop.

I feel their unblinking stares on me and my ears fill with the sounds of sirens. Again and again, they watch me fall into nothingness.

The Lilies killed me . . . if you could call this death.

And to this day, they keep the school's biggest secret: at Archwell Academy, sometimes names are erased—

—sometimes girls disappear.

Drew

DEATH GRINS UP AT ME. Mocking. For a moment, I'm so angry to see it that I think about sliding it back into the beaten-up tarot deck. But I know that won't change anything.

Have you ever had a card that just won't leave you alone?

Death, number thirteen in the Major Arcana, is hounding me these days—ever since Grandma Simmons died and I transferred to this school. *I dare you, Drew. I dare you to ignore me*, it rasps.

The Death card can be a sign of new beginnings and endings. But I know—sitting here in the Archwell Academy library—the symbol is literal.

At first glance, the library seems an unlikely place for death to occur. Monday-morning sun penetrates the stained-glass windows. It shoots rainbows across the library's Victorian arches. The shelves of the stacks wrap around me, deadening any outside noise. The books make a heavy, mildewy promise to keep me safe from violence. The library wants to be my hiding place, a place where I can be myself. But I know better than to trust it. October glow spills over Death's sneering face.

I know what happened here, Drew. I know what you did, it taunts me.

Cold anxiety slithers through my veins. Before it can lure me into the memory of everything that happened last Friday, the sound of encyclopedias thudding to the floor makes me jump. I lean back in my chair and peer through a slat in the bookshelf. In my first couple of months at Archwell Academy, I've learned to watch my back. I wish it were something I didn't have to do, but as a nonbinary kid, I'm already used to looking over my own shoulder.

I can't see much through the gap in the bookshelf. Just someone with dark curls, bent over a mess of paper and books splayed all over the floor. They pause, tense, and, finally, lift their head. Pleasantly disorganized curls frame their round face. Their skin is a light shade of brown. Their eyes are a sparkling umber. They have a look about them that's both sincere and a little chaotic.

"Sorry," they whisper to me. "I didn't mean to bother you. I thought I could reach, but . . ."

"No big," I say. "Need some help?"

"Oh no," they mutter as they stoop down again, frantically gathering their papers. But I'm already on my feet and rounding the corner of the bookshelf to help clean up.

I catch the stranger's eyes as I stoop down next to them to pick up their mess. "I'm Drew, they/them."

"Huh?" The stranger's response is familiar. Because Archwell Academy is an 'all-girls preparatory,' people here sometimes get tripped up when I tell them my pronouns. It's something I wish Grandma Simmons had considered before she requested I transfer to her alma mater for my senior year. But, then again, she probably didn't even know the words *nonbinary* or *gender fluid*. It likely never occurred to her that I would be desperately out of place at Archwell with my buzzed head and faint little mustache (of which I'm very proud).

When I transferred, I expected people to look at me like I was beamed down to earth by my mothership, an effect I usually revel in, as I'd rather be in an other-worldly body than my own. But I've quickly learned what makes me alien here is not something to be celebrated. At Archwell, I'm an interloper, most easily defined by what I am not. Feminine. Familiar. Legible.

If I weren't a legacy student, I likely never would've been admitted to this school.

In the end, I don't care whether people at Archwell like me, but I hate being made to feel like a fly in the ointment. It takes me out of my body . . . makes me feel like I need to hide myself . . . to escape this place.

The library has generally been a good spot for that . . . at least until today.

Eventually, recognition spreads across the stranger's face and she speaks. "I'm Verónica . . . Well, Veró. Never

Verónica, unless someone's calling roll. She/her pronouns are good for me."

"Hi, Veró," I say, offering her a handful of pages and rising to my feet.

"Hi," she says, fumbling with the last of her papers. For the first time, I notice that they're all the same: mostly white space with the words *Error 404: Page Not Found* artfully scrawled in calligraphy letters. Veró's brow clouds over as she sees me eyeing her stuff. She resists my gaze as she tries to stash the papers out of sight. I wish she weren't so pretty. It would be easier to look away.

"Feeling retro?" I ask, bending down to flip the last of the fallen books closed.

"What?" Veró's voice is low and edgy.

"You were pulling down encyclopedias that were printed in 1999. That's some pretty old source material."

"Oh," Veró says, returning two of the books back to their place on the shelf. She's taller than me, but only by a little. "I was just poking around."

She shoves the last of her papers into an overstuffed leather satchel. I recognize the bag. It's Hermès, the kind my mom was going to buy for herself with the inheritance money from Grandma Simmons. She changed her mind about the bag when she found out that the thing cost ten thousand dollars. The inheritance would've more than covered the cost, of course, but Mom refused to buy it on principle. Veró throws the bag over her shoulder like it's nothing.

Before the inheritance money arrived, a bag like that would have been out of the question for me and Mom. A million dollars is a life-changing amount for ninety-nine percent of people, and we were no exception. But Grandma Simmons left us more than a million . . . a lot more. All I had to do was agree to finish high school at Archwell Academy and the money was ours.

"It was your grandmother's last wish. Her only condition," the estate lawyer explained. "It's your call on what you'd like to do, but it's a no-brainer if you ask me."

Mom didn't pressure me to transfer to Archwell, but . . . I mean . . . did I have any other choice? I would've done anything to wipe away her worry lines. Anything to nullify the threat of those red-edged envelopes with *Final Notice* printed on the outside. I knew the cash from Grandma Simmons would change our lives—but I didn't realize it would end the world as I knew it.

Veró snaps the authentic silver clasp of her bag shut. "You're Charlotte Vanderheyden's friend, right?" she asks.

The muscles in my neck tighten. I close my eyes for a split second. Death smirks at me from behind my eyelids. *I know all about Charlotte*, it croaks. *I know what you did.* But I don't have a choice. I open my eyes and look at Veró.

"Charlotte and I aren't friends," I say. It's the truth. Charlotte Vanderheyden was the only sophomore at Archwell who would dare treat a senior like dirt. You can guess some of the reasons why a girl like her might treat a senior like me that way. "We were assigned to the same room in Chatham House. Turns out when you transfer in, you're sort of at the bottom of the barrel when it comes to roommates."

I'm surprised when Veró's caginess melts instantly. "I hear that." She laughs. "I transferred in last year. I lived in Chatham House then too. Whew . . . they put me with a freshman. She was a Park Avenue princess. We did not hit it off, to say the least. Did the chancellor assign you a baby-sitter too?" Veró doesn't have to explain what she means by babysitter. She's talking about an Archwell sponsor: a girl to help you "get acclimated" to the culture of the school. Read: someone to introduce you to the pantheon of this place's unwritten rules. It's just one more of a thousand Archwell traditions—traditions that I'm mostly not a part of . . . not necessarily because I don't want to be. I just know that I'm not wanted.

"Charlotte was my sponsor."

"Was?" Veró asks.

I try not to react. I don't want to lie to this girl, but no one can know the whole truth about what happened to Char-lotte. And obviously, I don't want anyone to know how *I* was involved. Only Death knows.

I try to pivot. "I fired her," I say, forcing a smile.

Veró grins at me. "I bet," she says. "For real though, is she lurking around?" Her voice shifts, the hint of nervousness is back again.

"I haven't seen her since Friday night," I answer honestly.

"Her parents live just down the road in Potomac. I think maybe she went home for the weekend?" I make sure to say this last bit like I'm not exactly certain. Yes, it's misleading, but it's not quite a lie, so it doesn't weigh heavily on my conscience.

"Word," Veró says. "Just between you and me, I don't think she'd keep her big mouth shut if she saw me up here."

"Yeah? Why's that?" A touch of guilt twitches in my left eye.

Veró peeks around the shelves into the aisle to make sure we're truly alone before she starts to whisper. "Pretty much all the librarians, except for Ms. Katz, refuse to get rid of these reference books even though a lot of the information is outdated. It's also almost always patriarchal. Sometimes racist. You know the drill. So, I have this little project I've been working on."

She opens an encyclopedia that's still lying on the polished mahogany desk. "Go ahead and look up Christopher Columbus." Her smile gleams. I take a step toward the desk and leaf to the *C*s. There, pasted over the encyclopedia's Christopher Columbus entry, is the message *Error 404: Page Not Found*. The ink of the swirling letters is fresh on the parchment pasted over the entry. I turn to Veró, who is holding a finger to her lips as she pulls a tube of stick glue out of the side pocket of her bag.

"Dude!" I laugh.

"Shh!" she insists. "You never know who's around. Your

roomie is the kind of Archwell girl who would for sure narc on me, ya know?"

I nod and latch my lips closed with an invisible key even though I absolutely know that Charlotte is not around to expose Veró's prank. My left eye twitches again. I rub it away with the heel of my hand.

I exchange social media handles with Veró. Mine is @much.gay.very.enby. Hers is @therealvero. I get a little zap of excitement as I scroll through her photos after she leaves. Cool girl. Arty. I've finally met someone who is interesting in this purgatory of a place.

I take a moment to scroll through my feed. There's a new post from @QueerCovenMD. Next, there's a clip from my favorite astrologer about Scorpio season. Then I see her. Charlotte. Her red hair is gleaming in the sunlight, offset by her caramel-colored coat. My heart starts racing. In the video, she's standing on the central quad, smiling at the camera. The muscles in my chest tighten. She throws a fistful of fall leaves into the air. The tight, jittery feeling spreads to my fingers. The eye twitch passes from my left lid to my right. "Happy Founder's Night," she shouts. Her smile seems to stretch across her skull.

The video is a few days old. Founder's Night was last Friday. The clip was posted before the Founder's Night party . . . before everything that happened. I try to steady the tremor in my fingers as I silence the screen. The phone goes black. Still, I can't quite shake the feeling that Death has found me again.

It's strange to watch a person pass from one realm into another. At least when I watched Grandma Simmons die, I was expecting it. She was gray faced in her hospice bed. When she pulled me in close, her breath was shallow and sour. She whispered something to me. "Look . . ." She gestured for me to lean in close. "The Lilies." Her hands shook as she slipped off one of her gold rings and pressed it into my palm. Her fingers felt papery against my sweaty hand.

Grandma Simmons had never given me anything before. Mom had seen to that. It was only when she went into hospice care that we started to visit. The shadow of death forced Mom to bury the hatchet with her. She never said what exactly had gone on between the two of them that caused the years of silence.

"Go find the Lilies, Drew," my grandmother croaked.

"You want your flowers, Grandma?" I asked, motioning to the vase of white lilies sitting on the windowsill. They'd arrived the day before and were already starting to wilt.

"She's not lucid," my mother whispered to me, but Grandma Simmons continued to speak.

"Find the Lilies. It's your birthright. Your duty."

I let go of her hand and walked over to the floral arrangement. It seemed wrong to send a dying woman funeral flowers. There, embedded in the leaves, I noticed an unmarked, unopened card.

"You want this, Grandma?" I asked, picking up the envelope and unsealing it. The first strange thing appeared on the inside flap—someone had drawn an infinity symbol.

9

"Sacram memoriam," Grandma Simmons wheezed. Mom lifted a cup of water to her lips.

"It's okay, Mother," she said. "Just try to relax."

Without having read the card, Grandma Simmons had called out the second strange thing—whoever sent the flowers included a very weird note:

Ut sacram memoriam.
Her memory is sacred, beyond the bounds of time.
But as the clock hands turn, memory erodes the mind.
Her secrets are best buried in a loop that turns to dust,
where the present turns to past and past remains unjust.
Therein lies infinity—the place where she survives—
while we protect our sisterhood, our secrets, and our lives.
For only when her sisters' wrongs are once again made right
will she escape anew and take her place within the light.
And so shall four return again beneath the waning moon
to resurrect the memory, or find our way to ruin.
Ut sacram memoriam.

I don't get poetry . . . and I don't know Latin. So, I didn't understand what any of it meant. But later I noticed the phrase *ut sacram memoriam* was cast into the bottom of the gold, crested ring my grandmother had given me. Above the words was an infinity symbol, a double loop set in delicate diamonds.

I didn't realize the ring had something to do with Archwell Academy until the reading of the will. Along with her

dying wish for me to transfer to her alma mater, Grandma Simmons wanted me to wear her ring everyday "for protection."

"Apparently, the ring promises you entrance to the Lilies
Society," the estate lawyer explained.

"What's that?" I asked.

"It's one of the secret sororities at Archwell Academy," my
mom sighed. "I can't believe she wrote that in there. That
is *so* her . . ." I watched as my mom gulped down whatever
else she was about to say. She wasn't going to speak ill of the
dead, but I could tell there was more to all of this.

"It says here your grandma was one of the founders of the
Lilies Society," the lawyer continued, pretending as if my
mom hadn't said anything at all. "That makes you a legacy
member."

"She always wanted me to join and I never did," my mom
muttered. "This is her way of getting what she wanted all
along." She turned to me then, jaw locked and arms crossed.
"You don't have to do this, you know," she said. "Transfer-
ring schools, accepting the ring . . . you don't have to do any
of it if you don't want to." I could tell Mom meant what she
said, but money was money. And I couldn't refuse a request
from beyond the grave.

I agreed to wear my grandma's ring, even though I didn't
know what it meant. It was probably worth more than
Mom's and my house at the time. Wearing it still makes
me feel like I am committing some kind of crime. It doesn't
seem right for a seventeen-year-old, white enby kid to go

around wearing inherited diamonds while most other folks are barely getting by. And it *really* doesn't seem right that something like my grandmother's death would solve so many problems for me and my mom. But then again, it created some problems too: I had agreed to transfer schools without knowing what Archwell Academy was like. I wish I had read the fine print.

My invitation to join the Lilies Society never arrived. More accurately, it was never sent. It wasn't the first sign that I was not wanted at Archwell, but it was somehow the most noticeable. Following my grandma's conditions, I kept wearing the Lilies ring but . . . I can't say it has had any of the protective qualities she promised.

The first bell sounds. It's time for class. I stash my phone, pack up my tarot cards, throw on my Archwell blazer, and head for the stairs to the main atrium. As I pass the circulation desk, I see Ms. Katz—she's the librarian on duty on Mondays and Fridays, and the only teacher at Archwell that ever uses the right pronouns for me. She has a dog named Mort. Sometimes she shows me pictures of him and her family, including Scout. "My favorite nibling," she says. "They're just a couple years younger than you, Drew."

Today, Ms. Katz looks a little worn. Her eyes are missing their usual brightness. Maybe she had trouble sleeping this weekend. If so, she wasn't the only one.

"Drew, I was keeping my eyes peeled for you, dear." Her voice is heavy and strange. Something cold and stony is pushing its way into her words. Something is worrying her. "The chancellor would like to see you in her office this morning. She told me to write you a pass to excuse you from first period."

"Oh . . . um . . . okay." Death reappears in my mind. The skeleton from the tarot deck scowls at me. The same scowl that Charlotte had on her face the last time I saw her in person. "Am I . . . like . . . in trouble or something?" I ask.

"I doubt it, honey, but she didn't say. She just mentioned it was a 'roommate situation.'"

My stomach fills with acid. Breath leaves my body. The chancellor knows something. Something about Charlotte. Maybe she knows about what happened the last time we saw each other. The twitch worms its way back into my left eye. My vision blurs.

You're trying to ignore me. It won't work, Death breathes.

"Are you okay, Drew?" Ms. Katz asks. I nod and snatch the pass from her outstretched hand as I hustle out of the library. But Death follows me.

I know what you did.

Rory

WHEN I WAKE UP, THE taste of Caitlin Callahan's strawberry lip gloss has gone stale. I run my tongue along the slick of it at the edge of my mouth. It's a bit crusty and gross. Completely unlike the smooth, tangy taste of Caitlin's lips. I use the heel of my hand to rub away the traces of last night's hookup. There's not much I can do about my bad breath until I drag myself out of bed.

I suppose this is what I get for taking Xan on a school night. When Caitlin asked for a double dose, I happily obliged. Maybe some girls wouldn't have—taking two Xanax late at night would definitely crush her chances of making it to our first-period exam. But, let's face it, I don't really care about Caitlin Callahan. And, at this point, I don't really have much to lose. If she misses the AP Bio midterm, that's one less girl in the running for valedictorian—the only other real contender is Blythe and I already have made moves to address that. So why wouldn't I give Caitlin the pills she asked for and better my odds at snagging the top academic spot at the same time? Even when I'm high, the logic is obvious.

I wriggle out of bed and switch on my desk lamp. The light burns my pupils—a sure sign that I need an Anny to start my day. The jewelry box on my desk is one of my favorite hiding spots. I dig through the necklaces, grab my stash, put two of the little blue pills on my tongue, and wash them down with some flat seltzer water that Caitlin must've forgotten about. I usually don't take speed within twelve hours of taking Xan, but I needed the downers to help me sleep after what happened this weekend . . .

My hands hover over the bottom drawer of my jewelry box. I let my fingers scrabble into its very back corner until they find my little crystal bottle. I pull it out and uncork the thing, gazing down at the sparkly powder inside.

Most girls try this kind of hallucinogen only once. It doesn't go well. I like to inhale a tiny bump of the stuff every now and then just to keep things interesting. I consider taking some now . . . but, then again, no. Sand is not a performance enhancer and it's been messing with my sleep since Friday night, the last time I took some.

Every time I've managed to drift off since then, I find myself in the same dream over and over. I'm in my green Lilies robe, standing in the initiation circle. Blythe is to my right. She catches my eye from under the hood of her cloak and smiles. The basement's low candlelight illuminates her dark brown skin. She whispers the Lilies vow to me. *Ut sacram memoriam.* Then she turns away. Someone else, face hidden by the hood of her cloak, taps me on the shoulder.

15

Her voice is high and seems to come from far away, even though she's right there. *Bury the secrets*, she says. *Remember the sisterhood. We protect our true sisters.* Then another, sharper voice comes to me. *I know what you did!* it shouts.

This is usually when I wake up, sheets sweaty. Eventually, when I fall back asleep, the dream cycles through again, except the shadows grow longer and the crystal pill bottle in my hand feels colder and heavier. Last night I knocked myself out instead of subjecting myself to the nightmare all over again.

So now it's time to face reality, or at least my version of it. I slip into my fitted sweater dress and top it with my Archwell uniform blazer and a plum-red lip. It's all dress code appropriate, of course, but I like to add a pinch of my own style. I look like myself again, even if I don't quite feel that way. It's almost time for morning check-in so I grab my backpack and head out. My room this year is in Dalton House, right on the central courtyard.

Being the chancellor's daughter, I get first pick on dorm rooms every year, even though I have to pretend I get assigned through the lottery like everyone else.

As soon as I'm out in the crisp fall air, I feel the Annys hit my bloodstream. The courtyard and surrounding buildings come into focus. The vines on the walls slither, animated by the breeze. Across the empty quad, I see a lone student walking up the path from the eastern side of campus. I start to wave, expecting to see one of the underclass presidents on their way to meet me and my mother at morning check-in. As president of the senior class, and the great-granddaughter of Archwell Academy's founder, I try to go out of my way to be friendly to the "littles." The student doesn't wave back at me.

Then I notice a flash of red atop their head and, for a second, I think it's her . . . Charlotte. But that's impossible. She's . . . Well, she's just gone.

No girl has ever just up and disappeared from Archwell. Certainly, no member of the Lilies Society. Everyone knows we're insulated from that kind of thing. The Lilies are special. Immune to all kinds of dangers that usually plague teen girls.

At least, I thought we were.

I suppose whatever happened to Charlotte could've been something unrelated to the Lilies or Archwell. I think I heard some of the littles talking about Charlotte having a shitty boyfriend over in College Park. Maybe her disappearance had something to do with him.

But at the same time, I know what I saw and what I didn't see last Friday. At least Blythe knows to keep quiet. If she does, my original plans just might work out after all.

The student crosses the courtyard and comes into focus. I finally recognize their dark red beanie, their long blue overcoat, and their rumpled dress shirt and uniform blazer. It's the new kid, Drew. I watch as they trot up the steps to the library and disappear behind the heavy lacquered doors. My mother says Drew is a legacy student—that's why they're

17

here . . . and why they are allowed to stay. I figured as much when I saw them wearing that ring. It's the same as the one I wear, the one I inherited from my grandmother. I can only assume that Drew inherited their ring too, although I'm pretty sure they don't know what it means to wear it. Seeing them wear a vintage Lilies ring is a little like seeing a tourist wearing a Harvard sweatshirt when you can tell they didn't go to college.

I know that sounds bad, but our society is secret. The rings are supposed to be for members only. Drew is definitely not a real Lily. They're just not . . . the type.

As usual, I'm the first class president to arrive at morning check-in. My mother is sitting in her office, behind her desk, eyes glued to the computer monitor. In the lenses of her glasses, I can see the reflection of Chassity Cantrell, host of DC Daily's *The Real Story*. The computer speakers are cranked up all the way. The talking-head chatter is especially sharp this morning. I wish I had taken an extra pill. Maybe the sound wouldn't be so harsh.

"We'll now hear from the Coalition of Women for Women to shed some light on the impact of this most recent attack."

My mother doesn't greet me. She doesn't acknowledge that I'm early and therefore, by her standards, on time. She just asks, "Did you see the news from Sunday?"

"I have my alerts turned off," I say.

"There was a shooter at the Women's March on the mall. The bastard fired into the crowd."

A familiar, heavy feeling returns to my chest. It's the feeling I get every time I hear about another mass shooting. But this particular bit of news begins to crackle against my rib cage. The Women's March took place on the national mall in DC, less than thirty minutes away. Close to home. Too close. The snap of pain fades into a deep, fearful ache. Tension mounts in my forehead, knitting my eyebrows together. I'm used to the feeling, but it doesn't change the fact that I hate it with every ounce of my being.

Some people would call this chronic anxiety. But I don't have time for all of that. I stay on top of the feeling with my own special remedies, hand-selected each day from my jewelry box stash. They keep my head above water. An Archwell woman is the master of her own mind. For us, therapy is a crutch.

The news anchor continues to squawk, and I feel sweat gathering at the nape of my neck. Some sand wouldn't be the worst thing right now, but I guess that wouldn't mix well with what I've already taken.

Instead of acknowledging my silence, my mother continues to list the facts. "Two dead. Eleven in intensive care. It just makes me sick." She mutes the speakers and sends the computer screen into sleep mode. "I could see the anchor's eyes moving. Clearly reading the prompter verbatim. Seems so insensitive given the circumstances." She shakes her head. "Remember, Rory, people will take underpreparedness as a sign of weakness."

I nod. She's not wrong. She might be tough, but my mother is never wrong. That's why people look up to her. She is the one and only Chancellor Eleanor Archwell, prep school president and feminist political commentator of cable news fame. By all accounts, the embodiment of excellence.

I know from experience: when your mother is someone like Eleanor Archwell, you will do anything—lie, steal, cheat, and kill—to be just like her.

She motions for me to sit down in one of the office's tufted armchairs as she continues. "It was a good thing I had to turn down that speaking gig. If I'd been at that march . . . I hate to think what might have—" She shudders. "They're having me on the show this afternoon to talk about women's responsibility to ensure the protection of girls."

"That old song?" I ask. "I thought you used those talking points last month when you went on *Good Morning, DC*."

"No. I used them in the profile *Dayline* did of me," she answers. "And it doesn't matter. After this tragedy, my points are more relevant than ever. Women are the most vulnerable members of this society. It's up to us to change that."

"I just wonder if the topic feels a little stale?" I say. My mother recycles this speech about feminism all the time. It's harmless, I guess, but sometimes I feel like she oversimplifies things.

I sit up straighter in my chair. "I mean, it's a little more complicated than 'men hate women,' right?"

"Rory." My mother takes her glasses off. She only does

this when she's dead serious. I like seeing the little flecks of blue in her green eyes. "There are many people in this world who don't respect the *real* struggles of *real* women: people that will stop at nothing to take women down a peg; people who are predators. If you let them, they will try to destroy you. Especially if you appear weak. So, at the risk of repeating myself—" She puts her glasses back on and turns off the desk lamp. Morning sunshine has flooded the room at last. "—preparedness is strength. Real Archwell women stay a step ahead of the game."

When my mother says *real Archwell women* I know she's not talking about the girls who attend the academy. She's talking about the women of the Archwell family: me, herself, and Grandmother Adeline—former school chancellor and a cofounder of the Lilies Society, may she rest in peace. I glance down at my Lilies ring and run my thumb along the smooth side of the gold band.

"I don't like that lip color on you," my mother says. She stands, then rounds the desk and hands me a loose tissue. "It's too purple. Makes you look ill."

I accept the tissue and dab the color away lightly, even though I completely disagree with her. This is my lucky lipstick. The shade is called Paramour. I've worn it every exam day since Blythe gave it to me last Valentine's Day. It was her last gift to me before we ended things—before I had to start pulling strings to make sure she didn't outshine me.

"I got in touch with Mrs. Masters," my mother pivots. "I

told her you would be missing your biology midterm today." My gut seizes for a millisecond. I was afraid of this.

Missing my exam wasn't a part of my plan. But after what happened Friday night, I anticipated some form of wrath from the merciless Eleanor Archwell.

And I suppose I deserve it, even though it wasn't my fault.

Ugh, this day is already a mess. It wasn't supposed to be like this. I was supposed to arrive early to first period, nail the exam, and knock Blythe out of the running for the top academic spot once and for all. Then Charlotte ruined everything.

"What do you mean?" I ask my mother. "I can't miss that test. It's twenty percent of my grade."

"Look at that ring on your hand, Rory. Grandmother Adeline's Lilies ring. I gave that to you as a deposit on your future. I trusted you'd grow into the responsibilities of being an Archwell. But you and I both know you're not up for it. Not yet."

She pauses, waiting for my response. She's gauging whether I already know what she has up her sleeve. She's trying to outplay me. Sometimes, Eleanor Archwell can be a real asshole.

I finally give in to her silence with a question. "What are you saying?"

"You think I'm going to overlook your little pill habit after what happened Friday? Certainly not."

Shit. It is just like her to start the conversation off one

way and make a hard left into the exact topic I don't want to touch. I'd managed to put everything that happened on Founder's Night out of my mind. Well, my conscious mind, anyway.

My flash of panic is quickly deadened by the memory of my dream looping around me: Blythe in her green Lilies robe, the circle of initiates, a body on the floor, and then the door into . . . No. I can't go back there. I can't think about it. I pry myself out of the jaws of my own mind. The only way to protect myself from the memory is to block it out.

"You're cracking under the pressure," my mother continues. "You're starting to abuse your prescriptions. You're faltering with your responsibilities. You need help. So, I put in another call to Northbridge Recovery. You're signed up for their three-week program."

"Well, I'm not going!" I raise my voice, unable to stifle my anger.

She grabs my chin between her thumb and forefinger, a bit rough. Then she meets my eyes with a cold stare. "You will go. Because from what I can see, you are high right now."

She releases me. I can feel my face flush red. Emotion wells up in me and strangles my vocal cords. "No. Let me explain." My voice shakes, a sign of weakness in my mother's book. I can't help but feel I've already lost this argument.

Her voice is a bulldozer. "A van will be here for you within the hour."

I grip the armchair, sinking my manicure into the leather.

I was worried she would do this. She's threatened before, of course. But I never thought she'd send me to rehab during the school year. It's so obvious. So imperfect. So *conspicuous*. I didn't think she'd actually go through with it, but here we are. It's her way of reminding me how badly I messed up, how greatly I dishonored Grandmother Adeline's memory on Founder's Night, and how I put the secrets of the Lilies in jeopardy.

She continues, "Of course I didn't tell your teachers *why* you'll be missing your midterms. I would appreciate it if you kept that to yourself as well."

So there it is.

She doesn't want anyone to know about this. It wouldn't be a good look for her or the academy if people knew that Rory Archwell is shipping out to rehab.

That means I still have a card to play.

My eyes slide down to my saddle shoes. Yes, I messed up, but my mother doesn't know what I'm capable of. She doesn't know how far I'm willing to go or how far I've already gone.

The conversation is over, but she hasn't won. Not yet.

Blythe

I DON'T HACK HER PHONE because I'm still in love with her.

No, that would be pathetic.

I hack her phone because I know she's slick. We're alike that way.

The Lilies like to get into other peoples' business while keeping our own secrets under wraps. The saying goes, *We protect our sisterhood, our secrets, and our lives.* It's meant to be interpreted as a message of solidarity, a promise of safety for members of our society. But I know what it really means: every girl for herself. Rory and I both understood that even before we became "bigs." Maybe that's why we fell for each other at first.

I'll admit, I was hacking her phone even before we broke up. When I was home for fall break, Salim caught me going through her emails. Hers and a couple of other Archwell girls'. And maybe some teachers' too.

"You still lurking around in white folks' inboxes?" he asked. "You gotta be careful, B. That principal of yours doesn't play."

"You gonna tell Mama and Daddy? Don't. Please." I made the word *please* an octave higher and a hint whinier than my normal voice. Salim would be less likely to rat on me if I played the baby sister card.

"Nah. I won't. But make sure Sean doesn't find out. You and I both know he's the family snitch." Sean is our parents' golden boy: a Howard junior, an Omega man, an intern on Capitol Hill. He's following in Daddy's footsteps. And I'm supposed to be using the same blueprint. First, become valedictorian at Archwell. Next, on to Spelman and rush AKA like Mama. After that . . . To be honest, I have no idea what I'm supposed to do after that. Be perfect, I guess.

But I am not perfect.

And Salim's warning was right: if Sean found out about my antics, he *would* rat on me. Just like Rory would if she ever found out I was sifting through half the inboxes on campus.

It's not hard to hack a phone remotely. I started dabbling with it in middle school as a means to revenge. To be fair, Dashawn Hall deserved the hack. He broke up with me in front of everyone in cotillion class, right there on the dance floor. Later, he told all the boys I was so greasy that he could feel the sweat on my hands all the way through my white gloves. He was lying, of course. He didn't know who he was messing with.

Dashawn's phone history made it obvious he was using his mama's credit card without her permission. He was paying for content that big-bro Sean would've called "salacious in nature." Salim would've called it "that X-rated shit." To me, it was the perfect leverage. I sent his mama anonymous screenshots of Dashawn's receipts. Then I erased all traces of the hack. I still get a little thrill, goose bumps up and down my arms, when I think about how I got away with it.

Here at Archwell, I'm not out for revenge—just inside information. It's easy to hack Rory's phone because I know her security code: 1952. The year her great-grandfather Edgar Archwell founded Archwell Academy. It's easy to remember, and it's not like she'd ever let anyone forget it anyway. I scroll through her messages. It doesn't seem like she told anyone else about the thing that happened on Friday after the Founder's Night party—the thing that I haven't dared to bring up since. The thing I'm trying not to worry about . . . even though it's driven me to snoop through Rory's messages.

The texts from over the weekend are all pretty standard. One particularly spicy message from Caitlin Callahan proves that she and Rory are hooking up again. I know you're supposed to be jealous when your ex gets together with someone new, but I don't feel that way toward Rory anymore. I'm sure I'll meet someone eventually, I don't care what gender. Still, I can't escape the fact that Rory Archwell will forever hold the title of First Girl I Ever Dated. There's no changing that.

One thing on Rory's phone seems a little sus. She made an outgoing call at 12:10 a.m. on Saturday. To make things even weirder, Rory called her mom. She *never* calls her mom.

27

The call lasted thirty-five seconds, no texts between them after that. I know this might be nothing, but it's making my brain run all the possibilities. Why would Rory make that call so late at night? Did she mention what happened after the Founder's Night party? What we did? What *I* did? If the chancellor already knew about what happened, she wouldn't be waiting around to call my parents. I would've been packing my bags over the weekend, headed home to Mama and Daddy to explain why I failed them, how I couldn't stay a step ahead, how I'm *not* going to be Archwell's first Black valedictorian, how I let down our entire family.

But, as far as I can tell, the chancellor doesn't know what happened. It's a new week and there's still hope.

In the hallway outside the biology lab, I close out of my Co-Spy app and slip my phone into my oversized Fendi. I pull out my tablet and one of the packs of gum I've been saving for today. Spearmint is good luck for my AP Bio exam. My jaw always aches during midterms because I try to chew gum instead of chewing my nails. But, inevitably, I run out of gum. That's when I end up ripping off my gel manicure and biting my nails down to the nub. Then I have to go get a manicure before I visit home on the weekends because Salim and Sean will rib me if I don't. That won't happen today though. I brought five packs of gum. I know I'll probably need every last stick.

"Good morning, Blythe." Mrs. Masters is standing beneath the Gothic arch of her classroom door, keys in hand. As usual, she looks a little rumpled in her tweed blazer and khaki skirt. It's the same outfit she wears every Monday. "First period doesn't start for another twenty minutes."

"I know, Mrs. Masters," I say. "I'm just doing some last-minute review."

"You know I can't let you into the classroom before the exam officially starts. It's one of *those* tests," she says.

"Yes, ma'am. I know," I say, turning up the brightness in my voice. "I'm cozy out here." I lean back in my seat on the mahogany bench, open my tablet to my ClassFace app, and pull up my virtual biology flashcards.

"The early bird always catches the worm," Mrs. Masters croons. "I suppose that's why you are on the cover of every Archwell Academy brochure, Blythe Harris."

I feign a giggle and nod at Mrs. Masters as she shuffles into the classroom with her travel mug and *Science Rocks* canvas tote. She meant what she said as a compliment, but there's a specific reason my picture has been all over the school's brochures since I was in first grade. It's not because I'm an early bird. It's because I'm one of the only Black girls in a sea of whiteness.

Last year, the school wanted to do a feature of me and my grandmother for the fall alumni magazine. The article they pitched was cringe worthy: *Rose Harris's Mother Was a Maid at Archwell. Now Her Granddaughter Is Top of the Class.* Thankfully, Grandma Rose wasn't having it.

"Those folks at that school of yours are damn fools if they

think they're gonna get one more millisecond of my time," she said. "Blythe, don't let them put you on display just to make themselves look good."

Grandma Rose had part of it right. But there's another part that she and I never had a chance to talk about before she passed. At Archwell, it feels like the students and teachers look at me but they don't . . . *see* me. I'm an invisible girl and I always have been. But I suppose there is an upside. If they're smart about it, invisible girls can get away with a hell of a lot of shit.

I open my GradeSnooper app and sync it to Mrs. Masters's computer. Her desktop is booting up in the classroom, just on the other side of the ornately paneled wall. Soon she'll download today's exam into the secure testing app. I'm not looking for answers to the test questions. I would never do that. I just want a preview—a sense of what I'm up against. At the very least, it'll help me lay off the gum.

As the first question loads on my tablet, my news app sends me a notification. *US Senate Anticipated to Pass a Federal Ban on Trans Athletes in Public Schools.* A groan erupts from my throat. Those motherfuckers. As I read the article, my teeth start to hurt. Anger is guiding the muscles in my jaw, grinding my molars together. My body is trying to find some way, any way, to reject the news.

Another notification materializes and the tension in my face spreads to my throat, knotting up my windpipe. *Two Dead After Sunday's Women's March. DC Incel Shooter Still at*

Large. Two sentences into the article and I've already lost the gel polish from my pinky finger. My little cuticle is bleeding. My breath is fast and hot. I swipe away the news. I shouldn't keep my notifications turned on in the first place. It always messes with my head, knowing that this world isn't safe . . .

I need to get my mind right—now is not the time to get trapped in fear and bad memories. I think about the way my feet feel in my loafers. I feel the pleats of my collar caress my neck. I sense the cool smoothness of my Lilies ring on my right hand. Class of 2024. Yellow diamonds in the loops of the infinity symbol. I'll wear it when I eventually cross the stage to make my valedictorian speech. Just a few more months to go, I promise myself. Just a few more tests and projects and presentations and events. "It's not a big deal," I breathe aloud. I just need to take the next step and conquer AP Bio. I can survive. I can.

My tablet buzzes in my lap. It's another notification. This one is a text. It's from Rory. Lord. I can't believe that girl really had the nerve to text me *now* after a weekend of silence. Still, I have to see what she sent. My future depends on it. I take a deep breath and open the text.

Morning B. Hope you're not feeling too guilty about what happened . . . I know if it were me I'd be feeling pretty shitty right now. Hope you were able to get some sleep this weekend. I bet it was hard. Just wanted to say good luck on bio today. ☺

And in another message on the heels of the first: Never forget, you're a Lily always. Ut sacram memoriam.

My whole body turns cold. My scalp starts to crawl. *Ut sacram memoriam*. Translation: *keep sacred memory*. It's the Lilies vow, or at least the first line of it. It's our pledge to keep our secrets. Even when the secrets play on a loop in your mind again and again. Even when the secrets torture you, haunting your memory all the way to the grave. Rory knows I'm thinking about what happened to Charlotte: my little, the newest Lily. She knows that the memory of what I did to her has been welling up in me like a sickness. She's trying to get in my head by not letting me forget what happened. And, in her own way, she's threatening me . . . She's reminding me that she hasn't forgotten what happened either. And as long as Rory knows what I did, there's always the possibility that someone else could find out. And that would mean . . .

Suddenly, I'm burning up. I take off my blazer and unfasten the top two buttons of my blouse, but it's no use. The Lilies vow is echoing in my head. I already feel my sweat pooling underneath my silk shirt. A thousand whispers loop around each other. *Ut sacram memoriam—sacram memoriam—sacram—*

The hallway starts to curl around itself. I can't breathe. I undo another button and try to stand, steadying myself against the cherry woodwork. My lungs are burning. My face is wet. Tears and perspiration run together. I lug myself down the hall to the bathroom and steady myself against the porcelain sink.

"You're okay," I tremble. I run the water and watch it

twist into the bottom of the basin. It disappears down the drain. "You're okay, Blythe. You're okay." My voice is thin. I barely have enough breath for the words. It's not my first panic attack. The hardest part is remembering that you are not actually dying. I splash water on my face then bend down over the sink so I can do the same against the back of my neck. "You're okay," I whisper. I keep my eyes fixed to a point on the emerald-tiled walls.

My mind tries to slip back into the memory. All the Lilies are in a dark room. They hold their candles away from their hooded faces as they form a circle around the—

"Don't go there, Blythe," I tell myself. "You are in this room. You're safe. You're in your body. You are not dying."

It's not unheard of to have a panic attack during midterms. To be honest, I think I've struggled every exam week since sixth grade. Knowing I have to be better than the best makes me feel like I'm lugging around extra weight all the time. It feels like Mama and Daddy, and all my uncles and aunties, and even Sean and Salim, are looking over my shoulder, telling me not to mess up. Well, I messed up. And Rory knows it. And now she's using it to her advantage. I know because, if I were her, I'd do the same thing.

"You're okay," I whisper to myself. "You're okay." I whisper the words over and over until Grandma Rose's voice floats into my mind.

"You'll be okay, baby," she always said to me. "Those girls at that school will make you feel like you lost your mind. But that's just their game. You're gonna be all right. Just watch yourself around them." Rose knew all about Archwell. She didn't go to school here, of course. Back in the early '50s, she wasn't allowed. But her mama was a laundress and a cleaning lady for the school and she had to clean up more than one mess made by an Archwell girl. If Rose had not watched her mother go through all of that, she might not have been as adamant about preparing me for Archwell. "You're gonna be all right," she would say. "Just remember to keep your wits about you."

I steady my breath. "I'm gonna be all right."

I keep my eyes on the tiles, following their geometry all the way around the perimeter of the bathroom. Eventually I turn the tap off and dry my neck and armpits with a paper towel. I don't know how long it's been, but the bell for first period probably rang already. I grab my bag and check the mirror before I go. I look a little wide-eyed but my hair isn't mussed too much. I smooth down my edges, button up my blouse again, and give myself a fake smile. Good enough.

The hallway is empty but the classrooms hum behind closed doors. First period has definitely started. I'm now late for my exam. I rush back to Mrs. Masters's classroom, but the door is closed and Ms. Sherman is sitting at my spot on the hallway bench. She's eating an English muffin and staring at her tablet. The screen is a grid of video feeds: Archwell's hallways, the courtyard, the front gate. Hall monitor duty here is on a whole other level.

34

"Blythe, you're late for your midterm." Ms. Sherman speaks with her mouth full. "The chancellor wants to see you in her office."

My heartbeat surges again. I ball my right hand into a fist. My pulse pushes against the Lilies ring. "I'm sorry I'm late. I was just in the bathroom," I say, my voice smaller than I mean it to be. "Why do I have to go to see the chancellor?"

"You're late for an AP exam," Ms. Sherman says, taking the last bite of her breakfast sandwich and wiping her mouth on a paper napkin. "It's the policy."

"Sorry, Ms. Sherman, but it's not. I was in AP Calc last semester and I remember Emily Crowler came in almost fifteen minutes late to the midterm. She didn't have a pass or any—"

"Just go, Blythe." Ms. Sherman hands me a hall pass to the chancellor's office. "I keep telling all you girls, your actions have consequences."

Bitch.

I take the pass and leave Ms. Sherman without saying goodbye. This isn't about being late. Something else is going on. Something that Rory might already know about.

I exit onto the quad. Before I can catch myself, I've picked the gel polish off my ring finger. Damn. My Lilies diamonds sparkle in the fall sunshine. The inscription catches the light. *Ut sacram memoriam.*

Veró

MALCRIADA IS EVERYTHING I'M NOT. Outspoken. Daring. Controversial. When I make installations under her pseudonym, I don't have to play by the rules. I mark each piece with my signature *M* and go about my business without any regret. After all, Malcriada has nothing to lose. No family. No history. When I install a new piece as Malcriada, it's art. But when I do it as Verónica Martín, it's vandalism. That's certainly how my parents see it anyway. It's how they saw it at Easton Academy too.

The dean at Easton explained the situation to Papi over the phone. "Veronica was found defacing a portrait that's been in the school's collection for over forty years." In addition to mispronouncing my name, the dean failed to mention that the "portrait" was just an old poster, the kind they used to hang in classrooms back in the day. Still, I don't think that added detail would've changed the way Papi felt about the whole thing. My design adapted the old poster of Ronald Reagan into an image of el diablo. Over the words *Ronald Reagan—40th President of the United States of America*,

I superimposed the words *Ronald Reagan—Imperialist, Capitalist, White Supremacist Patriarch.* Papi *really* didn't like that.

"What you did was un-American, Verónica," he screamed into the phone.

I scoffed.

Papi is very concerned about appearing "American." The story he tells on the campaign trail is an "all-American" tale of "rags to riches," a man born in East LA to parents who immigrated from Campeche for a better life in California. He lets people believe that his parents were campesinos, but it's just not true.

The year before my father was born his parents sold their vast waterfront property to American developers and made for the States. The story goes that my grandmother went into labor while they were stuck in traffic on the 710 so they wound up at a hospital in East LA, even though they were Downey residents. Papi never dives into the fact that he basically grew up in what is now one of LA's fanciest suburbs. Some of his biggest donors are other Latinos from Downey and they eat Papi's rags-to-riches story right up. People will believe anything if you say it with enough conviction.

"Positively un-American, Veró," Papi shouted again. In the background of our phone call, I could hear the roar of the crowd from his campaign event in God-Knew-Where. "This kind of thing does not reflect well on the Martín family, mija. Not during the midterms. We raised you to be respectful. I don't know where this behavior comes from."

37

He didn't show up to move me out of the Easton dorms. Neither did Mami. They sent Troy, Mami's assistant, instead.

"For what it's worth," Troy said as he loaded the last of my bags into the rental car. "The illustration you did over President Reagan's face was very good. You've got talent, Veró. You've just got to be strategic with where and how you use it."

There's nothing that makes my skin crawl more than a patronizing adult offering unsolicited advice to the Impressionable Youth of America. As Malcriada, my approach is *all* about strategy. A big part of that strategy is not getting caught . . . Well, at least not again.

At Archwell, I've been smarter about when and where I make my Malcriada installations. People know the work by now, of course. It stands out on the school's otherwise pristine campus—a lime-green stencil on weathered sandstone, a fake flyer calling all "miscreants" to report to "Miss Understood's" classroom for a meeting of "the Ouija Club." People know that each piece is by the same artist because I sign all the work with Malcriada's anonymous M. Nobody but me knows her name. I make it my business to keep it that way.

I always have an alibi. It helps that I also have first block as my free period. In the early morning light, Archwell girls are either in class or sleeping in. The teachers are slower and less vigilant. Some buildings are completely silent and empty. I never run into anyone who would suspect me as the artist known only as Malcriada.

Today, I make sure that Ms. Katz sees me come into the library at seven forty-five a.m. "Can you look up a call number for me? I lost my copy of *For Whom the Bell Tolls* and I need it for Mrs. Holloway's class."

"Let me see," Ms. Katz taps on her keyboard for a moment. Her eyes dance across the desktop screen. "Second floor. Under PS351 . . . I'll just print the number for you." She fires up the little printer on her desk and gets a funny look on her face. "Hemingway, huh?"

"Yeah," I answer. I want to say, *Yeah,* Hemingway, *that misogynistic drunk* . . . but I don't.

"Great writer . . . and a total putz," Ms. Katz mutters. "A landmark in American literature, sure. But definitely a major putz."

"I know, right?" I say. "Mrs. Holloway isn't having any of that though. She's got this whole thing about separating the art from the artist."

Ms. Katz sighs as she grabs the printout from the tray. "Well, that's Mrs. Holloway's opinion. But some of us have different thoughts." She winks at me as she hands me the little slip of paper with the call number. Sometimes it seems like Ms. Katz is the only adult at Archwell who is normal.

In many ways, Archwell is like any other prep school. There's all the typical bs: white ladies pronouncing my name wrong, the "classics" syllabi from last century, and social cliques based on whether you're a legacy student, a field hockey player, or a foreign exchange student. Before I transferred here from Easton, I mostly hung out with the exchange kids from Ecuador and Venezuela. They liked to tease me with all the usual brown-on-the-outside-white-on-the-inside food metaphors. I pretended like the jokes didn't hurt. Still, it never feels great to be reminded that I'm too much of a "no sabo" kid for the other Latinas and too "ethnic" for the white girls. At Archwell, I keep to myself. Not just because of the jokes, but because some of the girls here are weird as hell.

I've been to my fair share of prep schools, and I can honestly say that the vibe at Archwell Academy is off. Well, the vibe at *all* prep schools is always a little off, but at Archwell it's on another level. Graduating from Archwell anoints you for the Ivy League, so girls here deeply believe they are the Chosen Ones. The superiority complex is turned up to a thousand. Some of them speak in riddles and whispers. And from the perspectives of the legacy students, anyone who has spent fewer than five years at the school is an outsider. The legacies have their own secret club, I've noticed. I like to think of them as Chancellor Archwell's minions. They have matching rings. They dress alike. They mutter in Latin to each other. It's funny how easily white people fall into culty shit. Sometimes I wish that all the legacies would just get it over with and all make out with each other in one of their secret meetings like I know they want to. That would definitely improve Archwell's vibe.

It's good to be an outsider at Archwell. Good for me at

least. Making art as Malcriada has taught me to embrace the benefits of being on the margins. It's where I do my best work. But today's installation doesn't just require anonymity. I need stealth. What I'm working on this morning is big: a piece that will tear the mask off Archwell Academy and its so-called legacy.

Upstairs in the stacks, I run into the new kid, Drew. Seeing them spooks me—the library is usually empty at this time of day. And, yes, they catch me with my 404 pages. The 404 project is a side hustle. It's not really what I'm here to do. My encounter with Drew solidifies my alibi, though. At eight a.m. Monday, October 9, Veró Martín is on the second floor of McClure Library, with her copy of Hemingway, up to some low-level mischief with the old encyclopedias. Once I leave Drew behind, no one sees me take off my Archwell blazer and pull Malcriada's black hoodie over my collared shirt and top tie. No one sees me climb one of the library's many spiral staircases.

On the third floor, I steal through the reading room, my footsteps dampened by the sprawling oriental rug. I reach into my bag and remove my extra-long extension cord before plugging it into the outlet nearest to the little door. I don't think most people know about the little door: the one that leads to the tower's top level, where the old school bell used to be. The belfry, I think it's called. The space is rarely used now, despite its sweeping views of the campus. Autumn chill rushes through the cased openings. Leaves wave to me from below, all turmeric and ruby. It's a painter's dream landscape. But I'm not here for the views.

I drop my bag and lay down the extension cord. It trails neatly behind me, linking me to the power source back inside the reading room. My bag has two sets of old school speakers. They're not ideal—rechargeable and cordless would've been better—but they work just fine and I got them for free. I don't buy supplies. And if I do, I buy them in cash. Malcriada can't leave a paper trail.

I plug in the speakers, set the volume extra low, and sync them to my phone. I place them around the edge of the belfry. When I hit play, the tower will act like an old gramophone, sound booming up into the conical turret and across the campus. The noise will be the loudest in the room directly below the belfry: the chancellor's office. She won't be able to miss it . . . will no longer be able to deny her truth.

I pause for a second, shivering. I pull my hoodie closer to me. I tell myself it's because of the cold. It's not because I'm afraid. It's also not because of what will happen if I get caught. And it's definitely not because something is haunting me: the memory of what happened last time I did a major installation. Sure, someone got hurt. And, yes, it was my fault. But I'm trying to not get too caught up in it right now. This installation is going to fix all of that. Maybe then I'll be forgiven.

I return to my bag, pull out my banner, and start to unroll it. A bright green letter *T* appears against the black fabric. The painted letters are dry but are still off-gassing. I unfurl the next letter: *E*. The chemical smell makes me gag before the breeze carries it away. Then excitement bubbles in my throat. With the second-to-last letter revealed, an *R*, I can see now that the banner's green-and-gold border will really pop against the stone facade of the tower. Once I hang it from the belfry, everyone on campus will see the truth. Archwell's biggest secret will be out. I just need to get the thing rigged up and I'll be—

"Excuse me." A voice cuts through me, sharper than the morning chill. "What are you doing out here? Students aren't allowed up here unsupervised." I'm frozen, still kneeling over the unfurled banner. "What do you have there? What does that say? Oh my."

Shit. My banner and I might be caught. But that can't happen. That would ruin everything. My hoodie is still covering my face. I don't think the person recognizes me as Malcriada. Or even as Veró Martín. To her, I could be anyone. I could try to make a run for it—but where would I go? When my gaze flits over to the little door, I see that the person is blocking my way out. She's wearing worn-out flats and white stockings. Damn. It's Ms. Steiner, one of the librarians. She must've been on hall monitor duty or something because it's not her day to be at the circulation desk. I kick myself for not thinking to check where *all* the librarians would be during first block on a Monday. It's a stupid oversight. Not up to Malcriada's standards.

"Veronica," she says, mispronouncing my name. I wince. "Stand up." I rise to my feet slowly, eyes hot. Everything is about to be ruined.

"So you're the one who's been behind all the recent vandalism, hmm? You're M?"

M for Malcriada . . . Shit. She knows. It's all over now.

Before she even says it, I know what Ms. Steiner is going to say next. "I think we better go to the chancellor's office."

The words slash across my chest, a fatal blow. My hoodie falls back and Malcriada evaporates. It's over. I am hollow now. The death of Malcriada might as well be the death of me.

Papi already told me what would happen if I got into trouble again, and he's not known for making empty threats. "Not one more time, Veró," he said, "or you're going to Fort Hancock until you graduate. Then we'll talk about which options would be appropriate for college. Your mother and I would hate to see that college fund go to waste."

Military schools like Fort Hancock aren't known for their art programs. And with my college choices left up to Papi, art school is definitely off the table. In a matter of minutes, I've managed to obliterate my entire future.

"Veró," Ms. Steiner repeats. "Gather your things. Now. I'll walk you to the office."

I pick up the banner. The fabric is heavy in my hands. It's just a painted sign, I try to convince myself, but the word the banner bears is damning. When I made it, I knew it would destroy someone. I just didn't think that it would destroy *me.* I fold the banner up so its acronym is no longer visible. *TERF.* A trans-exclusionary radical feminist. Ms. Steiner knows the word as well as I do. And the chancellor . . . Well, she definitely knows what it means. Her army of minions do too. Papi probably won't know it, and even if I explain it to him, I doubt he'll understand.

I created Malcriada so I could be free for once. Free from family. Free from history. Free from consequences. But Malcriada was never real. There was only ever Veró, Senator Martín's daughter. And Veró is not an artist. She's a vandal at the very least. And at most, she is much, much worse.

Drew

THE DOOR TO THE CHANCELLOR'S office is the color of blood. It's the same color as the emergency exit doors at Dundalk High, a shade of red that screams for mercy. It's the only thing the chancellor's door has in common with those heavy double doors back at my old school.

Those old doors lied to us: *Alarm Will Sound If Door Is Opened.* Nope. The wire that tripped the alarm was frayed beyond function. So the doors became an escape hatch. A portal to the outside world. A world beyond security cameras and bag searches. Beyond the metal detectors that greeted us when we arrived at school. We kept the emergency exit doors propped open when we could. We didn't want anyone to get locked out, but we didn't think about who might be able to get in.

Outside the chancellor's office, I pause, not sure if I should knock or take a seat on the hall's glossy wooden bench. If I knock, I'll have to face the reason why I'm here. If I sit, I'll prolong the torture.

My fingers resist as I curl them into a fist. I knock.

Someone shuffles around inside the office for a few seconds before unbolting the lock and squealing the wooden door open. I recognize the girl, but I don't remember her name. She's tall and slender with an ombre-blond dye job. It's supposed to look natural, but I have a good eye for roots. I've been doing Mom's hair since elementary school.

"It's Drew, right?" she says. Her voice is crisp and candied, but her eyes narrow in on my buzzcut. She's thinking that my hair is not very Archwellian. I have to agree, but that's one of the things I like about it. It's cyberpunk meets newborn baby. It's spring chicken meets Dominic Torretto from the Fast & Furious movies. I love being all these things at the same time . . . but the girl at the door isn't vibing with it. Unsurprising, I suppose.

"You're here to see my mother?" she asks.

"Your mother?" I say, stepping into the office. The room is lined with built-in bookshelves, all washed in the same bloodred varnish as the door. There's a heavy mahogany desk, a credenza crowded with black-and-white photos, and half a dozen tufted leather chairs. An iron sculpture of Athena has been converted into a table lamp. I've entered some kind of sapphic lair.

"Chancellor Archwell," the girl answers. "She just stepped out for a minute. She's with Mrs. Pendleton."

"Your mom is the chancellor?" I ask, taking a handful of peppermints from a crystal bowl perched on the credenza. "Huh, I thought arachnids mostly ate their young."

The girl glowers at me for a moment. "Yes, my mother is the chancellor," she says, unamused. "And you've got your science wrong. Spider cannibalism is reproductive. The females eat the males after mating."

I'm so thrown off by the specificity of this comeback that I struggle to rebound. After a beat, I manage to ask, "Who's Mrs. Pendleton?"

"Mrs. Pendleton is our head of security," the girl says, watching me closely as I settle into one of the armchairs.

"Your family has a security team?" I ask. I unwrap two of the peppermints and pop them both into my mouth.

The girl makes a face again. I can tell she's annoyed by me—probably for all the same reasons most Archwell girls are annoyed by me—but she keeps her tone cheery. "Mrs. Pendleton is head of security for *the school*."

"Gotcha. When do you think the chancellor will be back? I can get out of your hair if you think it's gonna be awhile." I try not to get too attached to the idea of just getting up and walking out of the chancellor's office. It would be way too easy. And, again, I would just be delaying doom, maybe even making it worse. There's no place to go, no point in resisting the inevitable.

Death's voice whispers in my ear again: *I know what you did. And so does the chancellor.* I try not to react to the premonition, hardening the muscles in my forehead instead of wincing.

"She should be back any minute," the girl says, taking a

seat in the chair across from me. Hers is the swivel kind. I watch as she reaches into her backpack and pulls out a tin of breath mints and a water bottle. The backpack is tufted leather—like the armchairs—but the bag's material is Pepto-Bismol pink. I can tell it's designer made, but the aesthetic of it sort of reminds me of the kind of bag they have in the Target children's section. It doesn't fit this girl at all. My second-grade cubby mate, Tanya, had a backpack like that. Unlike this one though, hers was made of plastic.

That bag caused a lot of drama. It was the bag where our teacher, Ms. Terry, found the gun. When I think of it, my ears start to feel like they're full of water somehow. I saw Ms. Terry pull the thing out of the pink backpack at security check and my body got really cold. She gasped and lowered the gun back into the bag. Seeing an adult like that, all flustered and shaky, made me scared. It felt like the world had fallen off its hinges and everything was sideways.

Later, Ms. Terry came to pull me out of specials. She wanted to talk to me. "Drew," she said, "did Tanya tell you she was going to bring a weapon to school?" I gulped down my fear and lowered my eyes, trying to memorize the floor's blue tile pattern. Then I shook my head no.

"Really? Not a word at all?" she pressed.

"Well, she just said that some of the older kids were giving her problems in the cafeteria and she was gonna get them."

Ms. Terry inhaled slowly through her nose. "I see. Thank you for your honesty, Drew."

I'd told the truth, but something made me feel like I was in the wrong no matter what I said to Ms. Terry. I shoved the inexplicable shame into the pit of my stomach.

After that, all the kids at school had to get clear plastic backpacks. Tanya got suspended. I fed my shame M&Ms and tried not to let the memory play out in my mind on a loop. Some memories have an undertow. They can carry you away no matter how hard you fight against them.

In the chair, across from the chancellor's daughter, I try to shake off the thought of Tanya's gun. I follow the floral pattern of the woven carpet with my eyes. I eat two more of the chancellor's peppermints and pocket another handful from the bowl. They're supposed to settle anxious stomachs.

The door handle turns. The hinges squeal. "That must be her," the chancellor's daughter tells me, but then her face falls when she sees that she's wrong.

"Rory?" Blythe Harris from my third-period French class is standing in the office doorway. "What the hell?" She's shouting for some reason. "Are you behind this?"

"Behind what, B?" The chancellor's daughter's voice stays sweet. "Are you in trouble or something?"

"You tell me." Blythe's words are sharp. She troops into the room, flings the office door closed behind her, and shoves her bag into one of the chairs. She doesn't take a seat. "Hi, Drew," she gruffs, meeting my eyes for a half second before she starts to pace around the carpet's edge. "Ms. Sherman sent me up here on some bullshit." Blythe does not say this to me. She's speaking directly to Rory. It's weird to see her like this after half a semester of watching her ace all her conjugation drills. I'm not sure if I've ever seen Blythe speak anything other than French.

"That's odd," Rory tells her. "She wrote you up?"

"She said I needed to come here 'cause I was late for the bio midterm. You *know* that's not a thing," Blythe says. Then she stops midstride and turns to face Rory. "Why aren't *you* in the bio midterm, Rory? Did you tell the cha—" She cuts herself off, eyes darting to me for a split second. She revises, "Are *you* in trouble too?"

"Me? No." Rory takes her phone out of the pink backpack and starts scrolling. She keeps her eyes to the screen as she speaks. "I was here for the class presidents' morning meeting. After it was over, the chancellor asked me to hang back. She just stepped out with Mrs. Pendleton for a minute. Something to do with campus security cameras."

One thing Dundalk High and Archwell Academy have in common: security cameras. Archwell has a lot more though, and I don't know where they all are. I suppose it's to make the Archwell parents feel like their kids are in a safe place. But it's hard for me to feel safe anywhere at Archwell, particularly here in the chancellor's office. The color of the walls hurts my eyes. I shut them and try to rub the sting away. I consider again if it's worth it to slip out of the office with my pocket full of peppermints. But then the crimson door flies open again.

It's Ms. Steiner, my least favorite librarian. Brisk and serious, she holds the door open with her left hand as she checks the alerts on her phone. Veró steps into the office, her hair glowing mauve against the office walls. At first, I smile at her, but then I see she's crying. Her face is streaked and shadowy. It's been only about twenty minutes since I saw her in the library stacks. What could have gone so wrong in twenty minutes? I hate to think.

"Good morning, girls." Ms. Steiner's voice is a little jittery. She doesn't catch her error. We aren't all girls here. I try not to let it bother me, even though it does. I counteract the dull ache of Ms. Steiner's casual misgendering by thinking of all the times Mom has called me her "precious they-by" instead of her "precious baby." The thought of it makes my whole body smile. It's a gender euphoria magic trick that I keep in my back pocket, but I can do it only so many times in a day before it loses its potency.

"Are you all waiting for Chancellor Archwell?" Ms. Steiner asks.

"Yes, we are," Rory answers.

"Didn't she tell you to lock the office door?" she asks Rory in a low voice.

"Yes. People kept showing up though."

"I see." Ms. Steiner looks back at her phone before lowering her reading glasses and looking the office door up and down. "I need to return to the library and check in with Ms. Katz, but you better lock up behind me," she says. "I just got a staff alert saying we're going into Code Emerald right now. So the door should be locked."

"What's Code Emerald?" I ask.

"Campus-wide lockdown. Like the one we did last week," Blythe murmurs to me before speaking to Ms. Steiner. "Is this a planned drill?"

"Well, dear, I didn't receive prior notification of it, but that doesn't mean it's not planned. Sometimes they do these lockdowns without warning to keep the staff on their toes. You can never be too careful about campus safety."

I know from experience that real lockdowns are different from drills, faster, more confusing. Still, I feel a tremor creeping back into my hands. I rub my palms together and try to unwind the tension.

"I'll text the chancellor. I can get us a time estimate on when the drill will end," Rory says. She's steady and buttoned-up, unphased by the term *Code Emerald*.

"Wonderful," Ms. Steiner whirrs. "If you girls will excuse me, I have to secure the library doors."

"You girls *and* Drew," Blythe corrects Ms. Steiner. I'm not expecting this from her. After all, we only know each other from French: a language where even the lamps and tables fall into the gender binary. La lampe et le canapé. Hearing someone acknowledge me, even just a little, calms the tension in my hands and shoulders.

Ms. Steiner screws up her face as if she doesn't really understand Blythe's comment. She turns to leave, but her phone shrieks another alert just as she pulls the door closed behind her. Before she shuts it entirely, she peeks her head in and says, "You might consider moving a piece of furniture or something heavy to block the door after you've locked it. Just a thought." And with that, she leaves. The door closes and my tremors return, creeping from my fingertips up into my arms.

Lockdowns mean danger. And even if a Code Emerald is just for practice, I know that there's real danger out there. When Mom and I moved to Montgomery Avenue, back when I was really little, we kept hearing the *pop-pop-pa* out on the street every other night. The sound made my bones rattle. Mom sat me down to have a talk. "All guns are bad, Drew," Mom told me. "Even unloaded guns. Even toy guns." Still, I cried when Mom threw away my one and only Super Soaker. I won the thing fair and square in a raffle at my school's spring carnival. But Mom wasn't having it.

Later, when I enrolled at Archwell, she said, "That campus is way out in the sticks. No one will be able to just waltz in off the street out there. No guns. It'll be safer than Dundalk." I heard her voice snag on the word *safer*. She shook her head just a little, as if she didn't quite believe her own words. Then she stiffened up and spoke again, trying to convince herself of something. "You'll be safer," she repeated.

The cold, jittery feeling that's slithering through my body tells me that Mom was wrong.

"How often does Code Emerald involve barricading the doors?" I ask the others.

"Never," Blythe says. "Rory, you said your mom left with security?"

"Yes," Rory says as she crosses over the blossomy carpet and bolts the door shut. "I'm sure it's just a regular drill."

"Does she usually walk the grounds with Pendleton when it's a drill?"

"Yes . . . At least I think so," Rory says stiffly. Her cheeks look more hollow than I first realized. She's weary looking, almost skeletal. Death's skull superimposes itself over Rory's face and the cold feeling spreads to my gut.

Blythe looks unconvinced and shifts her eyes onto the heaviest-looking armchair. "Can one of you help me with this?"

Veró, still wordless, rises to help Blythe shove the thing across the carpet against the office door.

"That's unnecessary," Rory mutters. But by the time she says it, the scarlet door is blocked.

Veró breaks her silence. "Did your mom text you back yet, Rory? Is this a drill or what?"

I try to ignore the fact that the room feels so much smaller now that we're sealed into it. I sink into my seat, pretending I'm anywhere but here.

Blythe returns to pacing, audibly breathing in and out. I am being consumed by the cushiony leather chair. The cold has gripped the bottoms of my feet.

Rory looks at her phone again. "She hasn't texted," she answers Veró.

"Rory." Blythe pauses in front of her. "Could this have anything to do with . . ."

"No." Rory's voice is a bracing wind. "It's a drill," she insists.

"But what else could it be . . ." Blythe mutters, returning to her pacing.

"The alarms just haven't come on yet. I'm sure every girl on campus is safe." Rory says that last sentence with a little lilt in her voice, like maybe there's more to the story. Maybe she knows what I know: that we're not really safe. We never are.

My legacy membership to the Lilies Society was supposed to guarantee me safety at Archwell, but look how that turned out. I suppose I should've known better, should've known that I'd be on my own here.

In the end, no one can really protect you.

Death rudely hisses in my ear. *Not every girl is safe.* I put my hands on either side of my head, trying to push the memory of Charlotte out of my mind.

You're not safe. Not ever. Not as long as I know what you did.

The room shrinks again. I close my eyes and Death is there to greet me once more.

Then a new sound shakes the office.

BLEEP-BLEEP-BLEEP . . . BLEEP-BLEEP-BLEEP . . .

I am expecting the alarm, but it still paralyzes me. The sound is deafening. Louder than at Dundalk High. Louder than the roar of memory. Somehow louder than the alarm that blared through the campus during the lockdown drill last Friday.

A robotic voice shouts underneath the sirens: *Warning. Warning. Lockdown. Shelter in place. Secure doors. Warning. Warning.*

"Are you still sure this is a drill?" Veró asks Rory. "Or is there something else going on?"

Rory is a stone wall. Blythe says nothing, but she looks like she's about to cry.

Death's voice is an echo in my head: *Not safe. Not ever.*

Blythe

YOU'RE IN THIS ROOM.

You're in your body.

You're not dying.

You're safe . . . but actually.

Warning! Warning!

Shelter in place! Secure doors!

Warning! Warning!

The chancellor's picture frames are trembling against the walls. The robo-voice on the intercom is too loud to block out. I feel the tide of panic swelling in my throat again.

The curly-headed girl called Veró speaks. "Seriously, is this for real or what?"

"I told you. It's just a drill," Rory insists, her voice a knot of thorns. "We had one just like it on Friday night, remember? The exact same sequence. Alarms on. Intercoms on. Shelter in place. This is all normal . . . And even if there *were* a real threat, this office is still the safest place on campus."

My pulse doubles. I glance at the red, barricaded door. The office doesn't feel safe, at least not for me—not as long as Rory is holding the secret about Charlotte over my head. If *I* were to go missing, I would hope they'd send the campus into a lockdown and start a search. There's a part of me that hopes that this is what they're doing for Charlotte . . . even though it's over forty-eight hours later. Maybe they are looking for her. Or maybe they are looking for the person responsible for what happened to her. Maybe someone called in a tip. The thought pushes hot tears against my eyelids.

I have to get out of here. Away from Rory. Away from this room.

Warning! Warning! Shelter in place!

Panic washes me away, and I get lost in my memory.

I'm thirteen again, holding Sean's hand as we run through the crowded street. Riot cops are at the corner of Lafayette Park. We're not supposed to be here. Mama and Daddy said we couldn't stay at the protests past dark. But Salim wanted to stick around and Sean said okay. Now the air is filled with tear gas. I have to run faster, but it's hard to keep up. My brother's legs are longer than mine and my face mask is making it so I can't breathe. I have to get out of here.

Bing. Bing. B-bing. Every phone in the room wails an alert. Mine buzzes against my leg, dragging me into the present. I look at the screen. It's an all-caps push notification.

WARNING: ALL CAMPUS LOCKDOWN.

My hand trembles as I swipe the notification away. I can feel my heart in my fingertip, beating against the phone's gunmetal finish.

"Shit. What'd I tell y'all?" Veró holds up her phone. I can see she has the same notification. We all do.

"Does this usually happen?" Drew's voice quavers. "I've never gotten a notification like this before."

"It's just a system test," Rory groans.

"Then why didn't we get a notification like this during the last drill?" Veró asks.

"I . . . I don't know . . ." For the first time, Rory seems scattered. Her fingers are frantic, tapping out texts to the chancellor.

Veró picks up her bag and walks over to Drew, whose body has gone rigid in their chair. They have a funny expression on their face—half-frozen, half-scowling. She eyes them for a second. "You good?" she asks.

Drew gulps and nods, snapping out of whatever trance they were in.

I try to slow my breathing but my eyes are still burning. Then memory takes me again. I'm running through the DC streets, sweating in the summer swelter. Sean is too. Our hands are slippery. It's hard to keep my grip on him as we run. I turn around. Salim was right behind me. Where is he now? We have to get out together. Sirens wail. I can't think about this right now. I don't want to think about this. Not ever.

The voices in the chancellor's office sound impossibly far away.

"I don't see anyone out on the quad. No one is outside at all."

"Get away from the window, Veró. You're supposed to take cover during a lockdown."

"I . . . I really don't know if that's necessary . . . Once my mother texts back we'll know if . . ."

"Wait a second. Y'all saw the news this morning? That incel shooter on the national mall is still on the loose. What if this lockdown is related?"

Oh god. Another thing to worry about. I try to ground myself, leaning into my senses. My eyes land on an image framed in silver on the chancellor's desk—a photograph of Rory's grandmother when she was a student at Archwell. I inhale through my nose, catching a whiff of peppermint and mildew. I listen for a sound underneath the blaring alarm, searching for something, anything, to focus on other than the noise.

"You're gonna be all right, baby," I hear Grandma Rose whisper to me. "Just don't pay those Archwell girls any mind."

"You're in this room, Blythe," I mutter to myself. "You're in your body. You're not dying."

"What was that?" Veró shouts at me over the alarm and the drone of the security system's looped message.

Warning! Warning!

"We didn't hear you, B." Rory is at my elbow now. She can definitely tell I'm freaking out because she takes my hand. "Are you okay?"

I nod.

"I'm not playing with y'all anymore. This seems serious. Where can we hide?" Veró turns to Rory. "There's gotta be a spot for us to go. A secret exit or something?"

Rory shakes her head, her face ashen.

"Damn, I thought Archwell was full of secret rooms and trap doors and shit your weird-ass family put here. You're telling me we've got nowhere to take cover?"

The alarm continues to blare.

"What about in there?" Drew asks, nodding toward the extra-slim door behind the chancellor's desk. Finished in polished walnut, it can't be more than a foot and a half wide.

"We can't hide in there," I say. "We won't all fit."

But Veró is already at the door behind the chancellor's desk, rattling the knob. "What's back here?" she calls to Rory over the incessant beeping.

"We shouldn't go in there. It's . . . it's just a closet," Rory says. "Maybe it's better if we—"

"Come on, Rory. I'm not doing this back and forth with you. Not right now," Veró insists.

My phone buzzes in my hand again. Another push notification.

WARNING: CAMPUS INTRUDER. ASSUME LOCK-DOWN PROCEDURES.

"Shit," Drew says.

"I knew it," Veró utters. "Come open this door, Rory!"

"Seriously, trust me. You all don't want to go in there."

Rory's probably right. There's no way we're all going to

be able to squeeze into such a tiny space. But it's starting to feel like the only option.

Warning! Warning!

"Do you have a better idea, then?" Veró is almost shouting. "We have to do something!"

Rory glowers but she gives in. Behind the desk, she yanks one of her mother's drawers open and, hands shaking, takes out a ring of old-looking keys.

Shelter in place! Secure doors!

After fumbling through a few attempts, she finally unlocks the closet. "Happy?" she asks Veró as she holds the door open. Her face is a strange blend of fear and disgust.

Veró and Drew disappear into its darkness.

"Go ahead, Blythe," Rory says.

I have to turn my body sideways to successfully slide through the closet's opening. It's too dim to see inside. Rory stalks in behind me before she pulls the little door shut. Now we're in total darkness.

"I told myself I would not be forced back into the closet at this school." I recognize Drew's shaky voice in the dark. "Now look at me."

"Oh, so we're joking now? Okay." Veró's voice is rounder, a bit stronger than Drew's. "Can we get a light on in here, please?"

"I'm trying," Rory hisses. "There's a cord around here somewhere. Ah." Her tone softens. "There we go."

Click. I hear the delicate sound of the little metal chain igniting the bulb above. The glow is faint. The light buzzes. The sounds of the alarm and security message are muffled on the other side of the little door. My breathing slows as the inside of the closet comes into focus.

It's much bigger than I thought it would be, a little smaller than my freshman dorm room. But maybe that says more about the size of the dorm room than the size of the closet. The walls are lined with built-in shelves, just like the chancellor's office, but here, the shelves are painted black. They're supported by art deco–style arches, tiny women carved out of wood.

"What's with the costumes?" Veró asks, tugging on the velvet sleeve of one of the green robes hanging from a hook on the wall. I recognize the thing. It's a Lilies robe. But Veró can't know that. Every aspect of initiations, even the clothes, is supposed to be a secret. I glance around the shelves and notice they're stacked with the stuff we're not supposed to talk about. The rings, the candles, the blindfolds with the infinity symbols stitched on them. And then there's the army of alarm clocks strewn around the shelves, something that has nothing to do with the Lilies as far as I know. Maybe the chancellor is a collector? That might explain why there's a towering grandfather clock tucked in between the robes and gowns near the back of the closet.

Before Rory or I can think of a lie to tell Veró about the velvet robe, my phone goes off once again. Yet another push notification:

WARNING: INTRUDER PRESENT. ALL-CAMPUS
LOCKDOWN.

"Rory, look," I breathe, holding the phone up. "Wouldn't it say *drill* if it were actually a drill? It wouldn't say anything about an intruder."

I can see it in her scrunched-up face, the pale white of her skin turning pink. Rory is starting to panic. The others might not notice it, but I can hear it in her voice. I see it in her body. Something isn't right and she knows it. We all do.

"Ugh, this is so stupid," Rory says. "You all can do what you want. I'm going to find my mom and get the details."

"Don't go out there," Drew says. "It really doesn't seem like a drill. What if there really is a shooter?"

"They can't all be drills," Veró agrees.

Bong . . . Bong . . . Bong . . . Bong . . .

The sound of the grandfather clock ricochets around the closet like a bullet. We all jump.

"Damn," Veró says. "Why would someone keep something so loud in such a tiny space?" She eyes the antique's dusty mahogany paneling and brass pendulum like they're somehow responsible for the possibly-real-or-possibly-not lockdown.

It continues to chime. *Bong . . . Bong . . . Bong . . .*

The sound consumes us, and suddenly the closet's air feels stale. My skin is crawling now, itching to move around, move away, get out.

Rory ignores the noise and turns to leave, rattling the

doorknob. "C'mon," she mumbles, turning the knob in the other direction.

"Don't go out there, Rory." Drew's words are barely audible over the sound of the alarm, the security message, and the chiming clock.

She scoffs. "There is *no way* I am staying in *here*." She shoves her shoulder against the walnut finish. "Freakin' stuck. C'mon you piece of crap!" She kicks the wood with her unscuffed saddle shoes.

Bing. Bing. B—

Our phones all sing together. My device buzzes in my hand, pulsing against my skin like a bird beating its wings. Then the screen goes black.

"My phone just died," Veró utters.

"Mine too," Rory says.

My thoughts mingle with the sounds from outside the closet. *Warning. Warning. You're in this room. You're in your body. Secure doors. Lockdown. Warning. Warning.*

IT ALWAYS STARTS AND ENDS with the sound of the alarm. My memory reanimates, engulfs me, and then sends me reeling. After a while, it deposits me back in the closet. I can find some solace here for a moment before the clock chimes and the cycle repeats.

I pass the time between by collecting things, like a crow, amassing treasures that feel important: my lipstick, my journal, my letters. I also steal things. My only excuse is knowing these things will never be missed. They'll be replaced when everything starts over. They always are.

Sometimes, I find new things in the closet. Things I've never seen before. A single earring, a jacket, a doll. Once I found a newspaper. Each one is a clue that time is moving forward somehow, somewhere.

I reach into the folds of my dress and take out the timepiece I swiped from my father's desk. I've stolen this thing so many times, I probably have eight or nine identical ones. I rest the clock on the shelf with all the others and hold the hands still, stopping time for a moment, but eventually the alarm starts to buzz. The mahogany clock chimes in and the memory starts again.

For the Lilies, memory is a weapon.

For me, it is a dead end.

Rory

I HATE MY MOTHER'S CLOSET. It's filled with clutter and malice. This has been the case ever since I was little. I would never tell her this directly, of course. I would never let on that the closet holds more memories than I care to revisit.

The first time I was here was in second grade. I remember how the shelves were stuffed with pennants from the 1950s and '60s, letterman-style jackets from the 1980s, and even some Archwell-branded field hockey masks from the late '90s. There was also a quiver of white cocktail dresses from past Founder's Nights. At first, I thought it was a treasure trove. The emerald and gold memorabilia made for the best game of dress-up ever.

Then I found the Lilies Society stuff. I thought the blindfolds were spooky, but I liked trying on the strange green robes with the gold-ribbon trim. The best was the collection of diamond rings, one from each Lilies cohort, dating back to the society's founding in 1958. Dozens of sparkling infinities. I remember trying to fit all the rings on all ten of my fingers at once. My hands were small back then. They sparkled in the dim light.

Then something shifted.

The clock chimed.

Terror set in.

"What's in that closet is not for public consumption," my mother told me afterward. "The Lilies are a secret society for a reason. And a real Archwell woman never shares her secrets." I remember these words and my mouth goes dry.

I don't know why I let them in here. Between the blaring alarm, the shouting, and the weird phone notifications, I couldn't think straight.

Now, there's no avoiding it. They're going to find out about this place. Their eyes run over every inch of shelving. Every heirloom. Every secret. Each one is a memory, threatening to descend upon me . . . threatening to trap me in my own head.

I wet my lips with my tongue. Try to act normal, I tell myself.

"Don't. Touch. Anything. Please," I say, vocal cords scraping together.

My head is beginning to pound. When you're a Lily, only two things are sacred: memories and secrets. This closet has both.

"I can't get my phone to come back on. Anyone know what time it is?" Blythe directs her question to the others.

"Well, we've got an abundance of antique timepieces in here," Drew says, picking up an old-fashioned metal alarm clock with bells on the top. "And yet . . ." They look the grandfather clock up and down. It's ticking but the hands aren't moving. ". . . yet, we're out of time."

"All the clocks are stopped," Veró says. "But they were ticking a second ago. We can't have been in here that long."

"Feels like forever," Blythe says. I have to agree.

"You hear that?" Drew stiffens and holds up a finger to signal silence.

We wait for a beat and listen. "No," I say. "I don't hear anything."

"Exactly," they answer. "The alarm stopped."

"You mean out there?" Veró says.

"For real?" Blythe stands and leans in close to the slim shadow of the door, listening again. "You're right. I can't hear it. The security message is gone too."

Instinctively, I reach for my cell phone, but the screen is still blank. I hold the tiny power button down but the thing is completely dead. This isn't good.

I stare at the blank screen, willing it to brighten up with a message from my mother. I wish she'd texted me something by now.

This is just a drill.

Everything is fine.

The rehab van is here to get you.

Any message would be better than no message at all.

My tongue is rough and heavy in my mouth. I swallow hard, holding back the fear. If I pretend it's not there, it might go away. Sometimes, I can trick my brain into feeling nothing, into forgetting the difference between what's real and what's not.

"You think we should go out there?" Veró asks. "Or . . . should we wait?"

I conjure the numbness, trying to focus my mind on anything but the closet door. I feel the rub of my school blazer against the back of my neck. I sense the weight of the diamond Lilies ring on my finger. The memory of my grandmother Adeline returns. She tells me, "Archwell women have to be strong. So you need to be a strong girl, Rory. Just like your mother."

I harden my exterior and contort my face into cool, calm confidence. If I pretend to be strong, maybe I'll banish the feeling that I'm losing my grip.

"There's no use in hiding any longer," I say.

I try to stand, hobbling a little on my right leg. We've been crouched together for so long that my foot has fallen asleep. I join Blythe at the closet door and rest my hand on the knob. "There's no use feeling stuck in here when we don't know what's really going on out there."

"Except that, as long as we're in here, no one is gonna make us dead," Drew adds.

"Make us dead?" I ask. What does this kid think this is, a mob movie? "Where did you say you went to school before Archwell?"

"Aight, Rory. We don't need this from you right now." Blythe turns back to the door, shoves me out of the way, and jiggles the handle. "I'm out."

"Wait, don't," Veró presses, but it's too late. Blythe shoves

71

the door ajar and evening sun bursts through the opening. I knew we were in the closet for a long time, but it definitely didn't feel like we were hiding all day. She steps into the light and I follow, squinting.

The room materializes around me. Carved arches stretch their arms up to meet the cathedral ceiling. A wrought-iron balcony keeps us from toppling down into the rows of bookshelves below. This is not my mother's office. But this room, wherever it is, is so familiar.

"Wait." Blythe is at my side. She grips the balcony's metalwork, steadying herself as she does a triple take. "Wait. Hold up."

"Whoa." I turn at the sound of Veró's voice. She is peering out of the closet door behind me, eyes the size of silver dollars. "Where are we?"

"Dang. It's . . . I don't . . ." Gazing out from over Veró's shoulder, Drew wriggles the words out finally. "It's . . . the library. We're on the second floor of McClure Library."

They're right. But my head pounds against the idea that we've emerged from the closet somewhere totally different. This can't be happening. Did I get my morning pills mixed up? Am I seeing things? My eyes scan the room for a sign. I look for crawling walls, angels in the beams of sunlight, beetles marching along the bookshelves. Everything is looking distinctly unpsychedelic. Below, I zero in on the circulation desk. Ms. Katz is sitting there, packing up her belongings for the day. She doesn't see us. Beside her, I can make out the digital clock: *5:12 P.M. OCT 6.*

Oh god. Now I know for sure what this is.

I'm not high anymore. Though I wish I were. I wish this weren't happening. I wish I could go back and change everything.

"I . . . I don't get it. This part of the library is not even on the same side of the building as the chancellor's office. It's . . . it's not close at all," Veró says. "How can we close a door in one place and have it open in another?"

I brace myself. The truth is hard, but there's no avoiding this part of it. "*Ut sacram memoriam*," I mutter to myself. "*Her memory is sacred, beyond the bounds of time.*"

"Huh?" Veró says.

Drew's eyes narrow in on me. "Say that again. *Ut* what?"

"*Ut sacram memoriam*," I repeat. I watch Blythe's jaw clench. Before she can open her mouth, I give her an icy look that says *don't say anything*. We're in uncharted territory now. We should reveal only what we absolutely have to.

"What does that mean?" Drew asks.

"Keep sacred memory." I try to explain, but Veró and Drew are blank. I don't know what I expected. They don't know about our vow. They don't know what it means to go "*beyond the bounds of time.*" They don't keep secrets to survive. They aren't Lilies. But Blythe's face falls, so I know *she* understands what has happened. *She* knows where we are just as well as I do.

"Rory." Veró speaks slowly. "What is going on?"

"We traveled," I say. "We traveled through time."

"No." Blythe starts mumbling to herself. "No, no, no."

73

She balls her right hand into a fist and rubs it against her forehead. Her Lilies ring flashes stars onto the vaulted library ceiling.

"Look at that clock over there." I point to the circulation desk so the others can see. "It's October sixth. Friday evening. We've gone back to last Friday. Founder's Night."

"No. No. No. No. No." Blythe's pacing now, rubbing the band of her ring against her forehead.

"Wait. Hold on. You're telling me that your mom has a *time travel closet*? In her office?" Veró's voice is flat. Her tone matches the side-eye she's giving me.

"That's messed-up," Drew mumbles.

"It's not like that. This is . . . the Lilies Society calls it the memory loop. Or just the loop. Memories are sacred. But they can be dangerous. Sometimes you get caught up in them. You can end up reliving the past in an infinite cycle. The same memory again and again. *The present turns to past.*"

"No, Rory. No." Blythe's voice has tears in it now. "This is not for real. I'm not doing this again. This is not a real thing."

"What is the Lilies Society?" Veró asks. "Is that what you call y'all's secret club?"

"What's this gotta do with the closet?" Drew asks.

"I'm not doing this. No." Blythe grabs me by the arm and yanks me back toward the closet door. My shoulder nearly dislodges against the door frame as Blythe pushes Veró and Drew back into the dim and pulls me in behind her. The

74

closet slams shut and we're in total darkness again, bodies piled together on the floor.

"Ew, get off me, Rory." Veró's voice is a dart in the dark.

"Gah, I'm trying. It's not like I would try anything gross at a time like this," I spit back.

"Ugh . . . help." Drew's muffled voice emerges from the bottom of the pile. "Please get off."

Someone pulls the light switch and we untangle ourselves. Blythe curls into a ball, blocking the door with her body. Sweat makes the deep brown of her skin glow. The rest of us sit on the floor, resting our backs against the shelves.

"I'm not going back out there, Rory," Blythe whispers. "It's bullshit. I never believed the legend about the loop. If I don't believe in it, then I shouldn't have to deal with it. Y'all can do what you want but I'm staying right here."

"So . . . hold on," Drew says. "Do you mind bringing the new kid up to speed?"

"Yeah, a few of us are lost," Veró adds.

I let my eyes drift to the bare bulb on the ceiling. The glow creates a dark halo in my line of vision. I focus on it and try to keep my voice steady. I wish I had absolutely *any* of the little baggies in my jewelry box. An Anny, or even some sand. It would make it so much easier to explain all of this.

"Blythe and I are in the Lilies Society," I breathe. "We're not supposed to talk about it. But that's what half of the stuff in this closet is for. These robes, the blindfolds, the rings, the candles, the infinities: it's all Lilies stuff."

"So y'all are like cosplaying as the Illuminati?" Veró interrupts.

I scrunch my eyes closed. I can still see the halo of light, dancing against the back of my eyelids. "No. And the Illuminati is fake, Verónica."

"That's exactly what someone in the Illuminati would say," Drew chimes in.

Veró sighs. "I knew all y'all Archwell legacies were up to some old-school, culty shit."

"The Lilies Society is *not* a cult." I hear the edge in my tone so I try to soften it a bit. I'm going to need the others on my side if we're going to make it out of here in one piece. And I'm the only one who can get us out of here because I'm the only one who knows what to do before it's too late.

I was raised to do this . . . to be ready for anything. Being a Lily is in my blood.

I compose myself and try to explain. "Blythe and I have been with the Lilies since tenth grade. My grandmother Adeline and her friends started the society back when she was an Archwell student in the 1950s. Her father founded the academy back in '52 so his daughters would have somewhere safe to go to school."

"Gah. We already know all about your creepy family," Veró groans. "*Before the women's liberation movement, Archwell Academy was founded for girls to have a place to thrive away from the world of men.* We all read the brochure. Can you get to the point?"

I ignore the tone. What I have to explain next is too

important to worry about little slights. "It's tradition to have Lilies initiates explore their pasts. New pledges have to share their deepest secrets with the bigs. That's how we can tell if someone is serious about being a Lily: if they're willing to relive their worst moments and tell us their darkest secrets."

"So . . . you all know the worst thing about them. It's like blackmail." Veró's voice is stony.

"Not exactly," I answer, opening my eyes and zeroing in my gaze on her. Her brow is knitted, her eyes burning into mine. This girl has never liked me even though I've been nothing but sweet to her. She willingly misunderstands me. "Sharing secrets is how we bond with our littles. It's a supportive sisterhood."

Veró lets out a snort. "Sisterhood. Yeah. I'm sure . . . I suppose you have to be a legacy to join?"

"Not all Lilies are legacies," I say, eyes flickering to Blythe for a second. "But every descendant of a Lily is guaranteed legacy membership."

"Is that right?" Drew's voice has shifted from playful to poisonous. "Everyone?"

We lock eyes. I let my gaze glide over their unibrow, their unwaxed upper lip, their oversized oxford shirt. "Yep." I say, working hard to keep my voice even. "Everyone."

Drew looks like they want to say something else but they stay silent.

"How is all of this connected to this closet and the library?" Veró asks.

"Some of the Lilies say that the loop isn't just a symbolic

thing where they confess their worst memories during initiation. They relive those moments *for real*. It's an actual time loop where girls return to their worst memories again and again." My eyes slide over to Blythe, still crouched by the door, body rising and falling with every jagged breath. "I've only heard stories about it, but the legend has been handed down forev—"

"This isn't an initiation," Drew interrupts. "Veró isn't a Lily. And neither am I. So why are *we* in the loop?"

"I don't know," I answer honestly. "I just know there's only one way out." I reach over and touch Blythe's shoulder. She recoils. "The loop will focus on each of us, one at a time. We have to relive whatever memory it chooses for us. There's no stopping it. The only way to get out of it is to let each memory play out exactly as it happened and not change a single detail. Just like the initiates do at a Lilies initiation when they share their secrets."

"How do you know all of this?" Veró asks, her side-eye boring into my forehead.

"I just do, okay? I was born into all of this."

"Ah yes." Veró nods sarcastically. "Good old institutional prejudice at work. We've got a nepo baby on our hands."

"A what?" Drew asks.

"Nepotism baby . . . ?" Veró answers. "It's a *thing*, okay?"

"If you say so." Drew shrugs.

I brush past Veró's dismissiveness and Drew's ambivalence. "Listen to me! We just have to go out there, let each memory play out, and we'll all be okay. We do that, one by one, and we'll close the loop. We'll be able to get out."

"And if we don't?" Drew asks.

"Don't what?"

"If we *don't* relive our memories exactly as they happened . . . we *won't* get out okay?"

For a moment, no one says anything. Blythe stays curled by the door. Veró crosses her arms, as if to protect herself. Drew opens their mouth again. "I mean, I don't know about y'all, but I'd love to find a way to avoid reliving the worst night of my life exactly as it happened. Just doesn't sound like my cup of tea."

I shake my head slowly. They clearly have no idea what we're up against. *"As the clock hands turn, memory erodes the mind,"* I say. The line is branded into my brain though I've only spoken it aloud a few times. There's a big part of me that can't believe that I'm sharing this much with non-initiates. But since they aren't actually Lilies, they can't know what it all *really* means . . . which gives me an advantage.

"You can't subvert the memory loop," I explain to Drew. "It'll just keep repeating again and again until your mind turns to dust. That's the legend anyway."

There's a distinct click and all four of us turn toward the grandfather clock at the back of the closet.

"Did the big hand on that thing just move?" Veró asks.

Behind Blythe, the hardware of the doorknob creaks on its own and the closet door opens just a sliver. Before anyone else manages to react, Blythe reaches up and snaps the door shut again, holding the knob in her hand so it can't open without her consent.

Then the sobs come. "I told you, Rory, I'm not doing Founder's Night again." She gasps for breath, rattling into a higher octave. "You can say anything you want. I'm not doing it." She shudders through her tears. Her breath is ragged. Her panic attack is in full swing. I reach for her hand that isn't glued to the doorknob. "I don't care about the Lilies. I just want to get out of here and go home," she wheezes. "I just wanna go home." She rips her hand away from me and covers her face.

I hate seeing Blythe like this. It makes me want to break down too.

Grandma Adeline's words run through my head again and I find myself parroting them aloud. "We have to be strong," I murmur, trying to be gentle as I coach her to breathe. I rest my hand on her back. I'm careful to not muss her hair. We all sit there in silence for a minute, letting Blythe's energy swirl around the closet. Eventually she stops crying and her breathing calms.

I whisper to her. "Blythe, we have to be strong. The only way out is through."

Veró

GOOD ART WEAVES TOGETHER TRACES of open secrets: the truths that we live with but don't want to talk about. Folks don't always like what each piece has to say, but resistance is one of the ways you know your work is honest. You know a piece has been *really* successful when the art and reality flow together like two streams into a wide river.

I wish I could say that I learned about good art through creating it myself, but mostly I've learned through listening. You know how people say that a piece of art "speaks" to them? Since I was little, art has spoken to me. Not exactly with words . . . although I don't know how else to correctly describe it. I guess it's more like a mind meld. Murals come to life. Paintings invite me closer. La Virgen de Guadalupe, depicted as a seamstress by Yolanda López, winks at me.

At first Mami and Papi thought it was cute. "Look at Verónita! She thinks the painting is alive! She's talking to it." They didn't realize that I knew better than them about what the painting was doing.

The first time I got in trouble as Malcriada was at the Getty Center when I was five. We were in a gallery with gray walls and a high glass ceiling. We'd come to see a portrait called *La Revolucionaria*. Within seconds of walking into the space, *La Revolucionaria* locked eyes with me. At first she glared, the way she was glaring at everyone else. But when she recognized me, she started to smile. She didn't open her mouth—paintings rarely do—but I could still hear her speak to me.

It's impolite to stare, she said. *But you're not the first.*

"I'm sorry," I said.

I noticed how beautiful her skirt was, layered with a matte paint that almost looked like paper. It was the color of a watermelon-flavored candy. My favorite kind.

You want to touch? she asked me. *Go 'head, I guess. Nobody ever touches. It'd be a nice change.* I reached out and felt the texture of the paint beneath my fingers, smooth rivulets with rough, hardened edges. It felt like if I pressed hard enough, the globbed-on paint might give in to my little fingers, like hardened Play-Doh.

"Hey, she can't touch that," someone rumbled behind me. Then I heard the *BLEEPBLEEPBLEEP* of an alarm and someone was yanking me hard by the arm. I screamed, feeling my limb nearly slip from its socket. My eyes burned hot and I let out one long wail.

"Tranquila, Veró!" I recognized Papi's voice, hard and angry. "You can't touch. How many times do I have to tell you? Niña malcriada!" He swept me up in his arms. "Quiet, quiet now."

I caught a glimpse of *La Revolucionaria* as Papi whisked me out of the gallery. She was grinning at me, shaking her head as if it had all been a game.

Mi niñita malcriada, she clucked.

To this day, I will not go back to the Getty. *La Revolucionaria* is in their permanent collection and I don't trust her not to mess with me again. What happened between us stayed a secret.

I have to be secretive about art. It was the only way to make sure Malcriada survived . . . at least until I blew it with my installation in the belfry. I suppose the secrets remain, even if Malcriada doesn't.

I can tell that the chancellor's closet is full of these kinds of secrets, each one a loose thread on a silk gown. I can feel it. As Malcriada, I would have been able to weave all the threads together into a new garment and make sense of it all. But now that she's gone forever, the closet is just a wall of sounds that it seems only I can hear: a sea of wails welling up from the past. There's pain in these rings, these clocks, in the lining of these robes. Pain that means something, but I can't decipher it. It will not speak to me. It only cries.

I see that pain on Rory's and Blythe's faces as they huddle together in front of the closet's opening. It's the pain of whatever waits for them on the other side of that door: their worst memories, their biggest secrets. The muscles in my shoulders pinch. I know that *my* worst memory is waiting for me too. The realization fastens itself to my neck like a vampire bat.

I'm not proud of what I did on Founder's Night, and I'm with three people who are going to relive it with me. They'll see the truth, see me for what I am: a vandal and a villain. See the installation that went so wrong: the one for which I'll never be forgiven.

Drew will definitely hate me for it. And what then? We're the only two outsiders here. I need them on my side. I shiver and pull Malcriada's black hoodie closer to my body.

"What happens if we just stay in the closet?" I ask.

Rory shakes her head solemnly. "Same as if you stayed in any closet. Starvation? Death? The faster we can move through the memories, the faster we can get out of the loop. The Lilies initiation basically trained us for this. We just . . . didn't realize it wasn't a metaphor."

She stands and helps Blythe to her feet, rests her hands on her shoulders. "How are you feeling?"

"Fine," she says. She uses that word a lot . . . even when she's clearly not fine. But I can't blame her. If I got mixed up in all this secret cult crap, I would be beside myself too.

Wait. I *am* mixed up in it.

We're all in the same boat now.

"Are you sure?" Rory asks Blythe, genuine concern on her face.

Blythe takes a deep breath. "I don't have a choice, it

sounds like. We all gotta make it through the loop. I guess we're just starting with *my* worst memory. It's okay. I can go first. Really, it's fine."

It's definitely not fine, I think to myself.

"Wait," Drew says. "Your worst memory happened on Founder's Night?"

"Yeah." Blythe narrows her eyes. "Why?"

"Nothing," Drew shoves their hands in their pockets. "I guess I just thought we were going into my worst memory. I'm . . . not proud of what happened on Founder's Night either."

"Interesting," Rory says.

Something pricks at the back of my neck. I get a strange sense. Like déja vu, but not quite. Are *all* our worst memories of Founder's Night?

I envision a string invisibly tying us together. Each of our memories, a link in a chain. I see it so clearly, as if the image were painted on canvas. For a second I consider whether or not to keep the premonition to myself. Then I decide: in this situation, it's better for all of us to operate with the same set of information, at least for now.

"So," I cut in. "I had some pretty messed-up stuff happen on Founder's Night too."

"Are you saying that all four of our worst memories—"

"—happened within the same twenty-four hours?" Rory cuts Drew off, stating the truth of the matter before I can. "Yes."

"What exactly does *that* mean?" Blythe asks.

"Not sure." Rory is serious, her face clouded with confusion.

"I guess we'll find out," Drew says. "So . . . let's do the time warp?" they ask.

The four of us nod to one another, sealing our agreement to open the door.

"Whose worst memory started in the library at five twelve p.m.?" Rory asks.

I close my eyes and gulp as much air as I can. My fingers dig into my forearms. I steady myself. My body is already giving away a trace of my secret. Malcriada's ghost whispers to me. *Go ahead and say it.*

"It's mine," I say as I step toward the door and pull it open. "It's my memory."

I take a step outside of the closet. The library looks as it always has. But at the same time, the air feels heavier and colder than I remember. On the mezzanine of the reading room, the shadows are like storm clouds, dark and thick somehow. I notice the bookshelf at my elbow is littered with dead flies. Gross. I flick one to the ground and its little black body disappears into the plush green carpet.

From here on the balcony, I can see Mrs. Pendleton, the head of security, and Jerry, the maintenance guy, below. They're hauling in event tables, banners, and tablecloths—all in dark green and gold—for Founder's Night. An army of black-eyed Susans and calla lilies stands at the ready.

Something about the light in the room makes the white petals look a little gray. I catch a sickeningly sweet whiff of the floral arrangements. I gag.

Yes, this is Founder's Night as we all experienced it, but here in the loop, the memory is twisted into something else. Familiar but also . . . grotesque.

I glance at the clock. *5:15 P.M., OCT 6.*

"What now?" Drew asks, snapping the closet door shut behind us. "Veró, should we follow you?"

"I guess," I say. "I really don't know how this works."

I glance at Rory for a split second, the ringleader of this cursed quest. When I feel her eyes on me, I let my gaze float up to the ceiling. I don't want to give her the satisfaction of thinking that she's in charge here.

"Or should we split up?" Drew asks. "We weren't all together on Friday evening, obviously. If we have to replay the memory as it happened, does it make sense to stay together?"

"It all depends," Rory says. "It's five fifteen now. Do you remember where you were at this time last Friday, Veró?"

I hesitate. It's not that I don't remember. It's that I don't want to think about it. I summon the memory of my alibi reluctantly. *At five thirty p.m. Friday, October 6, Veró Martín is on the first floor of McClure Library, "volunteering" for the Student Activities Committee. No one sees her slip behind the swinging door marked* Girls.

But then the rest of the memory comes.

87

The smell of spray paint.

Charlotte's scowl.

The terrible, sinking feeling of being caught.

There's a new tension in my throat that wasn't there before. It's painful, remembering that you're the villain in someone's story.

I cringe and muster the guts to answer. "I was definitely in the library," I say. "As for my exact location at five fifteen sharp . . . I can take us to the general coordinates. I remember checking the time around five thirty."

"Why don't we all stick together, then?" Blythe asks. "The rest of us can duck out of sight when the time comes," she tells me.

I nod. "All right. Let's go."

The four of us slink down one of the spiral staircases. I grip the railing with both my hands, letting the extra-long sleeves of my sweatshirt slide along the cool wrought iron. We reach the bottom of the steps. To our right, there's the arched stone doorway. I know it leads to a hallway that connects to the library courtyard. Was I still out in the courtyard at 5:15 last Friday? I can't remember that part of my day. Out of curiosity, I turn the knob and push. The door doesn't open.

"That's weird," Blythe says, glancing up at the electric red letters—*Emergency Exit*. "Shouldn't this be unlocked at all times?"

"Could be a fluke," Drew says.

We steal behind a row of low bookshelves, toward the main library entrance. The sound of muffled voices and furniture dragging across the carpet has stopped. Pendleton and Jerry must've finished their part of the event set up. The rest is left for all of us on the Student Activities Committee. I glance at the circulation desk. Ms. Katz is gone for the day too. The library is empty except for the four of us.

No one says a word as we make our way to the double doors that lead out to Archwell's quad. As we walk, I can feel Rory's breath on the back of my neck. I tense and glance back over my shoulder. She's trailing behind me by at least eight feet. So why do I feel like someone's following close, watching my every move? In front of the double doors, Drew jostles both handles. They do not budge.

"They're stuck," Drew says. "Not locked. See?" They point to the latch at the top of the doorway that secures the entrance from the inside. It's open.

Fear loops around the nape of my neck like Mami's string of pearls. The doors *will* open. Just not for us. We're stuck in here. I suppose we all already knew that. But it doesn't make it any less frightening. The rules here are unfamiliar and unpredictable—it makes it hard for me to bend them.

In a panic, the others try to pitch in with opening the doors, struggling against the polished wood and hardware. My eyes pause on the gilded portrait above the exit. It's of a woman with a gray bob and beige pantsuit. The portrait's frame sports a shiny engraved plaque: ADELINE AMELIA

89

ARCHWELL, SCHOOL CHANCELLOR 1975–2011. She frowns down at me, and says, *Better watch yourself. You're not supposed to be here.*

"Listen," I say, speaking to the others but not daring to avert my eyes from the portrait's glare. "My memory happened here in the library before Founder's Night. And we have to let the memories play out exactly as they happened, right? So, maybe that means we can't go anywhere on campus that I didn't actually go to in my memory?"

"That makes sense," Rory says.

Blythe chimes in. "So, okay, let's go where you were. The sooner we're done with this the better."

Drew groans. "So much for getting some fresh air."

I lead the group away from Adeline Archwell's disapproving gaze. We end up congregating around the water fountain outside the girls' bathroom, at the edge of the stacks. Rory stoops to take a sip. I imagine the taste of memory water: bitter and congealed.

"Maybe don't do that, Ror," Blythe says.

"Yeah, you don't know what memory water will do to you," Drew adds.

Rory gulps the water down anyway. Watching her do it makes my intestines slither against each other. My stomach turns. "Mala suerte," I mutter to myself.

Rory scowls at me. "You wouldn't know anything about it," she snipes.

"No, I wouldn't! *You're* the expert on this creepy-ass

place. We get it," I spit back. This girl is really working on my last nerve.

Before Rory can get any uglier, the echoing creak of the library's main doorway makes me jump. It's strange to hear it open and close after all the efforts to pry the thing ajar. The sound announces something important: someone is in the main atrium with us.

"Veronica?" A tinny voice calls from a few bookshelves away. I can't see her face, but I recognize the vibration of Charlotte Vanderheyden's words. It makes my skin prickle. This is the beginning of something bad. All eyes are on me now as Charlotte calls my name again, drawing out the central *ó* sound into a long, Americanized *ahhh*.

"Ver-AH-ni-CAH?"

I hate it when white people say my name like that.

The others are paralyzed by the sound of the approaching sophomore. Blythe is frozen, as if she's heard the voice of a ghost brought back from the grave. Rory's glaring at me, but I see some fear underneath that poisonous look. Drew's face bears the shadow of betrayal, as if the sound of Charlotte's words has opened an old wound.

It's all kind of weird. I thought I was the only one who had beef with Charlotte . . . although I suppose Drew and Charlotte weren't winning any contests for best roommates.

I whisper my explanation. "Charlotte and I are both on the Student Activities Committee. We're supposed to be decorating for Founder's Night starting at five thirty."

Charlotte and I never really vibed, but I'll admit that she wasn't the worst person to have on the committee. Everyone else was deeply wrapped up in the nostalgia of Founder's Night. Silks, lace, pearls: it was all the usual prep school bullshit. But serving on a committee is a grad requirement and Student Activities seemed easy enough to coast through. Plus, the meetings were virtual so I could keep my camera off and work on my 404 pages in peace for most of them.

I'd pretty much completely tuned out of the last committee meeting when Charlotte interrupted Libby Hallsworth before she could move on to the next agenda item.

"What about the layout plan?" she asked.

"What do you mean?" Libby snipped.

"You have standing tables planned out and then those banquet tables with the little aisles . . . I'm not sure if that's the most accessible."

"We'll let maintenance figure it out. They're doing all the setup and takedown for the banquet." Libby was ready to move on, but Charlotte pushed.

"I'm not sure that's gonna be enough. I feel like it's this committee's responsibility to make sure the space is accessible."

Libby rolled her eyes. "Do you even know if anyone there is going to be a wheelchair user?"

Charlotte's nostrils flared, her cheeks flashing pink. She leaned into the camera. "Does it matter, Libby?"

At a loss, Libby countered. "If you care so much, then why don't you volunteer for setup?"

"All right," Charlotte said. "Sign me up."

So Charlotte and I wound up on setup duty together. Like I said, it could've been worse. But it also could've been better.

"Veronica, where are you? We need to get started!" Charlotte's voice carries over the tops of the bookshelves, closer than it was before.

"What do you remember saying to her when she first arrived to meet you?" Rory whispers. I think for a second. "Quick," she hisses. "It has to be exactly the same as you remember it or the loop will reset."

It's hard to ignore Rory's tone but I do what she says. I call out to Charlotte. "I'm just in the bathroom. Be out in a sec!"

"K. But hurry up though! After we finish setting up, I still need to get my hair done." Charlotte's voice doesn't come any closer. I hear the sound of a bag flopping onto a table and the groan of an old desk under someone's body weight.

Boo-boo-boop. Boo-boo-boop.

"Is she video chatting someone?" Blythe whispers.

Drew bends down, squinting through the gaps in the bookshelves, trying to catch a glimpse of Charlotte's deep red locks. "I can see her," they whisper. The rest of us crouch down next to Drew and peer through the bookcase. Sure enough, Charlotte is sitting there with her back to us. She is holding her phone out in front of her, angling the camera lens just so.

Boop. Someone picks up the call.

"Char, where are you? We're all here in Maddie's room getting ready to go to dinner." I don't recognize the voice on the phone, but I feel Drew stiffen next to me.

They catch me looking at them and whisper, "It's Faith Harlow. She and Charlotte are tight." Clearly, Drew isn't a fan of Faith's. It makes sense. Faith is one of the chancellor's minions and a royal pain in the ass. It wouldn't surprise me if she and Charlotte were quietly torturing a kid like Drew in the privacy of their dorm room.

Faith's voice rings through the cell phone speaker at a higher pitch than Charlotte's. Her words come out faster, almost gargled. "We need you over here, girl! It's a big night!"

Charlotte plays with a curled petal on one of the flower arrangements as she speaks into the phone. "I told you. I gotta set up at the library first. I'll be over soon—whenever this weirdo senior from the committee finishes dropping a deuce so we can get started."

Drew regains the twinkle in their eye as they peer over at me. "Is it true?"

"What?" I breathe.

"Were you dropping a deuce? Is *that* your worst memory?"

"Oh my god, Drew. Shut up." I knew I liked this kid. I don't think anyone else in the world would make a potty joke at a time like this.

"Must've been an epic deposit," Drew continues.

"For real, Drew, shut up. I'm trying to hear." Blythe's voice is low and sharp. She and Rory wear permanent scowls.

Charlotte and Faith yammer on for a while about what they're going to wear to Founder's Night, what booze they're going to try to sneak in, and the "top-secret thing" they're going to do after. "My mom's a legacy and she said that it's not so bad," Faith explains on the phone. "She said the hardest part for her was staying up super late."

"Yeah? My grandma Evelyn's stories are way scarier," Charlotte says. "Initiation is no joke. She told me all about it. Every detail."

"Oh my god, Charlotte. Your grandma is totally not supposed to talk to you about initiation," Faith shrills into the phone.

"So what? Neither is your mom! Plus, I'm her granddaughter. She's not gonna keep secrets from *me*. She's just trying to prepare me for what I'm getting into with the Lilies."

"Gah! Don't say the name. Like, just stop talking right now."

"What's the deal with the initiation thing they're talking about?" Drew whispers.

"It's more freaky, culty, secret society shit," I answer.

Rory keeps her mouth shut, even though I can tell it's taking every ounce of her willpower.

"Don't talk about what you can't understand," Blythe says. I don't expect the jab, and before I can respond Rory springs for the jugular.

"What happened between you and Charlotte?"

"What do you mean?" I try to stall. She's about to see the

95

whole thing play out anyway. No use in rehashing what I'm about to relive.

"You *do* realize that Charlotte hasn't been seen since Friday night, right? You were clearly one of the last people to see her."

The memory of Charlotte's scowl reassembles in my mind. Then her frown twists into a new shape. Her red hair fades to gray and suddenly I can see the portrait of Rory's steely grandmother hanging over me again. Something is really, really wrong here. I feel like I'm losing it. Charlotte is . . . missing?

I turn to Drew. "I thought you said that she went home to Potomac over the weekend?"

"You know Charlotte too?" Blythe turns to Drew. "Who told you she went home? Did you see her? Like, in the flesh?"

Drew seems to crumple under Blythe's rapid-fire questions. As I watch them silently wither, my stomach twists. I resist the urge to tell Blythe to lay off. Finally, Drew manages to squeak out a partial response. "Charlotte was my roommate."

There's that word again: *was.* Past tense.

Before I can totally spin out about all the reasons why this situation is deeply not okay, Malcriada's ghost comes to me. *Keep it together,* she says. *Gather your thoughts. Get caught up. Then get ahead.* I breathe out and review what I know.

One: Drew and Charlotte were roommates.

Two: Charlotte was a Lilies legacy member.

Three: Charlotte has not been seen since Founder's Night.

I breathe in and choose my next words carefully. "Didn't Charlotte just say that later tonight—aka Friday night—she's going to join the Lilies for an initiation? Wouldn't that suggest that *you two* were some of the last people to see Charlotte?" I gesture to Blythe and Rory.

"Oh man," Drew says. "That's right! She never made it back to our room after Founder's Night."

Blythe opens her mouth but no sound comes out. Rory speaks for her, "Nice try, Veró, but you're barking up the wrong tree. You don't know what we saw or didn't see on Friday night."

"I bet I will know . . . pretty soon," I say. "I bet I already know about some of the secrets that your little society might be hiding. I can think of at least one secret about your mommy, the chancellor."

Rory screws up her face. "What's my mother got to do with it?"

"Cool it, y'all," Drew says. "Regardless of what happened, all our memories overlap with Charlotte somehow. That's gotta mean something . . . right? What happens next in your memory, Veró?"

I sigh. Things were just about to get juicy. "Charlotte gets restless," I answer. "She starts to wonder where I am, so she—"

Charlotte appears at the end of the corridor of shelves.

"Uh, Veronica, what the hell? I thought we were gonna set up the space together. Wait, why are all of you hiding back here?"

BONG!

The sound of a clock chime reverberates from the library rafters. Charlotte has found us, *all* of us. This isn't how the memory played out the first time. I was supposed to be alone in the bathroom when Charlotte found me.

BONG!

I feel my body seize and thrash and then I'm disintegrating, flying apart in every direction. We're falling away. We all are. Together, we are pulled back into darkness.

BONG!

Rory

I KNOW THIS FEELING—THE FEELING of falling apart and coming back together again.

My molecules are suddenly rearranged.

I'm both fragile and elastic, delicate and invincible. It's the all-too-familiar feeling of coming down from a high—a telltale sign that a dose of sand is starting to wear off. It's the same feeling that I get now as I'm sucked out of Veró's memory and spit back into the closet where we started. The four of us are left sprawled out on the floor, breathless and queasy. It doesn't feel great, but at least we're all alive. For a second, I wasn't sure whether I'd make it through.

"Everyone okay?" I rasp.

"What *was* that?" Drew asks, rising to their feet. "I hated it."

"That was the loop," I say. "It reset."

"Oh lord," Blythe mutters. She is sitting on the floor, leaning against the closet door, looking like she's about to lose her lunch.

"We've gotta do that *every* time?" Drew asks. "That felt like being in a blender."

"More like a hurricane," Veró says, coming to a stand. She massages a knot on her shoulder.

I shrug. "Hate to say I told you so, but . . ."

"You didn't exactly mention being ripped apart at an atomic level. I would've remembered that." As Drew speaks, they finger the sleeve of one of the hanging white gowns. In the dim, I can make out the lace pattern overlaid on the satin. My stomach clenches in on itself and the words fly out of my mouth before I can think.

"Don't touch that," I say. "It isn't yours."

Drew yanks their hand away, as if my words have turned the white satin into hot coals. "Sheesh," they say. "Sor-ry."

"It's not yours either by the look of it." Veró swoops in, reaching around Drew to pluck the gown's hanger from the rack. She holds it out in front of her, examining the dress's tapering neck and A-line '50s skirt. Some of the ivory crin-oline petticoats start to fall out of the bottom of the dress, and I flinch.

One time when I was little, I pulled that same gown from the hanger and laid it out on the floor as a blanket. I don't really remember why . . . maybe to ground myself or something. I could've been protecting myself from roving spiders . . . or intrusive thoughts.

When my mother came to get me out of the closet, she looked absolutely horrified. "What are you doing?" Her voice was the sharpest it had ever been . . . at least up to that point. She would get even sharper with me later, her words cutting deeper and deeper with each passing year. "Lilies things aren't toys," she said. "Family heirlooms aren't toys."

"Put it back," I growl. "It's a family heirloom. It belongs at the back of the closet."

"Then why was it hanging right here?" Veró asks.

"Because it belongs with the other Lilies stuff," I say.

"Which is it then?" Drew asks. "A family heirloom or a Lilies thing? Does it belong up here or does it belong in the back of the closet?"

I don't know why, but the question makes me so angry. It's a stupid question, really. It's not an either/or answer. For Archwell women, there is no difference between family heirlooms and Lilies things.

There's no use in arguing. I yank the hanger out of Veró's hands and hold the dress close to my body. It's laced with the smell of lilacs and radiates an unexpected warmth.

My mother made it very clear that I was never supposed to touch this gown again. Not after she found it on the floor. "It isn't yours to play around with," she said. "It's not mine to handle either. It's all your grandma Adeline had left of her sister. It's special. I don't want you to ruin it."

Now, smoothing the wrinkles from the gown's skirt, I'm surprised to find that it's already ruined.

"Oh no." Just below the gown's neckline, I see the flecks of blood. Bright crimson dribbles down the front of the dress. My heart starts to pump harder as my fists clench the bodice of the gown. This is really bad, the kind of bad I might not be able to get around.

"What's this? What did you do?" My voice barely sounds like my own. It comes out as a low growl.

Veró stands between me and Drew, shielding them from my words. "That stain was already there. I saw it when I pulled it off the rack."

"Impossible," I say. "This gown belonged to my great-aunt Lillian. It never had a stain on it before."

Drew checks their cuticles before holding their fingers up for me to see. "I'm sorry, Rory, but my hands are clean. I have no idea how that got on there. Must be old."

"If it's old, then why is the blood fresh?" I ask. "Old blood dries brown. Everybody knows that."

Veró and Drew steal a quick glance at each other. I know what they're thinking: that I'm overreacting, that I'm being over the top. But when my mother sees this, she is going to kill me. They may think they know the wrath of Eleanor Archwell, but they have no idea. As soon as I notice I'm digging my nails into the fabric, I loosen my grip on the dress. My tongue is as dry as a mothball. I need water and about five Annys.

"Rory," Blythe says. She stoops down and snatches something from underneath the rack of cloaks and gowns. "This fell off the hanger."

At first it looks like Blythe is handing me a Lilies robe, but when I get ahold of the thing, I realize it's softer and a bit smaller. It has no hood, but the color is identical.

"I think it's a blanket," Blythe says. And as she does, I realize there is some wetness to it. I hang the gown from one of the shelf ledges and hold the blanket up to the light. It is dark green, so the stain isn't as obvious, but it's there. Fresh blood.

Drew says, "That's really weird."

"Do you think someone used the blanket to clean up blood?" Veró asks.

I lower the blanket and meet her eyes. "My mother is the only one who uses this closet," I explain. "She's the only one with the keys. I don't think she would use something like this to clean up blood, of all things, and then just throw it on a family treasure to dry."

Veró shrugs. "You said yourself that this closet is filled with Lilies stuff. Do you think someone from the Lilies Society put it in here?"

"What are you implying?" Blythe narrows her eyes at Veró.

"Only that y'all trade in secrets. It just seems possible to me, since most of the stuff in this closet has some relationship to the Lilies, that this might too."

"What would a Lily be doing cleaning up someone else's blood?" I ask. I hate the implication Veró is making, but I am trying to see if she's brave enough to put it into plain words. I know it's a gamble, but I like my odds. Verónica Martín doesn't have the ovaries to accuse the Lilies of murder. She doesn't have the guts to say that she thinks this is Charlotte's blood.

My bet pays off. Veró says nothing.

Instead, Drew breaks the silence. "Are we ready to go back out there and find Charlotte?" Some may find it endearing, but I swear, Drew has the tact and cunning of a Great Dane. It doesn't matter, though. It's easy to use to my advantage.

"Yes," I say, folding the blanket and placing it on a shelf. "Veró, take us to Charlotte."

I want out of this closet. True, I got us into this mess by agreeing to unlock the door and shuttle us all in here. Even though it was the *last* thing I wanted to do. But at least I haven't had to reveal all of my secrets—and I intend to keep it that way. As long as I can hold the memories at arm's length, I'll be okay. I have to be.

The loop is dangerous, yes. But if I've learned anything as a Lily, it's that secrets and memories are the most valuable currency.

THE GOWN WAS BOUGHT FOR my graduation. Yes, I got it nearly a year in advance, but it looked so picture-perfect in the shop window. I tried it on for Evelyn as a surprise. I paired it with a crimson lip and my class ring.

In my recollection, the dress is a perfect, silky ivory. But then the memory cycles through to its ultimate conclusion and the gown is ruined every time. It dies a thousand deaths, just like me. And every time I return to the closet, the stain from my blood is fresh.

My senior portrait was never hung. My graduation cap was never ordered. So, I put the dress in a place where they can see it.

I want them to know what happened.

I need them to remember that I existed.

I need them to sound the alarm.

Blythe

I'M THE NEAREST TO THE closet door, so the others look to me to open it. I don't want to. The memory isn't even mine, but it makes my fear swell inside of me just the same. Panic attacks are like earthquakes: once there's been a full-blown one, there's always the risk of aftershocks. It's when I'm at my most vulnerable that I'm most likely to be carried away by a memory or a feeling. I have to be careful about getting my mind right and keeping it that way, but it's really hard.

In my sociology class, we read about a famous experiment where psychologists asked participants to do a certain task while trying not to think about a white bear. But the people in the experiment said that trying not to think about the bear just made him appear in their minds even more.

For me, Founder's Night is a white bear.

Charlotte, my Lilies little, is a white bear.

Everything about the loop screams it at me.

"Blythe, you're going to hurt your fingers."

Rory's words make me think to look down at my nails.

Every one is chewed, three out of ten have no polish left at all. Sean and Salim will not go easy on me . . . assuming that I ever see them again.

I already lost them once before . . .

Oh no. I feel the memory rushing toward me like a tidal wave.

I'm running through the DC streets.

I feel myself losing my grip on Sean's hand all over again, and it feels like I'm falling.

I'm alone in a swirl of people, faces covered, eyes watering. Where are my brothers?

Careful, Blythe, I tell myself. *That memory's a white bear too. It's a trap your mind sets. You're not back there. You're here in this closet. Your hand is on the door.*

I try to ground myself, locking eyes with Rory, who's looking genuinely concerned. The doorknob feels like an ice cube in my hand. I breathe in the closet's staleness, mothballs and dried lavender.

"Are you okay?" Rory asks.

"I'm fine," I say.

Fine. It's the only acceptable way of saying *I'm scared.*

Scared of what I'm about to see. And scared of what's bound to happen—the others will see exactly what I did. Guilt clamps down on every muscle in my body. The closet door stays closed.

"Before we go out there, I wanted to ask—"

I'm relieved by Drew's interruption. I let go of the

doorknob and cross my arms, reminding myself that I am still in my body. The swell of panic subsides a little.

"—to avoid the reset, can we just take the most direct route to relive the memory as it happened?" they ask.

"About that," Veró says. "I didn't want to say before, but the whole thing actually happened in the bathroom."

"I knew it!" Drew grins manically. "The worst dump of your life. That's your horrible memory!"

"No." Veró smiles a little, but I can tell she's clouding over. The sorrow in her eyes softens my fear into sadness. I've been so caught up in my own insecurities about what happened on Founder's Night that I never considered that Veró would be dreading reliving her darkest moment, too.

"All right, then. Let's go and get it right this time," Rory gruffs. Her tone is a machete slashing at everything and everyone in her path. "Move." She forces the closet open and leads us back out into the library.

But it doesn't really feel like the library anymore. While it's definitely the same room, the light has a strange green tinge to it now. A horrible rotting smell worms its way up from the bookshelves below, collecting into a cloud under the cathedral ceiling. I recognize the odor of flower stems decaying in water.

"What's with the nasty smell?" I murmur. "I thought the memory was supposed to stay the same. Or did we already move on to a different one?"

"Most memories are distortions of what happens in real

life," Veró says. She leans on the railing of the mezzanine as if to steady herself against the tide.

"So, like, your memory is decaying?" Drew asks Veró. "Like you're forgetting a part of it?"

"No," Rory cuts in. "The loop warps your memories. They get more and more twisted every time you start over. The saying goes, *Memory erodes the mind . . . in a loop that turns to dust.* If you spend too long replaying memories again and again, you break. The loop turns to dust and there's no way back."

It's strange to hear Rory quote the Lilies vow so openly, but she doesn't have to explain further. I know exactly what it's like to feel trapped by your own mind. Maybe that's what made me a true Lily: sometimes I get in my head and it really feels like the past is present and *the present turns to past.*

I hold my nose to dampen the smell of rot and follow the others. As we cross the library's main atrium, I glance up at the portrait of Rory's grandmother Adeline. The original Lily. Her jaw is clenched. Her expression is serious, almost sad. She had her own secrets, I'm sure. Did she experience her own version of this loop? Did guilt threaten to break her, too?

On the west side of the main atrium, Veró pauses in front of the door labeled *Girls.* She stares up at the word and the little skirted stick figure underneath. I can tell she doesn't want to go in. She doesn't want to face whatever is behind that door. She doesn't want to relive the memory. I know the feeling. She waivers a bit and for a second she looks like a little kid about to cry. I have the sudden impulse to hug her, but I don't think it would do any good. She's way too in her own head. She wouldn't be able to feel it, not really.

She pushes the swinging door open just a smidge and we all cover our mouths. The smell emanating from the bathroom is completely eye watering.

"I think we found whatever is rotting in here," Drew says, voice muffled. I turn and see that they've retracted their head into the collar of their oxford shirt to shield themselves from the stench. "Did you set off a stink bomb before Founder's Night or something, Veró?"

"No, it wasn't like this," Veró answers.

"I think the loop is deteriorating. The memory is rotting," Rory says. "The vow warned us about this. *The clock hands turn, memory erodes the mind.* If you had just let the memory play through as it happened the first time, it wouldn't be like this."

"It's not my fault that Charlotte caught us. And I didn't know it was going to be like this the second time."

"All the more reason to get it right this time," Rory says. "I mean, if we keep messing around, we might not be able to get out of here before the loop completely dissolves."

"We get it, okay? Jesus! Enough," Veró growls.

A question spills out of me. "Would you be willing to tell us exactly what happened in there? I know this is all a lot, but I think telling us what's about to happen might make it all easier and make sure that we get through this part without a repeat."

Veró's chin wrinkles. The curls around her face seem to lose their bounce. Her eyes close. I've touched a nerve, but it was unavoidable. We are all about to relive Veró's worst moment anyway, whether or not she decides to give us a preview. Drew and Rory freeze, waiting for her to answer. But Veró doesn't speak. I reach for her hand, clasp the fingers.

"It's gonna be okay," I say, even though I don't know if that's true. I've played the supportive sister at Archwell before, specifically with Charlotte as my little. But with Veró I actually get a chance to be genuine. I'm surprised at how good it feels to be real for minute. "What was so bad about setting up for Founder's Night with Charlotte?"

Veró gathers herself together and takes a deep breath. "It doesn't matter," she says. "It was a hard night for a lot of reasons." Then she turns to Rory with a treacherous look on her face. "Your mom didn't make it any easier."

"You know, Veró, for someone who has barely said a word to anyone in the two years they've been at this school, you've suddenly got a lot of opinions." Rory matches Veró with her own type of venom. Her fangs are out, ready to strike. I hate it when she gets like this. It happens very rarely, behind closed doors, and usually only with the littles. She can be vicious if you push her far enough. And Veró has definitely been pushing all of Rory's buttons today. "Why exactly would *my* mother be responsible for *your* worst moment? She's never

111

done anything to you except let your daddy buy your spot here as a last-ditch effort to keep you out of military school. Remind me, you got kicked out of Easton Academy, right? And what about the one before that? Was that expulsion from Madras Prep or Forrest Gable?"

"You're trying to mess with me, but it's not gonna work." Veró keeps her voice even at first, but I notice her flinch when Rory says the words *daddy* and *expulsion*. Her next few sentences spatter out like machine-gun fire. "You wanna know how your mom ruined my Founder's Night? All right, I'll tell you. When someone reveals herself to be a total, unequivocal TERF, it sort of ruins your day."

Rory crinkles her brow and tilts her head, confused. "What?" she says, quiet all of a sudden. "What do you mean?"

"Exactly what you already know, princesa. The chancellor, aka your mama, is a TERF. A big one. Capital T-E-R-F. You surprised? Huh. You're not as smart as I thought you were." Veró expels the words from her mouth and they thud to the floor. But that one word—*TERF*—echoes across to the atrium.

"That's . . . that can't be right. You just . . ." I can hear the tension winding around Rory's voice. No one has ever dared tell her anything about her mom, not even the bigs back when we were underclassmen. "You can't just throw around accusations like that, Veró. Calling someone like *my* mother a TERF is a big freaking deal."

"You'll see. Just wait." Veró motions to Drew and pushes

open the swinging door of the girls' room. "And don't worry, Ms. Archwell. Imma let the memory unfold exactly as it happened so you can see just how hateful your mom really is. C'mon, Drew." And just like that, she and Drew disappear into the bathroom, ignoring the smell of rot.

"She's lying," Rory says, turning to face me now that we're alone. "You know my mother. You know she's nothing like that. She's all about women's empowerment . . . I mean, she's a feminist talking head for cable news for god's sake. What Veró is saying is ridiculous, right?"

Rory is pleading with me to back her up. She doesn't want to be on the wrong team. She doesn't see herself as the villain here. At the same time, this situation is painfully familiar. If I had a dime for every time someone tried to smooth over a racist thing said to me at an Archwell alumni event, I'd be a rich woman. Every one of those things gets brushed off as a "misunderstanding" or being "out of context." Something tells me that Veró's experience with the chancellor might not be much different.

"I don't know," I say to her. "Veró clearly got that impression of your mom somehow."

"My mother is *not* a TERF, though. I know it. I mean, *I'm* not a TERF so . . ." The words spill out of her quickly—forcefully—as if saying them will protect her somehow.

Denial is a powerful thing, especially when it comes to white people and their families. Still, I feel for Rory. It's not like she brought this on herself.

"Look, I know it doesn't feel good to hear," I soothe. "But you're just gonna need to let the memory play out and see for yourself. It'll move us through the loop and get us closer to getting out of here. And we have to get out of here soon, Rory." I shiver away the thought of my brain slowly turning to dust as my worst memories play on a loop again and again. "I don't wanna be here. I don't wanna do this any longer than we have to."

She lets out a long sigh and is quiet for a beat. When she finally does speak, her voice is small. "You're right. It's just hard. I wasn't expecting . . ."

"Have a little empathy," I tell her. "We're all gonna go through this sooner or later." I'm right, but I wish I weren't. And I wish I weren't scared of what's bound to come.

The feeling forces the truth out of me. "Rory, we need to talk about what we're gonna do about the loop once it gets to *our* memories of Founder's Night."

We haven't talked about what happened, not directly . . . not unless you count the low-key threatening texts Rory sent me before our exam. It's time to be real with each other for a second while we're alone.

But before Rory can say anything, there's the creak and slam of the main doorway opening and shutting.

"Veronica?" Charlotte's voice reanimates my panic. Sweat begins to gather under my blouse again and my knees threaten to give.

I can't lay eyes on her. Not after what happened during

her initiation. Charlotte Vanderheyden might as well be a ghost.

"We need to hide," Rory hushes. "If she finds us, the loop resets again."

"Ver-AH-ni-CAH?" The voice wrenches my guilt back into my throat. The feeling chokes me. There's no avoiding this, no matter how hard Rory tries to resist.

"We need to talk about what happened to Charlotte, Rory. We never talked about what we did to her."

"You mean what *you* did to her," Rory snaps at me.

I'm speechless. Shame spreads through my body, replacing the tightness of guilt.

Rory continues, her voice rushed and harsh. "Listen, we don't have time for this, Blythe. We need to go in there and hide so the memory can move forward. I get that what happened freaked you out. It's understandable. But I need you to forget about that right now. The others don't have to know."

I break my silence. "They're gonna find out! The loop is going to show them. They're going to see how Charl—"

"Hello? Veronica?" Charlotte's voice is a bookshelf away. If she finds us, the memory is derailed and this all starts over. *As the clock hands turn, memory erodes the mind.*

Not wasting another moment, Rory springs into action. She shoves me with all her might against the swinging restroom door. I topple through the opening, body thwacking against the green tile floor. Rory is right behind me, pushing the door shut, and steadying it so it sits still on its hinges. My arm throbs against the cold tile. Pain shoots up into my shoulder.

"God damn," I groan. "What the hell, Rory?" Through the ache, I notice that it feels kind of good to curse at Rory.

"Shut up, Blythe. Just shut up," Rory whispers, pulling me to my feet and guiding me toward an empty bathroom stall.

Yep. I *definitely* should've started cursing this girl out a long time ago.

Next to the row of sinks, Drew and Veró are gawking at us.

"Charlotte's outside," Rory announces to them. "We have to hide. Not you, Veró."

Drew leaps into one of the other empty stalls as Rory faces me. "Stand on the toilet," she barks. "Don't let her see your feet."

And with that, she slams the stall door in my face.

Outside the bathroom door, I can hear Charlotte calling for Veró.

"I'm just in the bathroom. Be out in a sec!" she calls back.

But I know Veró won't come out to meet Charlotte. She'll stay in here until Charlotte finds her doing . . . I'm not sure what.

It was something bad that she didn't want to say.

But I can't blame her.

It seems we've all done something very, very bad.

Veró

GROWING UP, MAMI SAID I played too rough. I tended to get in the most trouble on Sunday afternoons after services ended and we went home but before the sun went down and family and friends parted ways. My cousins and I would get into a game of tag and someone would wind up falling on the deck and splitting open their lip while I was chasing them. We'd play chicken in the pool and whoever was bearing my weight on their shoulders would wind up underwater for a bit too long. One time I knocked the wind out of my cousin Julio with a toy golf club. I got sent to my room a lot.

"Vete a tu cuarto, Veró," Mami would say. "What you did was very bad." I'd stomp up the stairs and slam my bedroom door behind me. Then I'd spread myself across my bed and fix my eyes on Papi's poster from college that I'd commandeered from the attic. It was a museum print of Manuel Caro's *El Alma de la Virgen*. I sat and stared and fumed.

Outside on the pool deck below, I could hear my tías talking.

"La niña se porta mal. She doesn't *think* before she does things."

"I'm sure she'll grow out of it."

"You should be stricter with her."

La Virgen in the reproduced painting always smirked at me, amused by my predicament. One day, she asked, *Eres una niña buena o una niña mala?*

"I am Malcriada," I answered back. "I didn't mean to hurt anyone."

But you did hurt someone, didn't you? You do it often. Why else do they send you here?

"It was an accident," I said. "It wasn't my fault."

La Virgen didn't say anything after that. I filled in the blank of her silence.

I have hurt people. Malcriada has hurt people. And here, in the loop, I have to face that fact.

The air in the library bathroom is thick and pungent. It's hard to breathe normally. Or maybe I'm just holding my breath without realizing. It's about to happen again: my mistake, my shame. The worst damage I've ever done. I feel it building up. The memory is pressurized, ready to explode and set the loop on fire. I turn my back to the row of bathroom mirrors. I can't stand to look at myself. I don't want to see what happened again . . . what I did.

Dread is interrupted by a vaguely familiar wave of excitement. Something is materializing in my hand, molecule by molecule. Propane, butane, and pigment, all encased in a cylinder. Then I remember how all of this started—with a can of spray paint. I glance down and see that it's in my hand: Rust-o-Color, pigment #1356, Hot Pink.

But wait. I'm not the one holding the spray paint. Malcriada is. Relief washes over me. In the memory, Malcriada is alive. I feel it in my fingertips, in my legs, in my gut. She's here. I'm her again. Wrapped around me, her black hoodie is no longer a funeral shroud. It's armor. And in the next moment, I remember what I need to do. I reach out my hand and the paper stencil assembles itself out of a snow shower of tiny fibers. Yes, this is how it started.

Stencils aren't hard to make, but I'm quick and imprecise with an X-Acto knife, ruining designs with just one stray stroke. As Malcriada, my hand was always a little steadier. I breathe in the feeling of being her again, a surge of power burning in my belly. My fingers curl tight around the spray paint can, each of them individually resolved to carry out the mission. It's exactly as I remember it: the blank black expanse of the bathroom stall doors, the little blue shimmer of fluorescent overheads reflecting off the green tile, the feeling of total and utter belief in the work I've set out to do.

I lift the stencil and steady it against the door of one of the bathroom stalls. Inside, I hear Drew sniff. Once. Twice.

"Shut up." Rory's rebuke slithers beneath the dividers from two stalls away and silences Drew. What happens next has to be exactly as I remember. No disruptions, or the loop will reset. I hate that I'm relieved by Rory's correction, but I don't want to replay all of this again. Once is enough.

I lift the can of spray paint and compress my trigger finger. A continuous gust of magenta emerges, rushing to meet the back of the white cardstock stencil and the lacquered black bathroom stall. The smell of paint covers the stench of my rotten memory. I fill in the stencil's gaps then let both arms rest. Then I take a step back to review my work. Not the cleanest lines ever, but I'll get it on the next try.

"What's that smell?" Blythe whispers.

"If I have to shut up, then you have to shut up too," Drew says.

"Are you tagging the doors or something?" Blythe asks, ignoring Drew. I ignore Blythe. An eye for an eye. She knows better than to bother me right now when Charlotte is about to walk in. I move to the next stall door and press the stencil against the metal. I hold the nozzle of the can slightly farther away from the surface. No paint drips this time. The face at the top of the design is in sharper focus now, but my artistic rendering still pales in comparison to the inspiration for this particular piece.

The design was based on a photo of Gabe Lewis: my friend and Archwell's most underrated Underclassman, in my humble opinion. I screenshotted one of his selfies that was taken partially in shadow. As a result, the rendering of his face on my stencil was a bit minimalistic. Folks would definitely not be able to recognize Gabe as the muse for this piece—not unless they were already in the know. At least that's what I told myself . . .

A debonair sophomore with a flawless fade, Gabe was one of the only other art kids in Chatham House last year. We became friends shortly after he gave me his stash of his dad's old *GQ* magazines for a zine project I was working on.

Gabe was out to certain teachers—Ms. Katz naturally— and pretty much everyone who lived on the third floor of Chatham. Of course, being half out of the closet meant that Gabe had to be half *in* it too.

"This place is just painful," he said to me over a mug of peppermint tea. It was spring finals week and we were sitting in Chatham's velvety common room. Someone—we didn't know who—had just taken down the handmade *Gender Neutral Bathroom* sign from the third floor's single-stall restroom for the millionth time that semester.

"I'm still figuring myself out and that's hard enough . . . but it's basically impossible to do that when I feel like I'm not allowed to take up an inch of space at this school." He spoke into his tea as if it were listening just as intently as I was.

"I know, huh," I said. "Is there anything I can do to make it easier?"

He shook his head and stared out the window, examining the pollen collecting on the ledge outside. "I mean . . . something as basic as bathrooms shouldn't have to be a fight."

I agreed. And sometime over the summer I got the idea

for my installation. A surprise for Gabe: something that would change things for once.

Approving my own handiwork, I move on to the next stall and lift up the stencil once more.

"Veró?" Blythe whispers again.

"B. Shut up." Rory's voice is a curled fist.

I start a third time. Then I hear the squeal of a stall door. I resist the urge to stop and look, instead I keep my finger on the trigger. The third installation is the best so far, except for one drip dragging down one of the corners of the hashtag.

"'Justice looks like gender-neutral bathrooms.'" Blythe reads the words on the installation aloud for the others. She has her head craned at an unnatural angle to be able to see what I'm doing from her stall. "'#transinclusionatarchwell.'"

"Seems kinda wordy for a hashtag," Drew mutters.

"Who is the face on the stencil supposed to be?" Blythe asks.

"Will both of you shut the hell up?" Rory is desperate. "Charlotte could walk in any second."

I move to the next stall door and lift the stencil. "She's right," I admit. "Y'all should be quiet now."

"Now?" Drew asks.

"Charlotte will come in just after I finish the fourth installation."

"So we need to hide, like now!" Rory barks.

The silhouette of Blythe's head bobs back into the stall and the door quietly shuts behind her. I hold my can of magenta steady.

"I know exactly when it happens," I say, more to myself than to any of the others. "I finish the face," I say, holding the stencil in place. "I start on the words." The paint particles make contact with the metal door, clinging to the black before emulsifying together. I squint, the way I remember doing. I didn't bring eye protection when I did this the first time and I don't have it here in my memory either. "I finish off the word *bathrooms*. Then I start on the hashtag and she'll be here in five . . ."

The pink meets the black.

". . . four . . ."

My lungs burn. A combination of paint fumes and Malcriada's fire.

". . . three . . ."

It's intoxicating.

". . . two . . ."

And terrible. Terrible to be back here again.

". . . and . . ." I whisper.

The door stirs behind me.

"What exactly are you doing?" Charlotte's tone is as noxious as paint thinner. "What the hell? You're vandalizing the bathroom right now? We're supposed to be beautifying the place for Founder's Night, Veronica. Not messing it up."

My shoulders are at my ears. What do I say to her next? Suddenly, I don't remember how I phrased it. My pulse pounds against the can in my hand. It falls to the floor with a clatter of metal on tile. The half-empty cylinder rolls away, a slow, aching sound.

I spin around and there she is, just as I remember her. Pretty, brows gathered, the sleeves of her black-and-yellow rugby shirt are rolled to her elbows. The fabric cinches her body into a knot as she crosses her arms and meets my eyes.

Then I remember what I said to her. The look on her face reminds me of it . . . of why I did all of this in the first place.

"You wouldn't understand."

"What's there to understand?" she snaps. "People are going to think that I helped you with this trash."

"It's art," I say, feeling the familiar heat in my face, the unmistakable strain in my throat. I turn away. I can't look at her anymore. It's her eyes. They remind me too much of Papi: angry and accusing. I follow the can to its resting place and stoop to retrieve it.

"Your weird art is about to get both of us in a lot of trouble." Charlotte's voice is rising.

I don't meet her eyes again. Instead, I locate my bag. It's perched on the counter near the paper towel dispenser. I grab it and unlatch the silver clasp. Inside the satchel I find the balled-up plastic bag I brought to secure the paint can. Malcriada plans ahead. She never gets paint residue on designer bags. She never leaves a trace of evidence . . . except for this witness . . . who's just standing here, waiting for the artist to respond.

"Well then, I guess you'll have to shut the fuck up about all this, won't you?" I say, my voice louder than I intend. Is it louder than I actually said it the first time? No, probably not.

Because the next thing I remember is a direct consequence of my words.

The bathroom door opens. The cycle continues. She's standing there again, tall and unflinching in her gray wool suit. Her hair is swept into a tight blond bun. Her jaw is wound, like always. It's Chancellor Eleanor Archwell.

I'm caught.

It happened just like this . . . but it also didn't.

Chancellor Archwell's square heels clack against the cold tile floor. She's trailing a noxious smell behind her, stronger than the spray paint. I choke on the air and notice how the loop has twisted my memory again. It's exactly what I remember, yes. But it's more how it *felt* than how it actually happened.

Charlotte and I are frozen. The chancellor's eyes, a sickly shade of green, slide from stall door to stall door, assessing the situation.

"I heard shouting," she says. Her words puddle into an oil slick on the bathroom floor.

She walks to the first stall door, striding right through the black puddle of her intentions and tracking greasy footprints behind her.

I hold my breath as she inspects my installation. The memory is brittle here. The loop threatens to skip and repeat like one of Mami's old records. I know that Chancellor Archwell's daughter, Rory, is on the other side of the partition, poised motionless above the toilet. But the chancellor

125

doesn't know that of course. I picture Rory's saddle shoes perched on the white porcelain toilet seat and pray that she doesn't make a sound.

After a long silence, Chancellor Archwell finally speaks. "I must say, Verónica, I was expecting something a bit more splashy from you after the report I got from Easton Academy. They made your antics seem positively diabolical. But this . . ." She runs her fingers across one of the paint drips, leaving a hot-pink smudge. "This is a bit more amateurish than I expected."

I know not to care about the chancellor's opinion. The moment she walked in, I expected an assault of some kind. But the word *amateur* stings more than I anticipated. The leaden lump in my throat leeches something toxic into my bloodstream. It's anger and it's sadness and it's fear all in one. It feels even worse than I remember . . . because I know what's coming next.

"We were supposed to be decorating together. We—we're both on the committee," Charlotte blurts. "I was wondering what was taking Veronica so long in the bathroom and then I smelled something funny and—"

"Who is this supposed to be?" The chancellor's silky, slick voice cuts Charlotte off. Her words fall to the floor and mix into the black puddle, congealing into a soup of toxic waste.

I summon my strength to speak, knowing now that what I'm about to say will ruin everything.

"Is this supposed to be G—"

Before the chancellor can use Gabe's dead name, I cut her off without thinking. "Gabe Lewis," I say.

Gabe's name echoes across the tiled room. The loop amplifies every syllable to a deafening tone.

Gabe didn't know he was the subject of my piece, the face above the hashtag bearing some resemblance to him and his signature fade. To be fair, I didn't think most people would recognize him. And I couldn't risk telling him. I had to stay anonymous.

Still, I wanted him to know that there was someone on his side at Archwell. Not just someone, a chorus of someones. That's what the hashtag was about. #transinclusionatarchwell was going to take off and the school would be forced to change its policies. Gender-neutral bathrooms. Inclusive admissions. Everything was about to change because of this. I just knew it. It was why I planned the installation this way.

And the best part was, to those who knew him for who he truly was, Gabe would appear to be the hero of it all.

But I was wrong. Malcriada was wrong. We weren't starting a revolution. We were starting a wildfire.

"Gabe Lewis . . ." The chancellor utters softly.

Just like the rest of her words, Gabe's name—a name that should be sacred—oozes into the black mass of bad intentions on the floor.

I remember this moment so clearly.

The moment when I realized the consequences of my actions.

"You seem to be confused, Verónica. Archwell is a school for young women. Your *subject*, I know, is also well aware of this. *All* Archwell students, and *parents* for that matter, are aware of our policies. This is a school for girls. A safe space."

Oh, no. Oh god. How could I have been so stupid? So careless?

I just . . . outed Gabe.

The nauseating realization mixes in with the sickening smell of the bathroom itself.

"Now that I've seen this, I'll need to make some . . . family phone calls."

This wasn't how this was all supposed to go down. In an instant, I have a splitting headache.

How did Malcriada get it so wrong? Why didn't I think? I don't have to search hard for the answer. The truth ricochets around my brain. I got myself here by valuing *my* anonymity more than Gabe's. I messed up because I treated Gabe like my *subject*, not like my friend. Like a cause, not like a person.

"Charlotte," the chancellor says. "You can go now. I will handle this. But mind I don't find you in another situation where you've run afoul of the rules. Especially given tonight's special event."

"Yes, ma'am." Charlotte practically sprints from the room, leaving the door swinging behind her. It flaps open and closed, open and closed, flashing the *Girls* sign again and again until it loses momentum.

I don't want Charlotte to leave. I don't want to be alone

128

with the chancellor. Not again. But now I have to face the fact that I've delivered Gabe to Eleanor Archwell on a silver platter. I hold my breath and brace myself.

"I have run this school for thirteen years now," the chancellor says. "I know what it takes for young women to be successful in this world. It's my responsibility to ensure I deliver on the promise of an Archwell Academy education." Her cheeks are more sunken than I remember. Her eyes are somehow smaller too. "That means I have a responsibility to remove anyone who poses a threat to our community," she continues. "You, Verónica, can thank your lucky stars that your father secured your place at Archwell through his generous donation. It guarantees you one strike. I can't say as much for your friend."

The chancellor's eyes flick to the stall doors and the stenciled rendering of Gabe's face. The magenta paint starts to coagulate and drip even more. The lump in my throat burns. I know what will happen next because I lived through it.

Over the weekend, the chancellor will call Gabe's parents and out him, exactly as I did, except she'll do it intentionally. By Monday, Gabe will have disappeared from campus. His parents won't come to get him themselves. They'll send a van driven by someone with a shirt that says *Youth Reparative Therapy.*

My heart has been swallowed by my stomach.

The chancellor's voice grows sharp. "Consider this your one and only warning, Ms. Martín. If you ever pull another stunt like this . . . Well, let's just say that'll be the end of a lot of things. Do you understand?"

My voice emerges in a gust of fury. "Are you threatening me?"

"I'm outlining the consequences," the chancellor says coolly. "I take anything that jeopardizes this community—this institution—very seriously. Those who wish to harm, those who disrespect the legacy of women who have graduated from this school . . . those people will be expelled." The chancellor waits for me to react somehow, but when I don't respond she continues again, shifting to a purposefully patronizing singsong tone. "If I remember correctly, your father has distinctly *different* plans for you should you not succeed here."

A new, thickly pungent smell fills the room. It takes me a moment to recognize it but then I know beyond a doubt. It's the scent of dead flowers in water. It's the scent of defeat. It's knowing what will happen if I'm expelled from Archwell and Mami and Papi send me to Fort Hancock.

"You can't do that," I say. But there's no point.

The chancellor has Malcriada by the throat. She can hold this over me for as long as I'm here at school. I guess I shouldn't be surprised. Her minions, the Lilies, seem to specialize in blackmail. I wish I'd dug deeper into the school's legacy when I had the chance. My Malcriada installations only scratched the surface of Archwell Academy's secrets.

Regret hooks its claws deeper into my legs. I'm rooted

130

to the spot. Frozen and small. My veins are filled with ice. Reality comes crashing down.

Gabe will be expelled because of me.

My art has hurt people.

I have hurt people.

The pain of this thought shoots from my legs into my pelvis. It winds around the bottom of my spine and travels along the nerves up to the base of my skull. I can't bear it. I don't want to relive the past anymore. It's the shame of it all. It's going to eat me alive.

I'm going to break apart. I'm going to fly into a thousand pieces. I'm going to—

Bong . . . Bong . . . Bong . . .

Drew

THE LOOP PULLS US AWAY from the memory. It feels like I'm being stretched: a part of me here and a part of me there. But fortunately, the world comes back into focus and I know that I'm back in the closet now. We all are. Yet there's still a part of me that feels like I'm hiding in that stall, trembling as Death stalks around outside.

I suppose our journey into the loop started like this as well. Hiding. Waiting. Hoping we'd all make it out in one piece.

I pull myself to my feet and come face-to-face with one of the alarm clocks perched at the edge of the closet's shelves. It's exactly at my eye level, old-fashioned with little brass bells on top. The little hand and big hand are pointing toward the twelve. Midnight . . . or noon, depending on your outlook on life. I can't say I'm feeling very optimistic at the moment.

"Was that it?" Rory's voice is muffled underneath the layers of hanging green robes and white gowns. She clambers out from underneath the clothing rack and stands. "Was that all there was, Veró?"

I can't help but snort. The notion that Rory was expecting something worse tells me everything I need to know about her. My anger is a black cloak, wrapping around my shoulders. My fists clench involuntarily.

Feel like fighting now, don't we? Death murmurs. *You like hurting people, huh?*

I relax my hands. I won't give Death the satisfaction of seeing me worked up any more.

"Yeah." Veró's voice is heavier than ever. "That was it."

"Great," Rory says. "That means we're through with the first loop. When we go back out there, we can tackle the next memory."

"Hold up." Blythe rises from a nearby spot and switches the closet light on. "We're not gonna even attempt to unpack that? What happened back there was messed-up on so many levels."

I try to breathe deep but I can't ignore my pulse hammering against my neck and wrist. The truth of what just happened pulls me back from the point of dissociation: I *should* be angry. All of us should be. Even though I'm a pro at it, I can't disconnect my mind from my body right now. There's fire within me . . . sooner or later it has to come out.

"Rory, your mom was way out of line," Blythe continues. "And Veró, you straight up outed somebody. What the hell were you thinking?"

"I don't know." I can hear the tears in Veró's voice. "I

wasn't thinking. Or I guess I wasn't thinking clearly. I'm sorry. I was trying to make things better but—"

Rage swells in my throat. "It's not just about that," I fume.

At once, the others are silent and I can feel their eyes on me. I take my hand and run it along the peach fuzz stubble growing on the back of my head. My mom used to do this whenever I buzzed my hair. Technically she buzzed it for me. The first time I asked her to do it I was in sixth grade. She finished the cut and cleaned me up, wiping away all the little bits of hair. "How's that feel to you?" she asked.

"Great." My voice was breathy, light with relief. "Really, really great."

I pet the back of my head the way Mom did and take a deep breath. I remind myself that I'm lucky. I know who I am. I'm loved. And I'm allowed to be angry.

"I don't get it," I finally say. "I don't get this school . . . It's like, how hypocritical can you be? If you're really worried about 'threats to the community' shouldn't you actually be worrying about protecting the students who go here, including the trans ones? I mean . . . c'mon."

I realize that I'm pacing only when I look up and find myself standing at the closet's polished wooden door. It's too cramped in here for this, but I have to move. I have to let this energy out.

"Yes, what Veró did was messed-up. She should've known better," I say. "And yes, the chancellor being a TERF is obviously . . . Well, it's shitty. But we already knew that about her. Well, I guess *some of us* knew it and now all of us have proof." I turn on my heel and let my hands run along the shelf ledge as I keep pacing. Dust collects on my fingertips. "But the *real* problem is that hateful people shouldn't be school principals. Hateful people shouldn't be making decisions for students. For anyone."

"You're so right, Drew." The way Blythe says my name makes me soften a little. At this moment, she sees me. And she's with me. And that counts for something.

My back is to Veró but I know she hasn't left her spot on the floor yet. She's crumpled in the corner and I can hear her sniffing back more tears. "Yeah, you're right," she says. "And I'm sorry. What happened is . . . Well, it's my biggest mistake. The worst thing I've ever done." Her voice is strained, as if the shame of the memory is blocking her windpipe. "But you all already knew that, I guess."

It's hard to accept the apology . . . Veró made herself out to be an ally, a friend. Her betrayal feels personal, even if it was unintentional . . . The *biggest* problem was that her actions *were* so deeply unintentional. So reckless and unthinking.

"What are you gonna do to make this up to Gabe?" Blythe says.

I turn to face Veró now, eyes downcast as she shakes her head. She wipes her nose on the sleeve of her hoodie. "I dunno."

"You gotta apologize," I growl. "And then you ask him how you can repair it. Don't assume that you know *anything*. That's how you got into all this."

"I realize that now," she sniffs.

I'll admit she's as pretty as ever, but this whole thing makes me look at Veró differently. Once the High Priestess from my tarot deck, she's been transformed into the Queen of Swords. Beautiful, ambitious, but able to cause harm.

On the opposite wall, next to the ticking grandfather clock, Rory is cross-armed. I know I'm not the only one who has noticed her silence, but I didn't really expect much else from her. She probably thinks that shutting up is the best move right now. If her first instinct is to defend her mom, then she's right to keep those glossy lips sealed. There is tension in her jaw and some strands of ombre blond have come loose from her braid. For the first time, I notice her hair is dyed the same color as the chancellor's. Was that on purpose? Or was it some kind of messed-up subconscious thing? Either way, I don't envy Rory for her shitty family's grip on her.

Thankfully, Mom is the total opposite of the chancellor. She's spent my whole life worrying over me, always trying to keep me safe. But I don't think my mom knew that Archwell would be dangerous like this.

Friday was the last time I talked to her. Charlotte had booted me out of our dorm room so she could get ready for Founder's Night. I heard her and Faith on the other side of the door as I closed it behind me.

"It's gone!" Charlotte gleed. "The room is mine again!"

I knew I was "*it*."

I went to hide in the stacks where no one would find me and video chatted Mom from there.

"What's up, Drew-bud?" she said. "I miss you. How's that school?"

I shrugged. I didn't want her to worry or make a fuss. After all, I'd chosen to be here. I had chosen Archwell and my grandmother's ring and all the baggage that came with it.

"Roommate problems," I sighed. "Nothing I can't handle."

"Oh, I'm sorry, sweet. Want to talk about it?"

"Not really," I said. "I just wanted to hear your voice."

"Okay," she said. "Listen, Drew, if you need me to come get you—"

"Gah, Mom, it's not that serious."

"I'm just saying. You know I always have your back."

"I know."

She studied my face on the screen for a second before speaking again. Then she said, "I know I've said it before, but hurt people *hurt people*. All you can do when folks act like jerks is just set a boundary and move on. Usually, people's jerky behavior has nothing to do with you."

"I know," I said. "I know about boundaries, Ma." In moments like this, Mom was always filled with platitudes. I'll admit, though, sometimes it helped to hear them.

"And when all else fails just say screw 'em. Put on your big-kid boxers and get out there and just say screw 'em, you know?"

I looked down at my baggy trousers, realizing that I was wearing my favorite boxers underneath (the ones with the corgis on them), and I smiled.

Mom always had a way of showing me how to tap into little joys. Here in the closet, joy seems hard to come by, but I try to feel it by scanning my body. I like the way my biceps feel against my oversized shirtsleeves. I look down at my hands and remind myself that I like the way they're shaped. Then I notice the Lilies ring, an infinity of diamonds sparkling in the dim. Compared to all the others on the shelf, the gold is starting to look a little dingy. Still, I can make out the inscription: *Ut sacram memoriam.*

I wear the jewelry, but I'm not a Lily. I was not given the opportunity. I don't have their privileges. Unlike them, I will never be safe here.

With my thumb, I turn the ring around so the diamonds are hidden.

Then I lift my hand to my forehead and press the infinity shape gently against my skin. I don't want to wrestle with memory anymore . . . not mine or anyone else's.

"I want out of here," I mutter.

"Well, we have that in common," Rory tells me. "But as far as I know, there's no way out as long as we're wasting time in the closet."

"But there's got to be, though," I insist. "The loop can't be this . . . this rigid."

Veró's memory was super difficult to navigate, and it wasn't even mine. But I suppose it taught me something about myself—I'd truly give anything to not have to relive *my* version of Founder's Night.

"What if we just stayed in the closet after all?" Blythe asks Rory.

"We've been over this. It's not an option," Rory answers forcefully. "We'd wind up stuck in here forever. The only way out is to let the memories play out."

"But there's got to be an escape hatch," I say, pressing the diamond infinity into my forehead a bit harder. "There should be a way to short circuit everything."

"I'm telling you, the Lilies vow says the longer we wait around, the more *memory erodes the mind*. The loop *turns to dust*. It's inevitable. We can't stop it."

Handed down from the dreaded Lilies, the words reverberate in my mind. I close my eyes and I see the letters form behind my lids in an erratic scrawl. They circle around each other, a jumble of lines and swirls. They're so familiar for some reason, but not because of Rory's incessant recitation of them. I just can't quite place them, though.

Then I remember—these words are only a small piece of the bigger puzzle.

"Rory, Blythe: Can y'all tell us the *full* Lilies pledge of allegiance?" I ask.

"It's called the vow," Rory says. "And no!"

I don't know why I bother with her.

I look at Blythe, who's glaring at Rory. She keeps her eyes fixed on her as she speaks.

"It starts: *Ut sacram memoriam. Her memory is sacred—*"

"Don't, Blythe!" Rory shouts.

"Shut up, Rory," Blythe says, and continues her recitation of the vow. *"Beyond the bounds of time. But as the clock hands turn, memory erodes the mind."*

I realize now that I know most of the words by heart already somehow, enough for me to start to make meaning out of them.

"Okay, yes," I say. "We're beyond the bounds of time in the loop. And the memories distort and restart every time we hear the grandfather clock." I gesture to our silent frenemy, the motionless timepiece at the back of the closet. "Keep going."

"Her secrets are best buried in a loop that turns to dust, where the present turns to past and past remains unjust."

"Yep, yep." I nod. "Again, the loop. We're stuck in a bunch of messed-up memories from the past."

"Okay, inspector." Blythe smirks.

Veró leans in, listening as closely as I am while Blythe continues the vow. *"Therein lies infinity—a place where she survives—while we protect our sisterhood, our secrets, and our lives. For only when her sisters' wrongs are once again made right will she escape anew and take her place within the light."*

I think of the note on my grandma Simmons's deathbed flowers. I know for sure now that the words in the Lilies vow are *exactly* the same as the words on the card. My grandmother was a cofounder of the Lilies—that, I already knew. But could she have known about the loop? Could Rory's grandmother have known? Are the original Lilies trying to tell us something?

"Escape," I say. *"When her sisters' wrongs are once again made right will she escape.* Are those the words?"

"Yeah," Blythe says, smiling a little as Rory fumes in the corner. "What about it?"

"What if the Lilies vow isn't telling us just about the loop but also about how to escape it?"

"You take AP Lit, don't you?" Veró says.

I grin. "Yes . . . that and I like a good riddle."

"Fair enough," Veró says. "Whatever butters your biscuit."

The phrase makes me smile. Seeing her memory bear out may have knocked Veró off a pedestal, but I can't avoid the fact that I'm still drawn to her. She knows what she did was wrong, but she's not groveling and she's not swerving out of her lane. In fact, she's gassing me up, propelling us forward.

"Maybe to escape we have to make the *wrongs* into *rights*, like it says in the vow," I continue. "We might have to change something about the past. Shift the history of what happened on Founder's Night." I fold my arms across my chest, satisfied. It feels good to have a possible solution to all of this, even if it feels like I'm grasping at straws.

"Oooo," Veró says. "I like it. Smash the time loop once and for all!"

"But there isn't any one thing that needs to be rectified, is there?" Blythe points out. "We all experienced different things that night. Wouldn't there be different *wrongs* that need to be made *right* again?"

"Well, you have to admit that there's still a through line," Veró points out. "I mean, don't you think it's weird that we

141

all had some sort of contact with Charlotte on the night she disappeared?"

I freeze up at the sound of Charlotte's name on Veró's lips. It seems that I'm not alone in this impulse. No one responds to Veró's question. No one wants to go there.

But the girl will pursue her version of justice at any cost. She presses me. "What's that phrase about infinity?"

I conjure the words: ". . . *therein lies infinity—the place where she survives—while we protect our sisterhood, our secrets, and our lives. For only when her sisters' wrongs are once again made right will she escape anew . . .*"

". . . *and take her place within the light,*" Blythe finishes the phrase out for me.

"All right, AP. Riddle me this," Veró says, turning to me. "What if the 'she' they keep referring to in the Lilies vow isn't just some girl, but is someone specific, like Charlotte? She disappeared, right? But the poem says she might survive in infinity . . . as in, she might be trapped in the loop or something. I mean, it really is all right there in the poem."

"It's not a poem, it's a vow," Blythe and Rory say in unison.

"Whatever," Veró gruffs. "All I'm saying is that Charlotte is the common denominator here. Maybe in order to escape we have to change the past, like Drew is saying. We have to right the wrong of Charlotte's disappearance."

"We can't do that!" Rory groans. "I'm telling you it won't work. I know way more about the loop than any of you ever will. The Lilies' lore is clear: You have to let the memories bear out. What happened, happened. You can't change that. None of us can."

"So, you want to stay the course? Qué sorpresa," Veró says flatly. "If we keep moving forward as planned, won't it all get progressively worse?"

Possibility stirs in my chest. Maybe Veró's onto something here. If we can just pause time, shift gears, change what happened to Charlotte, maybe I won't need to face my own memory at all. For the first time in a long time, I feel like I might have a real way to make things better—to undo what I did and get the hell out of here.

"Veró has a point," I chime in. "Won't the loop keep deteriorating as it repeats?"

"Won't it just reset and corrode if we try to intervene in what happened to Charlotte?" Rory responds. It's not really a question. She's trying to prove her point.

"I don't want the memories to keep deteriorating," Blythe mutters. "It's hard enough just wandering through them."

Blythe looks genuinely scared. I suppose it's not surprising that we're all meeting at this impasse. After all, we are four *very* different humans.

"Look. I don't know exactly what happened to Charlotte, and I'm pretty sure none of you wants to weigh in on how much information you have on the topic," Veró says. "But we should at least give it a shot, right?"

"Have you met Charlotte Vanderheyden?" Rory says. "It's no great loss not having her around. She just . . . didn't fit, you know? We can't change the past, so why don't we just try to move on and get through this."

Rory's words sit on top of my stomach like really old leftovers. Charlotte didn't fit. Just like I don't fit . . . but for different reasons. Reasons that are invisible to me. The notion knocks around the inside of my head as Blythe speaks.

"You better take that back, Rory. You're starting to sound like your mom . . . and not the way you would want."

Rory looks sad all of a sudden. She says nothing, but in the midst of her silence I get a whiff of regret. I consider whether that's possible.

Blythe brushes against something on the shelf across from me, and it makes a soft rustling sound as it falls to the floor.

She stoops to pick it up, then pauses.

"What is it?" Rory asks.

"This fell off the shelf. The one with all the rings. I didn't notice it there before."

"Need help?" I ask, and stoop down to join her, but Blythe doesn't move. She's holding an old, rumpled newspaper up to the light, studying the headline.

"I doubt that's more up to date than your news app," I say.

"Very funny," she says, not laughing. Then she lifts her head and meets Rory's eyes. "Is there a reason why your mom would keep this paper in here?" she asks. She holds up the paper for Rory. All four of us gather around to see.

The page is yellowing and has a slightly musty odor. It's

definitely from a long time ago. Near the top in black and white is a picture of a girl with softly curled hair. It brushes her shoulders just beneath her string of pearls, complimenting her white off-the-shoulder cocktail dress. Her face is shaped a little like Rory's, but the two don't quite look alike. One big difference is the girl in the picture is smiling.

I read the headline accompanying the photo. *Local Headmaster's Daughter Disappears.*

"Is this your grandma?" I ask Rory, pointing to the headline. "Your great-grandfather was the original chancellor of Archwell, right? Wouldn't the local headmaster be her dad?"

"My grandmother never disappeared. She took over the school from my great-grandfather and ran it until my mother took over."

"Yeah, *remember?*" Veró asks under her breath, with more than a hint of snark. I crack a smile at her. It's my subtle way of saying *We're gonna be all right, even after everything that has happened.*

Blythe reads a section of the article aloud. "'Lillian Archwell, the oldest daughter of the Archwell family, was last seen on October sixth, at a senior class celebration for Archwell Academy. Her parents, having founded a school for girls in part to ensure their daughters' safety and propriety, are distraught over the disappearance.'"

"What year is this article from?" Veró asks.

Blythe rustles through the paper to find the front page. "It says it was published on October ninth, 1958."

"That's so weird," Veró says. "That's the same day and date as today . . . But I guess 'today,' the day we're reliving, isn't Monday the ninth. It's Friday, so that makes it—"

"October sixth," Blythe interrupts. "The anniversary of the day Lillian Archwell went missing."

Something in my gut tingles as I gaze at the girl in the picture. Her face is starting to change, to sink into something else. Then I see it. Death. The familiar grin is plastered over the girl's soft smile, overshadowing the warmth in her eyes.

"Lillian was my grandmother's sister," Rory says reverently. "Grandmother Adeline didn't talk much about her. It seemed like it always made her sad."

"I can see why," Veró says. "Did they ever find her?"

"I . . . I . . ." Rory stammers. "I don't know . . . I always thought she had just died young. No one ever said that she disappeared . . . Adeline must've hung on to this paper for all those years."

"If this was your grandma's paper, then how did it wind up in here?" I ask.

"It's with the rest of the Lilies stuff," Rory explains. My blank look cues her to reveal more. "The Lilies Society was named after Lillian. In memory of her, I guess."

"Oh . . ." I say, ". . . uh . . ." I don't quite know how to respond. I can tell Rory's moving through some kind of feeling, but her face is too pinched for me to read it. Maybe she's inherited some family grief. Or maybe what she just told us was supposed to be secret. Maybe it's both. I study her profile and wonder if she was the one who decided not to invite me to join the Lilies. If Grandma Simmons helped start the secret society, then she must have known Lillian Archwell. I shudder a little, wondering what else I don't know about my grandma's history at Archwell Academy.

"And now Charlotte is missing," Veró says. "And the last time anyone saw her—"

"—was the same day that Lillian disappeared," Blythe finishes the thought, then keeps reading. "'With no sign of foul play, the students of Archwell Academy are left to wonder how one of their own might disappear without a trace. Evelyn Smith, a close friend of Ms. Archwell's, commented, "We love her dearly and we miss her every day."'"

I look back down at the picture of Lillian. Death is still looking back at me. I suppose I should *thank* Rory for excluding me from the Lilies. I don't want to be a part of *this* legacy.

"First, Lillian," Blythe says. "Now, Charlotte. I don't get it. Girls don't just vanish out of thin—"

Brrrrriiiiinnnnnggg!

Before she can say anything else, the closet is flooded with a shrill noise. I turn and face the alarm clock on the shelf, still set to midnight. It's vibrating. A very literal reminder that time will never stand still, not even in infinity. Its little hammer device strikes the alarm bells at a deafening decibel. I reach out and hold the clock still, pausing the little hammer, which silences the alarm.

"Sheesh," Blythe says. "Didn't expect that."

Brrrrriiiinngg! Brrrrriiiinngg!
Bzzzzzzzzzzzzzzzzz!
Brrrrriiiiinnnnnggg!

The closet erupts with the wails of every alarm clock in the collection. We start to scramble. All of us trying to make the noise stop. Rory punches a 1950s-looking flip clock again and again but it keeps screaming. Veró is busy trying to locate the old-school gears of every clock within her reach, but her hands are shaking too hard. The closet is just too loud. Blythe bangs another clock with alarm bells on top against the shelf to try to break it, but it just creates a loud repetitive *Clink! Clink!*

Twelve o'clock. Midnight. The last time I saw my roommate. My last moment with Charlotte. My brain took me elsewhere, to somewhere dark and unknown. Somewhere I don't want the others to see. Whether or not I have Rory's approval, I have to interrupt the loop. I have to keep the others from finding out what I did.

Brrrrriiiiinngg! Brrrrriiiiinngg! Brrrrriiiiinngg! Brrrrriiii-inngg!

The sound rattles my mind and the memory that I've kept at bay for so long comes roaring back. Everything red and black. The cold floor. The red box. Charlotte's hair spread across the tiles. How red her blood was against the delicate corner of her mouth.

Bong!

The grandfather clock joins the chorus.

Bong!

But my mind is elsewhere.

Bong!

Shaking Charlotte's rigid body.

Bong!

Thrashing her.

The closet door flies open.

It's time to do it again, Drew, Death whispers to me. *And it's almost your turn.*

AT FIRST, THE TERROR OF what happened twisted everything up. I barely recognized their faces. Adeline and Evelyn became ghoulish, barely shadows of their former selves.

But when I learned how the loop worked—when I finally understood that memories decay just like everything else—it started to all make sense. After that, reliving the horrors of that night didn't scare me anymore. They just made me angry . . . and that anger made me do things.

There were limits to what I could do, of course, but the safety of the closet became a means of playing with time's fringes. I started to arrange things. First, the diary. Then, the pipe from its hiding place in Adeline's bedside table. When I lived the memory again, I found another one in the same spot. An exact replica. How strange it was to return to my closet and find that the one I'd stolen was still safely tucked away. I tried to keep anything that would eventually reveal the truth. But time has a funny way of erasing people's stories. Well, some people's. And it didn't make an exception for me.

But even so, there's hope.

Some people have a gift: an ability to see beyond the boundaries. A capacity to unlock what is deeply true.

Others are too afraid to really look. To see themselves for what they are. They're too afraid of what time will do to them . . .

Rory

I HATE THE SOUND OF alarm bells, the collective blare of the closet's hundred clocks. I try to block it out by pressing my pinkies against each ear drum. It's something I used to do as a kid. When things got too scary, when I was alone in here for too long, I would plug my ears and spin around and around. I spun so fast that the corners of the closet would soften into a continuous, curved line. The four walls around me would become a circle. Then, when I could feel I was about to fall, I would stop in my tracks, crouch down, and shut my eyes tight. Being off-balance was a great distraction, as long as I was still in control.

When I realize the clocks in the closet have finally silenced themselves, I remove my fingers from my ears and find that a new noise has replaced the alarms. A low, growing hum is creeping in from the open closet door. Voices and laughter mingle with a strain of music threading through-out the chatter. Piano, guitar, and a woman's twangy vibrato keep four-four time.

I can't forget you. I've got these memories of you.

It's an old country song. An unusual choice for a party, but it's definitely memorable . . . Memorable enough that I don't have to leave the closet to know where the loop has led us this time.

Veró is the closest to the door. Slowly, she takes one step beyond the closet's threshold. I watch her head swivel, processing the scene. Then she turns back to the rest of us cowering in the dim.

"It's different," she stage whispers. It's the only way she can be heard over the hum of the crowd. "We're in the same spot but . . . it's all different."

"What do you mean?" Blythe says.

"Come look."

We follow Veró out of the closet. The door unceremoniously snaps closed behind us. No going back now . . . but at least I know what's coming. I remember being here.

The closet has ejected us into the same spot on the library mezzanine. But this time, the wrought-iron railings are looped with flower garlands and banners in the school colors. Outside, the sky is a deep blue-black, but the library is ablaze with the glow of iron chandeliers and votive candles in glass jars. I look down from the balcony onto the banquet tables where the candles are laid. Each one is decked out with forest-green tablecloths, fresh lilies, and black-eyed Susans. Between the tables is a sea of girls, each in their Founder's Night whites. It's a flood of ivory gowns, eggshell cocktail dresses, and pantsuits the color of snow. It's Founder's Night exactly as it happened three days ago. But it's a new memory altogether.

I check the clock above the circulation desk. *9:12 P.M. OCT 6.*

The party is in full swing.

"Shit," Blythe breathes.

"It's weird," Drew says, leaning closer to the railing. "I half expected to come out of the closet and have it be . . . I don't know . . . either back where we started at five o'clock or—"

"Midnight," Veró says. "All of those alarms were set to midnight . . ."

I nod. I understand the thinking, but I don't mention to the others that I knew better. The song playing over the buzz of the crowd already told me what time it was. The singer's lilting tone makes me shudder.

She's whining, almost begging. I resist the urge to plug my ears again. I've heard enough begging in my lifetime. Every year at initiation, there are girls who have bad trips. Every year, there are girls who want my help escaping from their memories. But I can't help them. Once sand hits your bloodstream, you are at its mercy. All you can do is ride it out.

I take a deep breath and try to tap back into what it means to be Rory Archwell. But that song. This place. This memory, again. I'm not in control, no matter how hard I try. And that scares the hell out of me.

"It's my memory this time." Blythe's voice is battering, the sound of a trapped bird's wings against a windowpane.

"It's mine. I know it." She backs away from the railing, resting the weight of her body against the closed closet door. Before she starts to crumble all the way, I grab her hand and squeeze it tight. I feel the stones of her Lilies ring press sharply against my palm, imprinting a tiny infinity symbol into my skin.

"It could just as easily be mine," I say. "Seriously . . . it might even be possible that . . ."

"That what?" Drew asks.

I look at Blythe and then down at the swirl of girls in white. "Blythe's and my worst memories. They . . . might overlap." The others look a bit confused by my suggestion, but I don't get into the details. I probably shouldn't have said anything. I press on before anyone can ask any questions. "We won't know until we get deeper into the loop and let the memory run its course." I try to sound convincing. If the others sense that I'm scared, this whole thing might go off the rails.

"What about trying to shift things?" Veró asks. "I think it's worth it if it means we can all break out of this cycle."

Oh boy. I was afraid of this, but I guess I was expecting it. "Trust me," I say. "I know how this works. I can get us out of here. But we all have to agree to stick to the original plan, okay?"

Saying "I know how this works" is only a half-truth, but the others seem to at least half believe me. They nod in agreement, hesitantly.

There's a fine line between a half-truth and a lie. But I've learned from my mother that even lies have a purpose. She taught me that Lilies need to lie.

The night before I was initiated, she called me into her office. The room was dark except for the desk lamp. Its low glow bounced off her nails as she drummed them against the mahogany desk. I knew about the Lilies Society already, but she'd called me there to tell me one more secret. The secret behind their name, the lie that started everything. When she told me, she kept her face in shadow, so I kept my eyes on her hands instead and pretended like I didn't have any questions. After she finished telling me she said, "Archwell was founded to keep girls safe and help them get ahead. As an Archwell woman, you stay a step ahead, even if that means stretching the truth. Understand?"

"Yes," I said, trying not to shiver.

"You'll be leading the Lilies someday," she said. "Just like I did and my mother before me."

Now it's on me to step up and lead. If I don't, then someone is going to try to change what happened on Friday night. They'll keep tripping wires, resetting the loop over and over, until infinity collapses in on all of us.

"Listen, we should just get moving and try to get through this as best we can," Drew says. "Let's at least see what we're dealing with, right? Blythe, you good to go down there?"

"What about our clothes?" Blythe asks. "If things have to play out as they really happened, we'll be out of place in the memory. Won't the loop reset once someone notices we're in our day clothes?"

"Oof, good point," Drew says.

I glance around at all four of our outfits. They are midterm chic but they are not right for Founder's Night. In blue, black, and brown, someone will spot us right away. But Lilies can always find ways to hide in plain sight.

I take a closer look at Blythe's ruffled collar. "Your blouse is white. You can probably get away with that if you keep it low-key and try not to draw attention."

Looking down at my clothes, I make the executive decision to slip off my Archwell blazer and lay it on the bookshelf behind me. "This dress is off-white but I think it's passable for now."

Veró takes off her black hoodie to reveal her white collared shirt with little black astrology symbols stitched into a design. "This work?" she asks.

I nod.

Drew takes off their uniform blazer and their long-sleeved oxford shirt. Underneath they are wearing a plain white tee. I can see the outline of their binder beneath the thin cotton weave of the shirt, but I don't say anything. At least it's white. Hopefully, if we stay mostly out of sight, no one will notice.

We edge over to the stairs and down to the library's main level. The music switches to something slightly less ancient: Frank Ocean. The chatter in the room grows louder. Laughter bounces off the vaulted stone ceiling.

At the bottom of the spiral staircase, two sophomores are sucking face in front of the emergency exit. I don't know their names, but I recognize one of them from Ms. Faulkner's theatre club. The other one is wearing a white spaghetti-strap maxi dress with a slit up to her thigh. I can tell from the way the fabric shines in the red light from the exit sign that the dress is real silk.

"Don't mind us." Veró smirks as we creep past them.

"Carry on," Drew chirps. As soon as we're out of earshot of the couple, they mumble, "If I have to relive someone's worst memory, at least it's a *gay* worst memory."

Veró laughs but Blythe doesn't. She has other things on her mind. I'm willing to bet we're worried about the same thing: How will the others react when they see the Lilies initiation? Who will they blame when they watch what happens to Charlotte? I try to ignore the feeling that's winding its way around my chest. I push ahead of the group and lead us onward.

We round the corner of bookshelves and find ourselves at the edge of the main atrium. The temporary stage and podium are to our right. The stage is encircled with flower arrangements, each carefully crafted into Archwell *A*s. Next to it is the Alumni Association table, where about thirty or so older women, also in white, are cackling over their champagne flutes. Their diamond rings sparkle in the low light, each a tiny infinity. I recognize some of the women from my mother's board meetings and donor meet and greets. Ms. Attmore, Class of '75. Ms. Williams, Class of '81. Ms. Livingston, Class of '01.

"We better move," I murmur to the others. "When the alumni get drunk, they like to give advice."

I try to be strategic with our moves, skirting around the edge of the crowd. We wind up over by the tables reserved for the class of 2025. I keep my gaze lowered, careful not to make eye contact with anyone. I can't have any of the juniors recognizing me. Instead, I focus on the dresses: a beaded flapper style with fringe, a long-sleeved wrap dress with a midi skirt, a sequined asymmetrical style with an off-the-shoulder cut.

Then in the crowd, I hear someone say it. Their voice is lower than the room's chatter, but I still hear it clear as a bell. "Ut sacram memoriam."

I lift my gaze in time to see someone pull on a dark green robe over their lacy minidress. From this distance, I can't quite make out who it is, but I know it has to be either Shelby or Courtney. Both of them are Lilies. Both wore identical lace minidresses to Founder's Night: an unintentional but minor fashion snafu.

The gathering will begin soon. I remember Friday's initiation started at ten o'clock.

Before I can follow the girl in the Lilies robe, she's gone. I stop in my tracks, scanning the expanse of candles and beauties.

"Where are we going exactly?" Veró hisses in my ear over

the noise of the crowd. "Should we be following you or Blythe? Whose memory is this?"

"Not sure yet," I lie again. "Just be patient. We need to be careful and make sure we don't derail anything."

Someone knocks against a nearby table and there's the sound of broken glass and the smell of spilled champagne. A lone lily falls to the floor and is trampled. A group of nearby freshmen breaks into laughter.

Then I hear the words again, this time louder. "Ut sacram memoriam."

I crane my neck and search the crowd for another girl in a green robe. I know where we need to be. The others just can't know it yet. If I can just hold on to the secret for a few more moments . . .

Someone bumps into me from behind and I wince, ready for the loop to suck me out of time and rearrange me back into the closet. But nothing happens. I look over my shoulder and find Drew and Blythe looking even more shabby than I realized in their barely passable Founder's Night whites.

"Where did Veró go?" I ask, anxiety straining my voice.

Drew says nothing. Blythe's eyes bounce around the crowd. "Maybe she saw something she wanted to check out," she says.

Shit. This wasn't supposed to happen. I'm supposed to lead them. I'm supposed to stay in control. Losing Veró is a liability. If she tries to find Charlotte, tries to shift the memory, the loop will definitely reject it. And what then? We'll end up right back where we started but in a much worse position: one where infinite memory starts to *erode the mind*, as the Lilies say.

I attempt to shake off the anger before I say anything.

Keep it together. Try to stay in control.

"She really shouldn't have done that," I say. "We need to stick together if this is going to—"

"Charlotte Vanderheyden?" Someone says from over my shoulder. I freeze. "Nah. She didn't really do that. No way."

I watch the other two as their eyes search the crowd for whoever uttered Charlotte's name.

"I'm telling you," someone else hushes. "She literally talked so much on that date that Margaret was like, 'See ya later, Char.' The girl has the subtlety of a parakeet."

"You're so bad," the first voice says. I peer over my shoulder to see who's talking and recognize Maya McConnell and Amy Yang. No sign of Charlotte, just gossip.

"I've heard that rumor before," Blythe murmurs, pulling us away from Maya and Amy so they don't hear us and throw the loop off course. "The one about Margaret and Charlotte."

"It's not true, though . . . Margaret didn't abandon their date," Drew says.

"How do you know?" I ask.

"Because after they got back to campus, they kicked me out of our dorm room so they could make out," they answer. "It wasn't the nicest thing anyone has ever done, but it doesn't warrant a nasty rumor based on—"

A familiar voice cuts Drew's sentence in half.

"And that's when I told her no way, you may *not* post pictures of us together. That's going to make things between us look way too official."

Fuck. Charlotte's voice is loud and close. Too close. Time to move.

"C'mon," I say, grabbing Blythe and Drew by the wrists and yanking them behind the nearest row of bookshelves.

"What?" Blythe says, shoving my grip away and peeking out from our new hiding spot.

"It's Charlotte," Drew says, their words rushed and urgent. "She's right there, see?"

Charlotte's hair shines in the candlelight. She's wearing a white-and-gold sequined dress. Her long bell sleeves scatter flecks of light. She looks beautiful. Prettier than I remember. But then again, the last time I saw her, her face was partially covered by a blindfold.

I steal a glance at Blythe and notice that some of her fear has melted away. She's watching Charlotte closely, just as Drew is. They're waiting for something: an opportunity to track her next move, a moment to possibly intervene. Like Veró, these two might be looking for a chance to change what happened. It occurs to me now that I can't trust either of them to do what I say and let things unfold, just like I can't trust Verónica Martín.

A dizzy, unmoored feeling starts to set in. And then the question appears in my head like a riptide, carrying me away: Was I ever in control? If I had been, then Charlotte wouldn't have disappeared in the first place. The thought echoes through me. I shake my head a little, but it doesn't dislodge.

Maybe I'm just as helpless as everyone else.

"It's like, I don't like you like that. We're just talking. Ya know?" My eyes dart back over to Charlotte and I recognize a telling slur in her words. "Some girls can't take a hint."

Charlotte's body shifts slightly to the right. She stumbles a little. Now I can see that she's talking to Katie Reynolds, who's wearing a chiffon dress and her Lilies ring. She taps her diamond infinity symbol against her little silver flask before taking a sip. Katie always made me feel bad for eating Annys like candy, but she never seemed to be without a little sauce. I'm not surprised to find out that she was the one who got Charlotte sloshed.

"Gimme," Charlotte says.

"No!" Katie bats her back playfully. "You've had enough. We've got a big night ahead of us. You're becoming a little tonight, remember?"

"Shhhhh!" Charlotte's shush involves some spittle. "You're gonna get me in trouble with them. You're not supposed to talk about you-know-what in public."

"Relax," Katie says. "You're a legacy. They have to let you in no matter what. It'll be a piece of cake. Nothing like what I had to do last year, I'm sure."

"They don't let every legacy in." Charlotte's tone is

suddenly serious, although her alcohol-induced slur is undermining every word she utters. "My roommate . . . you know, the weird one. Yeah, you know! Dre—"

She hiccups before she can finish saying Drew's name, but we all know who she's talking about. I steal a glance at them, noting a new tension in their shoulders.

"They didn't let Drew in. And they're a legacy, ya know? You know everything, Katie! I love you so much!"

Charlotte leans in and gives Katie a big hug. Katie rolls her eyes but allows it to happen. When Charlotte speaks again, her voice is too low to hear over the sound of the party. Just a few words come through.

"Drew . . . And so their grandmother was in with them, ya know . . . Double-crosser . . . That's what my grandmother Evelyn says anyway, but she doesn't remember much anymore. She has dementia. That's why she talks about the Lilies all the time. She forgot the rules."

I hate this—the way these girls throw around secrets like they're party favors. No respect at all. I knew Charlotte was a likely leak, but I didn't think Katie would be so cavalier on the topic of the Lilies. No matter what anyone says about womanhood, I know the truth: trust is hard to come by among girls.

"Wow." Katie sounds unimpressed by Charlotte's garbled story. "I didn't realize your grandmother was one of the founders too. So you're like a super-legacy. Is that why they put you and Drew together as roommates?"

"I dunno." Charlotte shakes her head. "One thing I do know, though—the Lilies control everything that happens at Archwell. Everything." With this she swishes her arm out to demonstrate the concept of everything. In the path of the swing, her arm collides with the table's centerpiece. It comes crashing to the ground, candles and all.

"Oop! We're starting a fire over here," Drew says as we watch Charlotte and Katie scramble to pick up the fallen arrangement. They're talking like all of this is a joke, but I hear the bitterness in Drew's voice.

"What does Charlotte have against you, anyway?" I ask.

"Dunno."

"Hmm . . ." I let my thoughts marinate for a moment, waiting to time my next question right. "It's pretty weird that Charlotte would bring up you and your grandmother on the night she disappeared, don't you think?"

"It's pretty weird that *you* belong to a whole secret society named after a girl who disappeared, *don't you think?*"

I didn't expect the clapback. I've pressed on a bruise. Good. Now I know how to hit Drew where it hurts. "It's a shame, really. Maybe you'd actually know something about the Lilies if your 'double-crossing' grandmother had bothered to tell you anything about us before she croaked. Maybe you'd have had a chance. Seems wrong that she didn't give you one."

Before Drew can answer, Blythe cuts in. "Rory, there is no way that Drew's grandmother did or said anything that was worse than what your mom did to Veró and Gabe. Like, c'mon. Let's be real."

Heat rises in my face. The back of my neck prickles. I'm boiling up, but it's not anger. It's something else. Something I don't want to feel.

"Listen," Drew says. "TERFs are TERFs. They're made, not born. TERF behavior is about suppression. It's about control. It's about wanting to maintain a facade."

My stomach lurches as I push the feeling as far down as I can. I wish I were somewhere else: another time and place, where I am safe, and small, and don't have to think about these things.

"Maybe the chancellor acts the way she does because she has something to hide." Drew's voice is as icy as the ocean in winter. I let it wash over me, let the hair on my arms stand on end.

Maybe my mother has something to hide?

Oh, the truth is hard. Harder than Drew or Blythe can comprehend.

Which is why I, like all good Lilies, need to do whatever it takes to maintain the facade.

Veró

IT'S NOT *MY* MEMORY, BUT I remember being there: feeling defeated, my mascara all smeared. It was not a good look the first time, but Founder's Night the second time around is not much better.

Archwell girls of all ages are packed together in their cliques. The bread is dry. The canapés are flavorless. There's a steady flow of champagne and gin. The students camouflage theirs while the alumni brazenly guzzle. We're all here to celebrate a white man, the founder of Archwell. Given how his granddaughter, the chancellor, and his great-granddaughter, Rory, turned out, I'm not so sure this dude is worth celebrating. There are toasts and speeches and grateful tears choked down to what's socially acceptable. A cacophony of caucacity. It's even easier to spot on the second go-around.

I traverse the crowd, finally on my own again. It's a relief to get away from Rory's bullshit and get down to business here in the loop. It's time to make things right, to fix what was broken. If I can just find Charlotte and interrupt whatever horrible thing happened to her, then we can all get out of here. It's not lost on me that saving Charlotte and freeing us from the loop will have side benefits too. Hopefully, it will give me a solid chance to prove to Drew that I'm not a total fuckup. After what happened with Gabe and the chancellor, Drew didn't exactly say that they hate me, but I don't know if they trust me anymore. And I'm realizing that I want them to trust me. I want them to like me. In some way, I feel pulled to them. More than any of the others . . . more than I'm ready to admit. But I can't think about that right now.

I set about looking for Charlotte, eyes flitting from redhead to redhead. She should be here, assuming she hasn't already disappeared. As I slide between cliques, I home in on different conversations.

"Jillian was going to let me borrow her Tom Ford for tonight, but Bettina said I could get my own from this year's collection."
"You're so bad, calling your mom by her first name."

"I felt like the thirty-year reunion was kind of a letdown. I was expecting more."
"Well, you know, it was a pandemic year. I think not everyone was comfortable . . ."

"Did you see Eleanor on DC Daily last month?"
"Ugh! Yes. Completely fabulous."

"It's gonna be huge, trust me. The bigs get together around ten, right after all this wraps up."

"Is that when I should show up?"

"Closer to eleven for new initiates. Don't worry about that though. Someone will take care of it."

"How will I know where to go?"

"We'll find you."

My ears prick up at the word *initiates*. I ease behind the nearest table and bend down to tie my shoe. Well, first I have to untie it . . . then retie it. It's not my slickest move ever but it works. No one notices that resident art freak Veró Martín is listening.

"Who all is coming?" This voice is high and soft. Freshman, for sure.

"I can't tell you that. Some new blood. Some legacies. It's always like that." This voice is smooth and slow. I don't quite recognize the tone. But it's definitely sus. This is obviously about some Lilies cult shit.

"Is Drew Simmons coming? I saw them wearing an infinity ring," the first voice asks.

The second girl doesn't respond immediately. She's calculating how to put this delicately. "The society is girls only," she says. "It's always been like that."

A flash of anger pushes its way through my chest. I pull my laces tight and listen hard.

"If they have a Lilies ring, doesn't that make them a legacy, though?"

The voices are beginning to fade. I stand and try to catch a glimpse of the girls, but their backs are to me. One has long, shiny black hair. The other has a blond pixie cut.

"I don't know . . . I don't know about that," the one with the long hair says.

With that, they disappear into the crowd. I try to follow but I can't move fast enough. Frustration pinches between my shoulders. I stretch up to my tiptoes and scan the room for the girl with the long dark hair and her short blond henchman. Instead, I see Rory.

Her hair is pulled back into an elegant ballerina bun she must've thrown together after I ditched her. For the first time, I noticed the rose tint of her lips and the graceful curve of her brows. She looks good. Better than I remember. At least more rested. She is talking to that girl, Caitlin Callahan. Her eyes flicker over to me but the expression of recognition never comes.

She's ignoring me. Good. I'm over Rory Archwell's shit anyway.

I realize that she probably knows my plans: to change what happened, to make things right. Not through an installation, but through direct action this time . . . although I don't really know what that looks like yet.

Of course, Rory doesn't want me to mess with her and Blythe's memory. She benefits from things staying the same, whether she knows it or not. For that reason, among others, Rory is dangerous.

Before she can decide to drop her silent treatment act and

come mess with me, I dart behind the nearest bookshelf and sink to the floor. The noise of the party is deadened, but only slightly. I rest my hands on the carpet on either side of me, noticing a trace of pink paint on my knuckle. Is it possible that this pink paint has been on my hands since last Friday? Or is it just a vestige of my replayed memory?

The shade of magenta takes me back to the memory of my bathroom #transinclusionatarchwell installation. I'm done with my part of the time loop, but the memory is still torturing me. Gabe's face materializes in my mind and I wince. He wasn't at the Founder's Night party. The chancellor had already dispatched him by then. I remind myself that, in his story, I'm one of the villains: a bad friend, someone who bulldozed his life in the name of art. Guilt wells in my tear ducts, but I try not to give in.

"It's atrocious," a voice moans from the other side of the bookcase, drawing my attention. "I would hope that Archwell's curriculum never would fall prey to those sorts of radical cultural politics."

"I'm not sure if accounting for historical context is particularly radical."

I recognize the second voice immediately. I can't see Ms. Katz, of course, but I can make out a librarian-shaped shadow from between the shelves.

"I think acknowledging an author's political and personal history to contextualize their work is a bare minimum for teaching high school students, wouldn't you agree?"

"Of course, Rachel. But that doesn't mean Fitzgerald and Hemingway should be written out of the curriculum."

"Even when there's anti-Semitism baked into their narratives? Come on now, Caroline. How do you think that made *me* feel when *we* were in school?"

I didn't realize Ms. Katz was an alum. I try to picture her as an Archwell girl fifteen or twenty years ago, maybe with bangs and a headband, probably with thick-framed hipster glasses. I wonder if she and this Caroline person—definitely another alum—were friends. The more I eavesdrop, the less likely it seems.

"Oh, don't be silly. None of us liked reading *The Sun Also Rises* and it wasn't because it was anti-Semitic. It was because we were kids and we didn't know any better."

I catch myself curling into a ball of anger. Caroline's dismissiveness is a bit too familiar. I can only imagine how many times Ms. Katz has had to wade through this sort of trash argument as a distinctly un-Archwell-y librarian.

"I'm saying that we all *should have* known better. The adults in our lives should have known better. Now it's up to us to live up to what this current generation deserves. Minimally, I think that means our idea of the cannon needs to evolve."

Before Caroline can get in another word, Ms. Katz maneuvers. "Ah, it's after quarter till. I promised the chancellor I'd help with dorm duty for the underclassmen. Good to see you, Caro." Except it doesn't really sound like it was good to see Caro at all. Ms. Katz's tone is more along the lines of *fuck you, Caro.*

I peek between the bookshelves and smile as I watch Ms. Katz walk away. For a second, I see her as she once was: Rachel from the class of '06. Brown curly hair. Gentle smile. I wonder why, after all this, Ms. Katz is still at Archwell. But then I remember that she's probably ensnared in the school's web just like the rest of us. I imagine that she also knows the strange feeling of being tied to a place that was designed to exclude people like you.

I glance at the clock above the circulation desk. It's almost ten p.m. The crowd is beginning to thin out but the music and chatter stay loud. I notice a white girl with silky black hair perched at a nearby table. She fingers the table's center-piece and shifts her eyes around the room. She's looking for someone, waiting for something to happen.

Nearby, a group of alumni hug their friends goodbye. Some of them take flowers from the tables and weave them into their hair. "For old time's sake," one of them says.

An upperclassman blows out one of the candles.

"Ut sacram memoriam," someone in the crowd murmurs. It's loud enough for me to hear, but probably too quiet for anyone else. I try to locate the speaker, eyes darting from girl to girl, but there's no sign of her.

My gaze falls back on the girl with the silky hair. She's still alone. Behind her, the library shadows grow longer as more candles go out, signaling the end of the Founder's Night party.

Then from those same shadows, a pair of hands. They clamp over the girl's mouth. Her eyes widen for a split second and then they're gone, covered by a velvety blindfold provided by a second pair of pale hands. She doesn't have time to scream. Somehow, I seem to have lost my voice too.

The hands wrestle the girl back into the stacks with little resistance. They pass by my hiding spot, nearly rounding the bookshelf corner and running smack into me. The two robed figures are a blur of dark green, faces covered by hoods topped by wiry flower crowns. The girl in their grips wriggles and resists as they drag her along the library carpet. I hear the dull sound of her heels against the floor. She's trying to stop them. Trying to pause time.

It's the Lilies. The beginning of their initiation. This is my first glimpse of it.

I rise to my feet and scurry after them. I know they'll take me to Charlotte if I can keep up. Then I'll find the right moment—the perfect window of opportunity—to pounce. To make things right.

I run as fast as I can, but that's not very fast. I've walked the mile for the Presidential Fitness Test every year, no matter how much shit gym teachers give me. Now I'm wishing I'd at least jogged a bit. It would've better prepared me for this.

By the time I've rounded the fourth corner of bookshelves, the Lilies and their captive are gone.

I freeze. Do I wander deeper into the stacks and try to find them? What if they see me and the memory resets before I can intervene? Or do I retrace my steps and look for more of their kind? The girl they took looked nothing like Charlotte, but I can only imagine they will do the same thing to her. If I can find a way to time it right, I might be able to disrupt the moment the Lilies take her away. With any luck, that'll launch us out of the time loop once and for all.

My breathing slows and so do my thoughts. I consider whether I'm getting ahead of myself here, like I always do. I'm quick, but I don't always think first. It's Papi's favorite and least favorite thing about me.

The first time I got kicked out of school, he came to pick me up from Forrest Gable himself. I was still young, barely done with the first quarter of seventh grade. He didn't talk to me for most of the drive home from NorCal, so I just stared out the window and took in the cliff views from Highway One, spotting swirling patterns in the clouds above and the waves below.

Papi broke his silence somewhere between Las Cruces and Santa Barbara. "I know you believe in justice, mija. That's a wonderful thing. But sometimes you have to take a step back to see the whole picture." He was quiet for a moment as we came to a traffic slowdown. "Getting expelled for fighting . . . it's just not you."

"I didn't start it," I insisted again. "Andy Corcoran has been bullying Teresa online all year and none of the teachers did anything about it. He deserved to get punched in the jaw."

"You inserted yourself," Papi said sternly. "And then when you blew up at Principal Foster you made it all about you and how he was being unfair to *you* specifically."

"It *was* unfair," I pressed.

"Where's your friend Teresa in all of this?" he countered. "Did she get justice because you got hotheaded? No. And now she has one less friend at school and you have an obvious smudge on your permanent record."

I crossed my arms and looked back out the window. Traffic had come to a standstill.

"Promise me you won't fight at school anymore, Veró. At least not with your fists."

"Fine," I huffed. Papi had a point. I had rushed into things. I hadn't asked Teresa before I confronted Andy. I hadn't asked Gabe before I made the installation. Now I was going out on my own to save the day . . . but did it make sense to go it alone?

You're losing time, the ghost of Malcriada whispers to me. *You can't wait around forever. You have to act.*

Maybe so, but it's probably better to work in solidarity with people I trust.

I turn back toward the main atrium to find Drew. We're more likely to uncover clues together. Plus, I'm better hidden in plain sight. The crowd is down to a skeleton crew, but the music is still as loud as ever. Whoever is controlling the playlist is obviously trying to clear the room. They're back to playing old songs.

Time is on my side. Yes it is. Time is on my side. Yes it is.

I emerge from behind the shelves and float to the silky-haired girl's table, now empty. Her half-full glass is still there. There's a partially eaten mini quiche on a napkin with a trace of lip gloss at its corner. The girl is gone, but somehow, I feel her here still. Maybe it's the loop, or maybe it's just in my mind. But if I'm being really honest with myself, I can feel all of them: the girl with the silky hair, Ms. Katz, Charlotte, even Lillian Archwell. Here one moment and then gone the next.

No, not gone, Malcriada's ghost breathes. *They're all always here. So are you. Memory is forever.*

I shiver the voice out of my head and back away from the table. My shoulder brushes against someone else's.

"'Scuse me," the girl says as I turn to face her.

Oh no.

I'm standing there in my Founder's Night whites, hair loose, mascara smudged.

I look a bit shocked to see me.

I can't quite blame myself.

I wasn't expecting it either.

Bong!

Time. Time. Time is on my side. Yes it is, the song croons.

Bong!

The colors of the room spiral into each other. The library becomes a massive pinwheel.

Bong!

All the oxygen concentrates at the spiral's center point. I can't breathe.

Bong!

Blythe

AFTER I KNEW FOR SURE that Charlotte had vanished, I called Salim. I shouldn't have, but I did. I didn't tell him about it, obviously. I never mentioned her or Rory. I didn't tell him about the Lilies and what they'd done to me . . . what I'd become. Salim didn't know that his baby sister was a monster. He just knew that my voice had taken on a particular pitch to cover the pain. He knew that something wasn't right.

"You want me to come get you?" he said.

"No," I said. "I've got midterms on Monday. I gotta study."

"Okay," he answered. "I know being at Archwell has been hard on you, Blythe. But you're so close to graduation. I promise it'll all be worth it. And in the meantime, you got me, aight?"

Except I didn't have Salim, not as long as I couldn't tell him my secrets.

At Archwell, I don't have anybody, a fact that is painfully clear in the loop of my memory.

We're barely back in the closet for thirty seconds before

Veró springs to her feet, throws the door open, grabs me and Drew by the hand, and marches us out into the library. I'm still nauseous from the violence of the reset, my stomach doing somersaults.

Then I take a deep breath and realize I'm not queasy just from lurching back to the start of my loop again. It's also the smell. The vaulted ceiling above the library's main atrium is abuzz with flies. Below, the room is still crowded with girls in off-white, gathering around tables of newly decaying flower arrangements. The aroma of lilies has been replaced by the smell of sludge at the bottom of a vase.

The music is strange. It's the same as before but somehow every note sounds flat this time. *I can't forget you. I've got these memories of you*, the singer pines.

"I think the loop reset us," Drew says. "This doesn't seem like a new memory."

"That was me," Veró explains. "I ran into myself before I had a chance to change anything."

"What?"

"Damn it, Veró." Rory's thorny words come from behind. Veró doesn't stick around to hear more. She leads the way along the mezzanine and down the spiral staircase.

"Where are you going?" Rory calls after us, but Veró doesn't stop.

We pass the two sophomores making out by the emergency exit. They're still at it. Or, I suppose, they're just at it again.

We head toward the crowd: a swirl of bodies, each with a distinct stench, as if each girl has started to decompose in my memory. Or maybe the smell is just my mind starting to go—like Rory said it would—as the loop degrades to dust.

In the throng of white gowns, I've lost sight of Drew and Rory. I want to get out of here, away from the thick of the memory. I yank my hand away from Veró.

"Let go."

"Sorry, Blythe. I'm just trying to get us to the right spot. Where did—"

"What spot?" I insist, running my hands over my wrist. It almost feels like Veró has left a rug burn.

"I saw them take someone," she says. "I wanted us to go find Charlotte together. I wanted us to follow the Lilies before they snatched her. I'm thinking it was close to ten o'clock when it must've happened, so we still have some time to get set up with a good hiding place. I need you to show me where to go to put a stop to all this kidnapping shit."

"Kidnapping?" It's hard to focus on what Veró is saying. The party is too loud, a collision of laughter and delighted squeals reaching a fever pitch. I can smell the buffet from here, the odor of singed catering pans and sterno cups. It melds with the rotting flower smell. My stomach roils.

"You need to show me where the Lilies take their initiates," Veró says. "It'll help us find out what happened to Charlotte and put a stop to it. It'll help us get out of the loop for good."

So Veró is playing detective, just like Drew. I suppose she has been this whole time. She's digging for the truth about what happened . . . except she still doesn't know that Charlotte was *my* initiate. Anxiety, refusing to leave me be, squeezes around my lungs.

"What about the others?" I ask.

"Rory's on some other shit. You know that already," she says. "She's not gonna try to disrupt the loop. She's too afraid of what will happen. And she's definitely not gonna tell me anything about the Lilies. Especially not with Drew around. But you . . . you already know a lot about them. You can expose them. Let people know what they're really up to. If we can get with Drew and find Charlotte, maybe we can put a stop to all this."

The tight sensation in my chest turns into an ache. The memory of Charlotte's initiation dangles in front of me. But I don't need to retreat into my mind to return to it. I'm here, about to live it all over again.

It's not so much what will happen next in the memory that makes me afraid. It's what will happen inside my mind: what will happen when the feelings force their way out again, breaking the dam.

I don't know if I can bring myself to see Charlotte again, not after what I did to her.

My eyes meet Veró's. She might be in my memory but thankfully she's not in my mind. She doesn't know that I'm starting to question the notion that saving Charlotte is our only way out of here. She thinks we're on the same team . . . and I hate to think about it, but Veró is naive. If I've learned anything from being a Lily—hell, from just being *me*—it's to never assume folks are on your side.

"Watch yourself around them." Grandma Rose's words return to me. "Those girls at that school will make you feel like you lost your mind."

"Please, Blythe. You have to help me do this," Veró pleads. "We have to fix this. I don't wanna live with this regret. If we can get out of here—stop whatever happens to Charlotte—then I can try to make things right with Gabe again and Charlotte will be back and . . . Please, can you just help me make it right?"

I take a deep breath and nod. I can empathize with how she feels, even though she's leading me deeper into a memory that I don't want to relive. Still, I figure it's better to go along with her for now, at least until the right moment.

Relief spreads across her face. "Thank you," she breathes. "C'mon, I'll take you to where I last saw them."

We cut a path through the party, skirting the wall, approaching the library's main entrance. As we get closer, Veró picks up her pace. She seems to think that we're going to somehow make it through this crowd without getting recognized. My stomach lurches and I stop.

"Hold up," I say, grabbing her by the hand. "We can't go that way."

"It worked just fine for me before," she says. "Trust me."

I feign a smile at her. Despite her years at Archwell, Veró's instincts tell on her. She's basically still a newbie here, someone with no idea how to navigate the school's unspoken hierarchies. "It might have worked for *you* before," I tell her. "But when your face is on the school brochure, you don't have the luxury of anonymity."

Recognition spreads across Veró's brow. She forgot that I'm an unwilling poster child. "Got you," she says. "We can go around the other side."

We backtrack and make our way around the library in the opposite direction, continuing to hug the outer wall, safely shrouded by a couple of rows of bookshelves.

"What exactly did you see before?" I manage to ask as we steal along.

"Two girls in green robes," Veró answers. "They had flower crowns on. Lilies and sticks . . . I dunno, they looked kinda like antlers? I couldn't see their faces. They had hoods on. I'm assuming that's them, yeah?"

"Mmm," I say. "That's them."

I stop myself from saying "that's *us*."

The memory of the flower crown is heavy, its wicker binding pressing into the skin of my forehead. I run my thumb along the spot for a moment, feeling for an impression that's no longer there.

"They took a girl and blindfolded her," Veró explains. "Covered her mouth so she couldn't say anything. I tried to follow behind but . . ."

I picture the blindfold, a heavy velvet with an embroidered infinity symbol. Veró must not have noticed the collection of them in the closet. She doesn't understand what the blind-folds are for . . . doesn't understand why someone would do such a thing.

The memory of the blindfold in my hand is so clear. It is a thing of power, suddenly transformed into just another loose strip of fabric the moment I take it off Charlotte's eyes. Those eyes, excited and scared . . . and then . . .

I run my hand along the wall, trying to steady myself. Gravity feels like it's shifting underneath me. The forces of nature are telling me to turn back. My head aches and I worry that my mind is turning to dust.

"It's just up here," Veró says.

But my feet won't carry me forward anymore. I can't do it again. Not with Veró watching. I can't let the memory carry me away.

All at once, I notice that my breath is ragged. My hand is leaving sweaty fingerprints on the polished wooden paneling. I slide my palm forward, willing myself to keep going. Instead, my fingers collide with something cool and metallic.

I gasp but I can't get any more air into my lungs.

I can't have another panic attack. Not right now.

I try not to think of Charlotte.

I try not to think of the Lilies.

I try not to think of the white bear.

Don't think about it, Blythe. Don't think about it.

I don't want panic to carry me away, but it does, and I wind up back on the tear gas flooded streets of DC. My face mask is soaked with tears. My legs won't move any farther. I'm thirteen again and I know that I'm dying.

I remember thinking it was just as well, since I assumed my brothers were already dead. They were certainly gone. And in a swarm of riot cops literally fighting with masked protesters, who could blame me for assuming the worst?

I barely felt it when Salim grabbed me by the waist, picked me up, and carried me.

He and Sean had found me. They weren't lost anymore, and neither was I. But I was numb to it all. The damage had been done.

You're in your body, Blythe, I call to myself from far away. *Ground yourself.*

Shaking still, overtaken by my panic, I turn to the library wall and come face-to-face with my savior: a little red box with white lettering.

Fire Alarm.

"You okay, Blythe?" Veró asks.

Maybe it'll reroute the memory. Maybe it'll change what happened. Maybe it'll just land us back where we started, but I have to try.

I have to get out of the loop before it can consume me.

I don't consult with Veró about my strategy.

Instead, I clamp my fingers around the handle marked *Pull Down.*

I do.

BAHNK! BAHNK! BAHNK! . . . BAHNK! BAHNK! BAHNK!

A moment after the alarm goes off, the hiss of the overhead sprinklers springs down to meet us.

Bong!

The room washes away.

Bong!

Books disintegrate into pulp.

Bong!

We're sucked out of the library and our bodies stretch between dimensions. The fibers of my muscles threaten to tear. A scream gathers in my throat—

Then we're back in the closet.

The passage doesn't get easier, just more familiar.

"Ucckk . . ." someone groans. "That felt bad."

"One of you reset us again," someone else growls. Probably Rory. It's always Rory.

"How can you be sure?" the first voice mutters. "Getting reset hurts just as much as an end to someone's memory."

"What the hell, Blythe?" This time it's definitely Veró. "What was that about?"

The tears are back, hot and determined. I can't hide them from her now. Maybe I was kidding myself that I ever hid them before.

The light clicks on and Drew is standing over me, steadying the swing of the bulb's little metal cord. "You okay?" they ask me.

"No! Obviously, I'm not okay!" The words come out louder and angrier than I intend. I'm so used to holding them down, so used to the lump in my throat. The sound startles even me.

I am a puddle of fury on the floor. I never let folks see me this way, not Rory, not even Salim. The tension in my body reminds me of why. I can't fall apart like this because it's not safe. Because I can't trust anyone at Archwell. Because I'm all I've got here.

I wipe the tears away with the back of my hand and try to get up.

"Whoa, hold on," Drew says. "We don't have to go right back out there. Just sit and catch your breath for a second."

But it's too late. I feel it. Something has broken inside of me. My reason? My sense of self? My grip on reality? It doesn't matter what has come unhinged because now that whatever it is has broken free, it's revealed a new truth: a way to bring all of this to a stop.

"I'm not going back out there," I say. "I'm done."

"We have to," Veró says. "We have to face the past in order to change it. It'll be worth it. I promise you."

"You don't know what happened," I say. "It's not *your* memory to change."

"It's *our* memory," Rory tells me. "I was there too, remember? I get that it's hard to face what happened, but we need to find a way to get through all this."

I attempt to wipe my tears away again, but they keep coming. No surprise there, I guess. I can't stand crying in front of other people, but I can't keep pushing all this down. It just makes it worse.

"I maybe didn't live through the same thing you did," Veró says, crouching next to me on the floor. "But I definitely know what it feels like. We all do."

"For real," Drew says. "This whole thing is a total—"

"—mindfuck," Rory finishes Drew's sentence. She waits a beat, giving me a moment to collect myself a bit, before speaking again. "I don't blame you for feeling this way about Founder's Night, Blythe. I truly don't. But we don't really have a choice here."

Then I'm back to crying again. The only way out *is* to face the truth, whether I relive the memory completely or I try to change what happened.

I catch my breath, preparing myself for what's about to come out.

"The initiation," I say. "It went . . . wrong."

"Okay," Veró says. "Wrong how?"

"Say more," Drew urges.

"I . . . I don't know . . . if I can."

At first, no one says anything. Drew shifts their body weight and bumps against the closet shelves on the opposite wall. Something clinks to the floor.

Rory reaches out, wrapping her manicured fingers around the little thing before she holds it up to the light. I half expect it to be a ring from the collection, but it's a weirdly shaped thing. Some kind of pipe.

187

"What is—? Oh my god, does the chancellor have a *drug habit* on top of everything else?" Drew asks.

Rory flashes daggers at them but avoids her attack instinct. "This is obviously an antique," she says.

"Yeah, but the bowl is black. It looks like it's been used," Veró adds. "What's it for, sand?"

"You don't smoke sand," Rory and I say in unison. Then I look at her, wishing that I didn't know anything about sand. Wishing that Rory had never introduced me to the stuff.

"That's an opium pipe." All eyes turn to Drew, whose expression shifts from confident to sheepish in a split second. "Don't look at me like that," they say. "My mom and I like to watch *Antiques Roadshow* together. One time someone brought on a snuff box and an opium pipe like that—for the appraisers."

"You really are a little weird one, aren't you?" Veró says.

"Oh, yes." Drew grins. "Very strange. But useful! I could come by your dorm some time and appraise some of your valuables if you want."

Veró blushes. These two have completely lost the thread of our conversation.

"GET A ROOM," Rory groans, breaking the spell.

"Huh? Whatever, Rory. Chill." Veró pretends like she doesn't know what Rory is talking about, but her blush deepens all the same. "Where were we? Charlotte. The Lilies initiation gone wrong. Blythe, you don't need to rehash it right now if you're not ready, but when we go back out there, we need consensus about our game plan. I say we keep trying to disrupt whatever happened to Charlotte. Maybe stop the initiation. But we need *everyone* to commit."

She directs a pointed look at me, and I wince. I need a fire alarm for *this whole situation*. But there is no escape hatch, not for me anyway.

"Only when her sisters' wrongs are once again made right will she escape anew and take her place within the light," Drew recites.

I give them side-eye. "You committed that to memory pretty quick," I say.

"Well, like Veró said, I'm an AP Lit kid. We memorize stuff." They say this as they fidget with their shirt collar. "More important, I'm serious about finding Charlotte," they say. "And I want out of this loop before . . . well, before—"

"Before it all turns to shit?" Rory interrupts. "Too late! We're knee-deep in it!" I realize now that Rory is pacing the closet. Something is winding her up. Maybe it's the fact that Drew can recite the Lilies vow from memory, maybe it's because we've been lingering in the closet for a while, maybe it's something else. All I know is that Rory is looking pressed as hell to get out of here.

"But we can at least—"

Before Drew can finish their sentence, Rory starts shouting.

"WE-CANNOT-CHANGE-THE-PAST." She claps to emphasize each of the syllables in her thought. "THE-LOOP-WILL-KILL-US-IF-WE-KEEP-TRYING. WE-WILL-ALL-TURN-TO-DUST."

189

Rory seems surprised when none of us are impressed by her rhetorical tactics. "AS-IN-FISH-FOOD," she adds.

That last bit makes some of us giggle. It's a wild kind of sound, like we're all just about to crack, but we tamp it down before Rory flies off the handle completely.

Suddenly, Charlotte's bright smile pops into my mind. I shut my eyes and the rest of her face appears to me as clearly as if she were standing right in front of me. Drew and Veró believe that she can be brought back. If time is infinite, if the present is the past, if I can relive more than one memory at once, then maybe they're right.

Maybe infinity is not rigid like the ring on my hand. Maybe it is flexible. I consider whether we can do what the vow says and right the wrongs to *escape anew*. There must be a hole in the loop. A loophole. Another wild giggle escapes my lips.

The Charlotte in my mind nods encouragingly. She's as earnest and open as the first day I met her, shortly after she was selected to join the Lilies.

When I found out she was going to be my little, I was genuinely annoyed. Pairing us was Rory's little way of playing a joke on me. I try to keep a low profile, but she was sticking me with a little Lily that had a reputation for being loud.

"I'm SO EXCITED you're gonna be my big sister, Blythe," she told me.

"Definitely, same," I said, adding honey to my voice. "I'll

always have your back. When you're a Lily, someone is always looking out for you." I left out the part about how someone also will always know your deepest secrets and not hesitate to lord them over you, but Charlotte was about to find that out soon enough.

Her expression shifted slightly. A flicker of sadness cut across her smile. "That's good."

I immediately sensed it: an opportunity to extract information.

I was always good at this part of being a Lily. It fit in well with my whole low-profile thing. I could make anyone feel like I was on their side. Girls would confide in me. I would collect secrets like currency.

"You okay, Char?" I asked, cocking my head to the side.

"Yeah."

"You sure, girl?" I said. "C'mon. You can tell me."

She exhaled as she spoke, like she'd been holding something in for a long time. "I mean, it just sounds nice for someone to support you . . . Sometimes I feel like . . ."

"Yes?"

She sighed a little and stared at the ground. "I just feel like I have to always watch out for myself, you know? Like, sometimes I get weird looks from other girls, like I'm being too much or something. I dunno. The rules are like . . . not innate to me, you know?"

I nodded and forced a smile. Charlotte was talking like she was the only one in the world with this problem. Like she was the only one who ever had to put on a mask to fit in. To survive.

"Sometimes I feel like I'm getting judged. I know there's a lot of lesbians here, but I feel like I get side-eyed for being . . . I dunno . . . a slutty lesbian."

"What?"

"I dunno. There's rumors going around about me," Charlotte said. "I'm sure you've heard some of them. People say that I just want to hook up and then be a loudmouth about it."

"Oh." I shook my head. "I haven't heard that," I lied.

"Well, I'm not slutty. I just like girls. And I don't mean to be a blabbermouth or interrupt people or whatever, but my brain just works differently. I feel like girls here don't understand what it's like to have ADHD. I'm getting judged for it."

I wasn't sure what to say to Charlotte. The best thing I could come up with felt hollow. "I'm sorry you feel like that's happening."

She said nothing in response and only turned away. "Anyway, I'm just really excited to be a Lily. You know, my grandmother, Evelyn Smith, was one of the founders. Have you heard of her?"

"Of course," I lied. At the time, I tried to fix my expression by biting down on the insides of my cheeks. What did Charlotte know about judgment? About prejudice?

Thinking about how I behaved toward Charlotte, even before her Lilies initiation, I start to cringe. If I had treated her like she was really my sister, things might have worked out differently. I might have been able to interrupt some of those sidelong looks. I could've squashed gossip and rumors about her. After all, wouldn't the girls who were being weird about Charlotte be even more likely to be weird about me? I remind myself that *weird* isn't the right word.

Time has a funny way of changing your perspective on things.

"*For only when her sisters' wrongs are once again made right will she escape anew and take her place within the light . . .* We have to change it," I mutter.

"What did you say, Blythe?"

I look up at Veró, Drew, and Rory from the closet floor. "I said, I want to try to change what happened," I say. "For real this time." I climb to my feet and meet Rory's bloodshot eyes.

"Let me try," I say. "It's as much in our vow as anything: I need to try to right the wrong I did. I want to stop what happened at initiation. I know I'll have an opportunity."

"What if it . . . What if it doesn't . . ." Rory's voice is way smaller than before. She sounds like she's pleading with me but I'm not sure why. She's holding something back . . . but that's just Rory being Rory, I suppose.

"You just have to trust me," I say. "Try to trust, Rory."

"Think of it like an experiment," Drew says.

Rory says nothing. Instead, she fiddles with her Lilies ring and avoids meeting my eyes. If three of us are resolved about changing the past, then she can't keep us from doing it.

"Fantastic. That's settled," Veró says. "Let's not waste any more time out there. Where does initiation take place?"

"The basement," I answer. The words pull at my throat. My body doesn't want to go back there. Neither does my mind. But my heart . . .

"Okay," Drew says.

"Okay," Veró says. "Then we'll go to the basement."

Rory stays silent. A storm is gathering between her eyebrows. But it doesn't matter what she thinks right now. Not when so much is on the line.

"Okay," I say. "Let's go."

I NEVER TRIED SAND BEFORE that night. I might have looked like a beatnik, a child of the underground. But really, it was a pose. I was just another high school girl.

Adeline was the one who liked the rush. She kept a stash of the stuff in her nightstand, along with all the trappings one would need to drop out of this reality—things that were mostly a mystery to me. My little sister was always the daredevil of the family, even though she masked it with her stringed pearls and tasteful hemlines.

Meredith was the one with the car, so she would drive us all to town: me, Adeline, and Evelyn. I went for the people watching. Sometimes I'd get a soda with Evelyn. It was all cool . . . until I learned to notice what Adeline was doing in town.

Meredith knew before I did.

Saint Meredith, who tried to help but made things so much worse for all of us. If only she hadn't written that letter . . . the letter that landed me in this nowhere place. The letter that tried to bare all our family secrets.

She could never, of course. She didn't know the half of it. But the note still makes my blood boil every time I see it.

I keep it where I keep all my secrets. Not because I want to hide the thing. Quite the opposite, actually.

If I'm being honest, I probably keep it out of pettiness. But if someone like Meredith Simmons tried to stab you in the back, you would be petty too.

16

Drew

MOM DID A READING FOR me the night before she moved me into the Archwell dorms. I cut the deck. She flipped the cards over and laid them out carefully on my bedspread.

The Moon, the Tower, Death, and the Ten of Swords. My past, my present, my future, and a bit of advice for good measure.

"It's a big transition," she said. "It makes sense that you have triple Major Arcana energy here. It looks scary, but maybe the reality of the situation is not as intense as it feels. Sometimes the Ten of Swords suggests that we're being overly dramatic about a perceived problem in our lives."

I looked down at the tarot spread, studying the illustration of the ten swords plunged into a person's back. Beside it, wolves lurked in the half-light of the Moon card. At the end of the spread, flames leapt from the windows of the crumbling Tower. And then, of course, there was Death. Things were not looking good, but Mom was trying to soften the message. She was trying to shield me from the consequences of my choice. I was throwing myself to the wolves, upending my senior year, all for us. Inheritance money was going to change everything. It was supposed to make things better . . . but the cards suggested otherwise.

I ran my fingers across the Ten of Swords, along the edge of the illustrated blood pooling underneath the tragic figure. "It's a *big transition*," I repeated Mom's words.

She offered me her little encouraging smile. "Don't worry," she said. "It will be okay."

It wasn't.

I am cold in the library in only my undershirt. It doesn't help that something has shifted in the atmosphere, a new humidity that sharpens the loop's penetrating chill. I'm almost grateful when Rory wraps the green hooded robe around me. Almost.

We're at the threshold of the library basement, a dim stone corridor tucked deep into the stacks. In this labyrinth, I can just barely make out the dull murmurs of the Founder's Night party winding down. Twisted snippets of music carry in from far away.

Time. Time. Time is on my side. Yes it is.

Rory unfurls the second robe she brought from the closet and drapes it over Veró.

"Make sure you keep your hood pulled over your face," she says. "We don't want you to get recognized as an outsider."

"Noted," Veró says, pulling the velvety hood over her

curls. "Do we say anything in particular when we get down there?"

"There's no password or anything. It's not like that."

"*Ut sacram memoriam*," Blythe says. "It's the beginning of the vow. When you're called to speak, that's all you should say."

My intestines start to crawl when I hear the Latin aloud. The ring on my finger, Grandma's Lilies ring, feels hot against my skin. My memory comes alive and I see my grandmother sitting up in the hospice bed, gray as a gravestone, wheezing the same words over and over. *Ut sacram memoriam.*

"You okay?" Veró asks me.

Blythe and Rory are already robed and hooded. It's time to go.

"I'm fine," I lie. I pull the hood over my face.

I'm not fine. But surviving at Archwell is an exercise in denying myself again and again—making myself smaller as a way to stay safe. This place is at war with me because of what I represent: a "threat to the community." A threat to their precious little rules, their understanding of the world, and their understanding of themselves.

I'm certain that this is why the Lilies didn't want me. And I'm certain that I will not be safe in their midst.

Find the Lilies, Drew, my grandmother whispers to me.

I know what you did, Death breathes in my ear.

"I'm fine," I say again. It doesn't sound convincing but

lying is a survival tactic. I'm willing to do it if it means getting to Charlotte before the loop can get to me.

We descend the stairwell, bare bulbs illuminating the brick arches overhead. The odor of decay strengthens as we go farther and farther underground.

"Why does it look like a crypt?" Veró asks.

Rory shrugs. "My grandfather really liked Gothic architecture. He wanted this place to look like it had been here for centuries. Every detail had to be perfect, even in the old servant corridors down here."

I steady myself, feeling along the cool condensation of the stone wall. Shadows gather around us and unidentified shapes start to congregate in the dark. I can't tell if my mind is playing tricks on me or if this is just the loop's way of exaggerating the past. I think about how many times we've had to dive into this memory in order to get to this point. I can't remember if this is the third go-around or the fourth. Either way, I would like it to be the last. I don't want to stick around to find out the true meaning of the phrase *memory erodes the mind.*

At the bottom of the stairs, there's an arched opening to a dimly lit room just out of sight. The flickering light suggests the presence of candles. I've been here before, but last time it was completely dark.

I hear a noise on the stairs behind us and my shoulders meet my ears. I'm frozen, expecting a ghost. Instead, Death brushes past me and every hair on the back of my neck pings up. I turn to the figure next to me on the steps, also robed and hooded. I brace myself for the hood to fall back and reveal the skeleton beneath. But Blythe's voice creeps out from beneath the hood.

"There are others coming," she whispers to me. "Just act natural."

What a thing to say.

I turn around and see that she's right. More robed figures are descending the basement steps. There are three of them. One is blindfolded with their hood slightly askew. The other two, crowned with flowers, flank their captive. They move slowly, guiding the blindfolded girl down the treacherous stairs.

"C'mon," Rory whispers. "And no talking now."

We follow her through the cased opening at the bottom of the steps.

The air is damp and stale. The loop's familiar smell of rot mingles with the regular basement smells. But there's another odor too. I know that smell. It's the smell from the dumpster behind Dundalk High. Rats.

The glow of the candles does nothing to warm the room, despite the fact that there must be a hundred or more. They line the space, spanning across stretches of the floor and the sheet-shrouded furniture. The floor is piled with wilted greenery. Magnolia leaves and tiger lilies. Calla lilies and those little yellow daisy-looking flowers with the black eyes. In the center of the room, the flowers are arranged into a figure eight on the floor. A handful of robed figures surround the figure eight, silently watching as we each file into the basement.

I follow the one who I think is Blythe to the far corner of the room, but as more and more robed figures emerge from the stairwell, I lose track of who's who. This is not good. How are any of us going to find Charlotte if we can't recognize each other? We'll never get out of here this way.

Still, I take a deep breath and remind myself that Blythe said she would have an opportunity to subvert the memory during the actual ceremony. I cross my fingers and pray that she'll keep her word this time. But I know I can't trust a Lily.

I scan the crowd, hoping to get a glimpse of someone's face. From this side of the basement, I realize that the flowers at the center of the room are not actually arranged in a figure eight at all. It's a ten-foot-long infinity symbol. Obviously.

Smart, Drew. Very perceptive.

Grandma Simmons's diamond ring simmers against my flesh. This all started with her. She and her friends formed a secret club and named themselves after a girl who vanished. It's a strange thing to do in the first place, but inventing this kind of ritual out of thin air is even stranger. I picture her in her hospice bed wrapped in a green hooded cloak topped with a flower crown. The mental image makes me shudder.

In front of the infinity of flowers, blindfolded girls are lined up and told to kneel. The voices from under the hoods are cold and sharp, not quite human. They seem more . . . feral.

The blindfolds stay on.

When I was here the first time, everyone was gone. Well, almost everyone. The place felt hollow. Empty.

The energy in the room now is solemn and fierce. There's something vicious about the slow movements and stinging whispers. It makes me think of pack animals, wolves surrounding their prey.

I avert my eyes, searching for something else to focus on, a momentary escape from this deep uneasiness. Then I see the door. I know the room that's on the other side. I know what happened there. Or, actually, what *will* happen there.

Death does too.

I ward the thoughts away from me. *That* memory isn't the one I'm reliving at the moment. If everything goes to plan, I won't have to relive it at all.

The memory I'm reliving at this moment, the one I'm standing and breathing in, fortunately, doesn't belong to me.

So why do I feel like it does? Why do I feel somehow responsible for what might happen to the girls in the blindfolds?

Because, Death whispers, *you chose to be here. You each chose to be here.*

I did it to survive, I argue. I chose Archwell because of my grandmother. She wanted the best for me and Mom.

She didn't know you, Death hisses. *She only knew this. She helped build this. And you are complicit in the horror reaped here.*

Suddenly I'm crying, but I can't make a sound, so there is no release. I let the tears collect in the crevices around my mouth, too afraid to move my hands and wipe them away.

I stare at a spot on the wall, trying to find a way back into myself. For the first time, I notice the large metal box inset into the brick. It's about as big as one of those fire extinguisher cases, but this box contains some kind of switch. One of the spiderwebs clinging to the heavy-looking handle flutters in the candlelight. The words *Duck & Cover* are painted across the top of the box in chipped, faded lettering.

Duck and cover? My brain conjures a mallard underneath a blanket.

Unhelpful, brain, I think.

Then I realize it's a reference to bombs.

The box is an old, defunct alarm system, likely from the time when Grandma Simmons was a student here. Air-raid drills, I learned in history class, were common then.

I think of the mallard's green figure one more time and shake my head at myself.

Smart, Drew. Truly visionary.

Someone steps forward from the crowd of robed girls. She is wearing a ring of flowers over her hood like so many of the others, but this one is particularly menacing. Pink lilies are woven in between branches that extend toward the ceiling, like points on a tiara. The pink tint isn't quite natural looking. The hue suggests poison.

This girl is an evil queen. When she speaks, I don't recognize her voice.

"Lilies," she says. "Reveal your initiates."

Several robed and crowned figures step forward and approach the kneeling, blindfolded girls from behind. They each pull back the new initiates' hoods, revealing the top of each girl's head. The blindfolds stay on, but without the hoods, I am starting to recognize the new crop of Lilies. There's Faith Harlow, her hair flat ironed into submission. Next to her is Alice Tran, who's biting her bottom lip. There are a handful of others who I don't know, but among them is the unmistakable red hair . . .

Charlotte is facing slightly away from me, kneeling in front of the infinity symbol and the queen. Instinctually, I look for Blythe among the girls in the inner circle, but I don't see her. Shouldn't this be the moment to strike? To right the wrong, save Charlotte, and get us the hell out of here? I remind myself that there's more to this. The initiation has to go wrong before any of us can make it right.

I look at Charlotte and I wonder if she's scared, like me. Or maybe she's excited. Some of these girls live for all of this, I'm sure.

"*Ut sacram memoriam,*" the queen says.

"*Ut sacram memoriam,*" the room responds in unison. I nearly forget to say the words. When I do, they are acrid on my lips.

Then the queen begins to speak the familiar words: "*Her memory is sacred, beyond the bounds of time. But as the clock hands turn, memory erodes the mind. Her secrets are best buried in a loop that turns to dust, where the present turns to past and past remains unjust. Therein lies infinity . . ."*

Here the queen pauses and gestures to the loop of wilting flowers laid across the cellar floor. *". . . the place where she survives—while we protect our sisterhood, our secrets, and our lives. For only when her sisters' wrongs are once again made right will she escape anew and take her place within the light."*

Her voice grows, hurdling from wall to wall. *"And so shall four return again beneath the waning moon to resurrect the memory, or find our way to ruin."* I catch myself thinking the words along with her and wince. I wish I hadn't committed the lines from Grandma Simmons's mystery note to memory. I wish I didn't know the Lilies vow by heart.

"Ut sacram memoriam," the queen cries.

"Ut sacram memoriam," the crowd echoes again. I can't bring myself to chant along. The feeling of being sick to my stomach is back.

Someone lays their hand on my shoulder. I've forgotten that I'm not invisible. I flinch away from the sensation.

"Drew?" I recognize the fearful whisper as Veró's. Thank god.

"How did you know it was me?" I breathe.

"You didn't say the second part of the vow along with the others."

I nod, careful to keep our whispers to a minimum. I would hate for someone to hear us and for the memory to reset again, only to decay even more. This gathering of the Lilies is already creepy enough.

I shift my position in the crowd so that Veró and I can stand side by side. The backs of our hands brush against each other. Electricity springs from my palm up through my arm. I don't want to pull away, but it feels impossible to focus on what the evil queen is saying. I think of what pulling away would mean. It feels like it would be closing a door, choosing to stay in the darkness of this basement alone. I've made choices like that so many times, mostly out of self-preservation.

This time I wonder what it would mean to make a choice based on what feels right, not what feels safe.

I grab Veró's hand and squeeze. She squeezes back and doesn't let go.

"Not everyone has what it takes to be a Lily," the evil queen says, distracting me from the sudden surge of euphoria flooding my brain. "Only a special kind of young woman is chosen for our society. Each and every one of you has something that sets you apart. Something that makes you exceptional."

I sense Veró's body tensing next to me, hardening against the evil queen's words. It's not just her icy tone, it's what she's saying. I don't know what she means by "special." I don't know what sets the initiates apart. But I do know that someone, maybe a host of someones, thought that I didn't have "what it takes" to join the society, despite Grandma

Simmons's hand in its creation. It occurs to me that maybe I'm glad I don't have "what it takes." Maybe "what it takes" is so much worse than anything I could imagine.

"With each initiation," the evil queen continues, "new Lilies must reveal their deepest secrets. Each revelation strengthens our sisterhood. Our pasts—no matter how horrible—bind us all together as we build a brighter future."

My ring finger aches as Grandma Simmons's diamond infinity symbol flashes white-hot again. Something horrible happened here. Something that planted the seed for the Lilies to grow. But this isn't just a memory: something horrible is happening right now, right in front of me. In front of all of us.

"Lilies," the evil queen calls, "form your ring."

The girls in the flower crowns step away from the blindfolded initiates and form a circle. They surround the group of new Lilies, the infinity of greenery in the center of the room, and the queen herself.

"To become a Lily," the queen goes on, "you must endure the trials of *your own* demons and be strong enough to relive your past. We Lilies summon our demons with this." She holds up a little crystal medicine vial above the crowd. Its silver cap nearly touches the arched brick ceiling. Pinched between the queen's thumb and forefinger, it catches enough of the candlelight to reveal that it is filled with something white.

"Initiates," she says, "I want to address something about sand. We use it during initiations because it enhances the experience. It brings your thoughts and memories to life. But I want to address the rumors you may have heard about it. Stories of girls getting lost in their own memories, their minds abandoning them. Those stories are false. Fairy tales designed to weed out the weak. Those who aren't cut out to be among us. Sand is a means to an end: it'll help you exhume your secrets. It'll open the door to relive your past."

With these words, three of the girls encircling the group break rank and take a step toward the queen. The others in the outer circle close the gap in the perimeter and drop to a kneel as if commanded. The woozy feeling descends into my legs. The Lilies were right, I don't belong here. Every molecule within me is screaming, begging me to push across the room toward Charlotte, grab her by the hand, and make a break for it. Something about this is horribly wrong.

The three girls face the queen and reach out their cupped hands. The queen lowers her crystal vial and uncorks it. The low ping ricochets around the basement. Then I see that the girl to the queen's far right is shaking ever so slightly. Her hood is beginning to slip back, her flower crown seems to be ill-fitting. My gaze lands in the shadows of her face.

Oh god. It's Blythe.

Finally.

A candle's flicker reflects against one of her cheeks. She's crying. Why is she crying? What does she know that I don't?

"Each of you will grow into a Lily tonight," the queen says to her initiates. "Remain in the circle and relive your past. You'll each take a turn recounting your deepest secret to your sisters. Your demons will come out to play, but you'll rely on each other, and push through."

As she speaks, the queen shakes out the sand into the outstretched hands beside her. Blythe takes her little handful of the powder and approaches the kneeling, blindfolded Faith at the far end of the line of initiates. The queen's other hooded helper does the same.

"Once you do this . . . once you pass this test—you'll have proven yourself: you will have shown everyone that you have what it takes to be a real Lily." The queen's voice seems to brighten as she finishes. Her words are poison honey.

I keep my eyes on Blythe, who is standing in front of Faith. She opens her palm and holds it in front of the blindfolded girl's face. "Breathe in," she murmurs. Faith does. The sand lifts into the air, grain by grain, forming a tiny cloud. The powder must be so fine. Faith inhales each sparkling particle. She coughs. Chokes. Blythe winces, but she doesn't intervene.

Silently, Blythe and the other hooded henchmen work their way down the line of initiates. Each new Lily takes a breath, freezes, then begins to choke. Some fall to their hands and knees. Others try to stand, but the Lilies surrounding them hold them back and force them down. Eventually the choking subsides and the girls grow silent and slack-jawed. Blank. The blindfolds, however, stay tied to each of their skulls.

My skin crawls as I watch Blythe move back and forth, slowly doling out breaths of sand to some of the kneeling girls. Her eyes are crinkled, mouth twisted into a repulsed scowl. I wonder how she's doing it. How can someone be so clearly disgusted by their own actions and keep going? Sometimes I forget how powerful fear can be, how quickly it transforms to self-hatred and shame. I see these feelings churning inside of Blythe, transforming into something sticky and toxic. Something that has trapped her from the inside. She's locked into the same pattern. The same thing, over and over.

She stands in front of her last initiate. Charlotte's hair gleams in the dim; a small flame, one that's about to be snuffed out.

"Wait."

Blythe stands in front of Charlotte, her face frozen.

"Wait . . . could I . . ."

The voice is high and scared in a way I don't expect. It isn't even Blythe's voice. She's not trying to right the wrong, to break the cycle. Charlotte is the one grinding everything to a halt. "Could I just . . . ?" she whispers, voice quaking, unable to finish her sentence.

The flowers wilt. Gazes sharpen as the queen of the Lilies bristles.

"Is there a problem?" The queen's words are a gutting knife. The question isn't really a question: it's clear that there better not be a problem. It's too late for that.

Charlotte can't pause her initiation now. It might as well have already happened.

I remind myself that all of this *has* already happened.

"Never mind," Charlotte rattles. "Go on."

I shut my eyes. I can't bear to watch and wait anymore. When is Blythe going to put a stop to all of this like she said she would? Veró squeezes my hand, signaling to me that we need to step in and do something. My breath catches in my chest.

No escaping fate, Death whispers.

"No!" Blythe cries.

My eyes fly open. "I reject this!" she screams. "I won't do this again!"

Bong!

It didn't happen like this.

Bong!

Time rips open.

Bong!

And swallows the room of Lilies whole.

Blythe

BACK WHEN I WAS INITIATED, the bigs didn't know what sand would do to me. Really, they didn't know what it would do to any of us. "You can't ever know another person's mind," Grandma Rose used to say. And she was right. The Lilies didn't know that sand would take me back to the protest in Lafayette Park. They didn't understand how—to me—the basement under the Archwell library was beginning to flood with tear gas. They didn't understand that the feeling of losing Salim and Sean in the crowd all over again broke something inside me. They didn't understand why getting lost felt like the worst thing that had ever happened.

They couldn't understand. They didn't know that I still felt lost.

You can't ever know another person's mind.

Not even when they take you by the hand and walk you through their worst memories.

I know that now.

I didn't know that when it was my turn to start initiating

new Lilies. I didn't understand what had happened to me. I couldn't see the Lilies Society for what it was.

Reliving the night of Charlotte's initiation brought the ugliness into new focus.

Laying splayed on the closet floor, I realize that we haven't escaped. Our plan didn't work.

"This fucking closet," Rory steams to herself.

"But . . . I don't get it. How are we right back where we started?" Drew says. "The vow says that escape is possible when the wrongs are made right. So . . . I don't get it. Blythe stopped the initiation before anything could happen to Charlotte. The wrong was made right . . . We shouldn't be back here again."

"Hold on," Veró says. "I just want to see . . ." She reaches for the closet door.

"Careful!" I blurt, but it's too late. Veró pulls the door open a crack, releasing the smell of decaying memory into the closet. Ignoring this sign, she leans into the doorframe and peers through the gap. "Shit," she says. "Party's still going. The clock says nine twelve p.m."

"We've been over this. Multiple times," Rory says. "Blythe's and my memory needs to play through all the way, as it happened, so the loop can close. I don't see why you would need more justification than that."

"It's not hard for you, is it?" Veró asks Rory, rustling some of the closet's hanging gowns as she shifts away from the cracked door.

"What's not hard?"

"It was like torture reliving my worst memory," Veró growls. "I could barely bring myself to do it all over again. But you . . . watching the initiation, seeing what y'all are doing to those girls. You like it, don't you?"

"For god's sake, it's *my* worst memory, Veró. Obviously, I don't like reliving it. Especially not when it keeps replaying and . . . you know . . . eroding." Rory is seething now.

She's skimming over the fact that the memory doesn't belong to just her—it belongs to me too. But that doesn't matter to her right now. I'm just as invisible as always. The realization reignites my anger, but I can tell there's trouble brewing between Rory and Veró right now and I'm just too tired to get roped into another fight. Let them have it out and exhaust themselves in the process. I just wish I could get the hell away from it all.

"I don't want to be trapped here any more than the rest of you!" she snaps at Veró.

"That's not what I'm saying," Veró claps back. "I'm saying you're out there with the rest of them in a hood and a crown. For all we know, you're the one who's pulling the strings in this whole operation."

Rory rolls her eyes. She grips one of the shelves, using it to quickly pull herself to her feet. The motion jostles one of the alarm clocks, but it doesn't start ringing on its own like before. "You wouldn't understand, Veró."

Rory's words have a bit of an echo to them. I think of

what Veró said to Charlotte in the bathroom when she was first caught. *You wouldn't understand.*

Rory couldn't understand me when we were together. Still doesn't.

The Lilies couldn't understand me when I was first initiated. Still don't.

Suddenly the closet feels very lonely. The words reverberate again: *You wouldn't understand.*

"I think I understand very well." Veró's voice is an icicle, deadly sharp. "I'm watching y'all *dosing* people."

"Possibly against their will," Drew adds.

"*It is not like that.*" Rory's voice is louder than normal. She's been forced into defense mode. "The initiates know what they're getting into."

I brace myself for what's next. These kids don't know it but they're playing with fire. It's never safe to back a girl like Rory Archwell into a corner.

The bickering builds for several more minutes. I try to tune it out, but my mind keeps retreating into the library basement. I ward off the stinging feeling in my tear ducts. Whenever I shut my eyes, I see Charlotte, her blindfold askew. Her fearful stare, pupils dilated.

"Wait . . ." she says.

Then she chokes. Blood begins to trail from her mouth.

No. I stand, ball up my fists, and press them against my forehead.

You're in this room.

215

You're in your body.

Stay in the closet, Blythe.

Just stay grounded.

I run my hands along the knobs of the black lacquered cabinets.

"Your plan isn't working," Rory growls. "Trying to find ways to save Charlotte won't work. Period."

"I don't wanna go back down there," Drew insists. "There has to be a way around all this. We're just missing something. I know it!"

"We need to stick together and let it ride. Trust me," Rory utters.

I begin to fiddle with the knobs. I pull a drawer open then shut it again.

Open. Closed.

Breathe in. Out.

"Have you given us a single reason to trust you, Rory?" Veró counters. "This whole time you've made it perfectly clear that you're just an agent for the chancellor. You love all this creepy exclusionary bullshit because it's the only way you can feel special. You're out here talking about who 'fits' at Archwell and who doesn't. Have you noticed that the pattern of who 'fits in" here falls perfectly in line with white supremacist patriarchy?"

"What are you talking about? You know Archwell's not like that. *I'm* not like that."

Anger roars through me, forcing me to break my silence. "But aren't you?" I scoff.

Rory wheels around to face me.

"Why did you give Charlotte to me as my little?" I ask her.

She frowns. "I . . . don't know what you mean."

I push the drawer closed with my fingertips.

It rolls open again.

Open. Closed. Over and over.

"Did you not *know* people were spreading rumors about Charlotte? That she was getting bullied for being different? By putting us together, weren't you telling us *both* exactly where we stood?"

"Where they stood." Veró picks up the thread. "As in, they might find themselves on their asses if they stepped out of line with the Lilies. Tell me, Queen Rory, was Charlotte grateful enough for the opportunity of breathing your rarified air?"

Drew narrows their eyes. They can smell the blood in the water. "Why *does* Archwell consider a person like Gabe a 'threat to the community'? Could it be because he disrupts your carefully protected order? The one with you at the very top?"

Rory shakes her head. "Wow. I get that you all have agendas here. But can you drop the crusade for like five seconds so we can *get the hell out of here*?"

I let go of the drawer again.

Open. Close. Repeat.

The others don't notice the sound.

We're right, of course. Right about all of it. But I know we are just wasting our breath at this point.

Rory's confidence made me fall for her, and her stubbornness kept us together for a little while. But in the end, it was her inability to see beyond herself that broke us up. At some point, way before we knew each other, she must've built a wall around her heart. Unfortunately, she can't see beyond that wall.

Open. Closed.

Breathe in. Out.

I withdraw into myself. The voices grow into shouts, but I try to keep them far away.

I get a brief flash of the contents of the drawer. Archwell-branded pens and face masks. More blindfolds. A tube of lipstick. Papers. A lot of papers.

Open. Closed.

Open.

I lift the yellowing files out of the drawer and begin to leaf through the pages. An old transcript. A handwritten homework assignment on weathered looseleaf with the word *Marvelous* scrawled across the top in red pen. No grade. No marks. Just *Marvelous.*

I sigh. If only school were that easy.

"We're wasting time," Rory says to the others.

"There *is* no time here," Drew retorts.

"That grandfather clock keeps saying otherwise," Veró points out.

I come to an envelope addressed in bubbly handwriting. Green ink announces the intended recipient is *Chancellor Archwell.* Not Rory's mom, I'm sure. The note feels too thin and delicate in my hand for it to be written recently. Maybe it was for Adeline Archwell . . . or maybe her father, Archwell's founder.

The top of the envelope has been slit open, no doubt with one of those fancy letter openers. I reach inside and unfold the letter. The date at the top is written in the same bubbly script. *October 6, 1958.*

Dear Chancellor Archwell,

I'm writing to you because I'm worried about your children.

Something catches inside me. I pause. I return to the top of the letter. *October 6, 1958.*

"I don't see why you have to make this so difficult!"

"*You're* the one who's making this difficult."

"Y'all?" I interrupt the shouting. At first the others don't hear.

"I withheld judgment when we were going through *your* memory. Can't you just do the same thing?"

"Y'all!" I bark. "Look at this."

"What is it?" Veró gripes.

"It's a letter."

"Who gives a shit about a letter?" Drew asks.

"Look when it was dated." I hold the paper out for the others to see. "And look who it's from."

The anger in Drew's eyes melts into worry as they focus on the signature.

Sincerely, Meredith Simmons

"Who is Meredith Simmons?" Veró asks.

"One of the Lilies founders," Rory says solemnly. Her eyes are glued to the letter, as if she's seen it before.

"She was my grandmother," Drew adds.

The two lock eyes for a beat. Both statements are true, they just hadn't been spoken aloud before. At least not here.

"Right." Veró narrows her gaze in on Drew. "I almost forgot that you're a legacy kid."

Drew glances at me and then back at Rory. "I mean . . . technically, I guess," they say. "I'm not a Lily, though. I wasn't invited into the group . . . thankfully."

My gaze lands on Rory. She's trying not to react to Drew's words—bottling something up all over again. Her cheeks are turning pink. To some, she might appear furious, but I know what's underneath all of that: years of maternal guilt trips and toeing the line, years of striving to prove herself worthy.

Yes, Rory kept Drew out of the Lilies. And, yes, her face reveals a flicker of embarrassment, even remorse.

Good.

She *should* feel bad about all the shit she does to please her mother.

I turn to Veró, holding out Meredith's letter. It's about time we were all on the same page. "You weren't with us when this happened, but we ran into Charlotte earlier in the loop at the Founder's Night party. She was talking about her grandma Evelyn and how she knew Drew's grandmother Meredith. They went to school together."

I steal a glance at Drew for a split second. Their eyes are traversing their grandmother's handwriting, puzzling the meaning of her words.

"She called her a double-crosser," I add.

"Why?" Veró asks.

"Look at the letter," Drew says.

We read in silence, anger draining away with every word. The note is a skeleton key.

Dear Chancellor Archwell,

I'm writing to you because I'm worried about your children. As you know, I often take Lillian, Evelyn, and Adeline into Georgetown. There, I have witnessed Adeline's habits in the company of nefarious gentlemen. I have spoken to Lil about Adeline, but he will not listen. He does not want to acknowledge the terrible truth that Adeline is an addict. He's too wrapped up with Evelyn.

I know you and Mrs. Archwell are good, concerned parents. Please know that I tell you this as a friend

*with the very best of intentions: please pull Adeline
away from this path that will surely lead to self
destruction.*

Sincerely,

Meredith Simmons

We finish reading, each of us shifting uncomfortably from side to side, piecing things together.

"So . . . hold on . . . your grandmother wrote this?" Veró asks.

"Yes," Drew answers.

"On October sixth," I point out. "The same date all this Charlotte stuff started for us."

"And the same day that Lillian disappeared in 1958," Rory murmurs.

"And she wrote it about *your* grandmother Adeline," Veró says and turns to Rory and continues, "who had a—a drug problem?"

"Yes," Rory admits.

"And she mentions Lillian, too. Adeline's sister," Veró says.

"But hang on a minute." I look back at the letter, zeroing in on the pronouns in the bubbly green handwriting. "I'm confused . . . She's talking about your grandmother's *sister*?"

We all look back at the paper. "'I have spoken to Lil about Adeline but he will not listen,'" Drew reads aloud. "'He does not want to acknowledge the terrible truth that Adeline is an addict . . .'"

"I'm confused," I say. "Meredith Simmons is using male pronouns when she's talking about Lillian . . . ?"

"Yes," Rory says.

"Is it some kind of mistake?" I ask.

Drew hesitates for a second, seemingly gathering facts in their head. "Wait. The way this is written . . . Could it suggest that . . . Meredith, my grandma . . ."

". . . outed Lillian as trans back in the 1950s?" Veró gasps.

The comment sucks the oxygen right out of the room. We all pause and consider. Trans girls "disappear" in America all the time. Lillian wouldn't have been the first, or the last, to "vanish." But my mind snags on all the details in the letter that don't add up.

"Meredith refers to Lillian by her name, though," I say.

"It's true," Drew says. "She doesn't use a dead name."

"And Lillian's parents *created* the school for their *daughters*," I add. "So they would have a safe place to go to school. *Away from the world of men*."

"And that makes it seem like Meredith is just messing up Lillian's pronouns without thinking of the consequences," Drew adds. "She's misgendering her . . . maybe not outing her though. We'd have to know more about the context to know for sure."

I watch as a flash of pain spreads across Drew's face. "But Lillian disappeared," they say. "Archwell wasn't safe for her after all."

"So how did it happen? And why?" Veró asks.

I think of the Archwell sisters, Lillian and Adeline. They

were students here just like us. It's almost weird to consider. The 1950s seem like so long ago. It was a time when my grandma Rose couldn't attend Archwell, not that she would've wanted to. Rose's mother, my great-grandmother, spent seventy hours a week cleaning the Archwell dorms and classrooms. Adeline, Lillian, Evelyn, and Meredith would've passed her in the halls . . . probably ignoring her in the process.

"Wait," Veró cuts in. "Is it possible that 'double-crossing' Charlotte's grandmother told her about has something to do with Lillian? Like maybe she and Meredith backstabbed Evelyn and that's why Lillian disappeared? Evelyn is responsible?"

"I don't get it. Are you suggesting that what happened to Charlotte is some sort of . . . intergenerational cosmic payback?" Rory asks.

"Umm. I'm not sure what Charlotte's grandma Evelyn's relationship was to all this," Drew says. "I suppose her granddaughter definitely inherited some TERFy tendencies."

"But Evelyn was Lillian's *friend*. She couldn't have been a TERF," I tell them. "They quoted her in that article we found about her disappearance, remember? She was devastated."

"She was *also* a founder of the Lilies Society." Rory sounds a little distant. It's almost as if she doesn't realize that she just made that comment out loud, because she startles and shrinks beneath our gazes. She's cornered again.

That's it. I've had enough of her secrets. It's time for the truth to come out once and for all.

"Is it true, Rory?" I ask her. "Did Lillian's parents found Archwell Academy for Lillian *because she was trans?*"

Rory inhales deeply through her nose, bracing herself for something. Instead of exhaling, she manages to squeak out one word. "Yes."

The closet trembles, swelling and expanding. The bare bulb above us buzzes a little louder. All of this seems so impossible in a place like this. A place where Gabe Lewis can't use the appropriate bathroom—can't use his proper name—can't be himself.

"It's not . . . It was something I was never supposed to tell anyone." Rory winces. "I didn't know about it for a long time . . . My mother only told me about Lillian the night before I was initiated into the Lilies. She told me that she was the namesake, the reason the school was started. She told me about all of it." Her face is pinched and pained. "I feel bad telling you all but . . . I dunno."

"Bad like ashamed?" Veró asks.

"Ashamed of what? Of Lillian?" Drew adds.

"No . . . it's just that, it was a family secret and . . ." Rory tries to finish her explanation, but she can't.

I turn the thoughts over in my head, replaying what I know.

The Archwells had a secret. At first, the secret was kept to protect Lillian, but then something shifted along the way.

225

The truth became twisted, distorting into something else entirely. The secret changed. Its purpose was transformed.

I think of the Lilies—of my initiation, of Charlotte's initiation—and my blood runs cold. Grandma Rose warned me about this. About these girls and what they might do.

This is what happens when someone deals in secrets for too long. They swallow shame. It turns them into monsters.

I understand, because I have choked down so much of my own shame: the shame of what I did to other girls, what I did to Charlotte, what I did to myself.

In this moment, inside the closet, the bulb growing brighter above me, I make a promise to myself: no more shame. I will not participate. I will not be a monster, not anymore.

I understand now that the loop has turned me hideous in my own imagination.

But I know my own mind. And now I know what I need to do.

Rory

I AM NOT ADELINE. I am not my mother. I could never be them, no matter how hard I try. But the closest I'll ever come to proving that I'm a real Archwell woman is standing in front of these girls, leading initiation. It's strange to watch myself do it.

I didn't have to say much else to get the others to dive back into the loop and let the memory run its course again without interruptions. No more trying to break out of the loop. No more attempting to change the past. No one wants to run the risk of having to relive the initiation anymore. Everyone just wants out, and fortunately, the others finally realized that I *do* know what I'm talking about.

Of course, I had to reveal more than I wanted to in the process, but at least I didn't give away *everything*. The truth of my memory thankfully stayed buried, even if I gave up a family secret to keep it that way.

Lillian deserved her due, I suppose. She deserved remembrance. I always thought that the way we conducted initiation honored her memory but . . . the loop is beginning to make me question that. To question everything.

Is this really how I remember it all happening? Am I the hero? Or the villain?

The basement is certainly darker than I remember. The arched brick ceiling bears down on me. The branches of my flower crown nearly scrape the mortar. The pink flowers smell sickly sweet, that same rotten smell from before.

I watch myself lift Grandmother Adeline's crystal vial overhead for the others to see. My hand grazes the greenery of my crown. I imagine what the wilted petals must feel like against the heel of my hand. They likely leave a slimy residue. In this version of the loop, my crown is rotting.

I go through the vow and my speech about sand. I've given it a few times now. It's a helpful reminder, even to me, especially as I know it really is starting to take hold of me. I didn't tell Blythe and Caitlin that I was going to dose before the initiation. It's a habit I got into once my bigs had graduated and it was time for me to step up and lead. Being on sand while the new littles go through their first trip into the loop helps me feel closer to them.

"Once you do this . . ." I say to the room. I listen to myself and my breath catches. My heart begins to sprint ahead of my words. "Once you pass this test—you'll have proven yourself . . ."

My words seem to speed up and run together, like an old video tape on fast-forward.

". . . you will have shown everyone that you have what it takes—"

The loop skips and zooms ahead, my voice takes on a Minnie Mouse pitch as the memory continues to distort.

"Whatittakes.Whatittakes.Youwillhaveshowneveryonethat youhavewhatittakestobearealLily."

I watch myself spring into frenzied action, doling out doses of sand to Blythe, Courtney, and Caitlin to give to each initiate. It's happening faster than I remember. I continue at a frantic pace until Blythe turns to me. Her hood slides back far enough for me to see the tears streaming down her face. She reaches out for the last time.

One more dose.

One more initiate.

This one is for Charlotte.

I watch myself pour the sand into Blythe's hand knowing what will happen . . . knowing what happened the first time . . . what keeps happening again and again in my mind. Blythe doesn't look closely at the doses I give her. Each one pours out of the vial like a tiny sparkling waterfall. The particles move in slow motion. Each one is a little orb, a world unto itself.

At this dosage, sand has the power to carry each Lily away into another time, back to when they—when *we*—were first broken.

"Wait . . ." Charlotte says. She hesitates and then . . . "Never mind."

She inhales her dose and chokes just like all the others, except I can't hear her coughing. I can only hear that strange buzzing noise of the bare bulb back in the closet, even though I know that I'm not trapped there anymore.

I'm here. In a memory of a memory.

The sound intensifies into a bright, deafening ping, like some kind of alarm clock from hell. And then it stops and the initiation keeps going. Charlotte is no longer coughing.

Anita steps forward and takes off Faith's blindfold. Her pupils are so impossibly dilated that her eyes are almost entirely black. Surely this wasn't how she looked the first time. The loop must be warping her face. Her gaze is vacant and blank when I prompt her to speak.

She is the first to dive in. Each will take a turn.

Faith tells the room of crowned and hooded figures her secret. It's a story we've all heard before, too many times from too many other Lilies. The kind of story where a relative or a neighbor or a so-called friend gets a girl alone. The kind of story where she's too young to know what is happening to her and too scared to call for help. And Faith is there in front of us, telling it all like it happened yesterday, even though her story takes place when she's barely out of elementary school.

I remember her crying the first time. And maybe she's crying now, but I can't tell, not with those eyes like that. Not with that blank stare. Is this what the Lilies do to people? Is this what it looks like to steal a secret? To extract someone's story in order to bind them to you?

My stomach lurches as the next initiate's blindfold is removed. I watch as I prompt her to speak. It's her turn now.

Alice's eyes look just like Faith's. I hear the tears in

her voice this time. She's afraid, but she tells us her secret anyway. This one is about what happens when you leave children alone. Alice and her sister were playing. Alice got jealous of her sister's toy. Alice grabbed her sister by the neck and squeezed until she couldn't breathe anymore. And finally, she let go when she realized what she could do, the power she had in her little hands. She could really hurt somebody. And, when there was no one around to see, and when her sister was too small to have the words to tell on her, Alice could have really gotten away with it. And she did! No one knew what happened. They just knew that Alice's sister was left wheezing and crying.

Nausea spreads from my gut down through my legs. My knees threaten to buckle. Is that the story Alice really told? And Faith too? I don't remember them being this horrible. I don't remember feeling like I was watching the specter of these memories play out in front of me. I don't remember feeling like I was living what the initiates were revealing. This is beyond what I can take.

But the cycle repeats. The memory moves forward. I have to keep prompting each Lily to speak, otherwise we'll have to start all over again, and I'm certain that, if we do, the loop will cave in on us all. I try to force myself to watch me as I do it. Never take my eyes off me. But I can't. I glance at the floor and see my saddle shoes peeking out from underneath my green robe.

I hear choking again. Gagging. I know the sound. I've heard it before.

We all watch as Charlotte falls to her hands and knees. It isn't her turn yet, but something has taken hold of her mind. Something is trying to force its way out from inside of her. She vomits, blood pooling on the floor in front of her. I remember her blood was red, redder than her hair. But in the memory, the blood is black and oily. If I were to touch it, I feel like it might be sticky. What is it? I don't have to ask. I know.

It's shame.

Charlotte vomits again. The sand Blythe gave her is too much for her little body. It was like this the first time. I knew it would be. Blythe didn't look closely at the dose. And now . . . watching it again, I don't know what to make of it. All I can do is stare and watch myself bark orders to somebody, who stoops down and drags Charlotte out of the circle.

I motion to the door, telling them not to take her upstairs. She just needs a minute to breathe. The sand needs to work through her system. Time needs to run its course. They take her into the next room. The door snaps shut.

I watch as my crown begins to seep down my face. It's falling apart, just like the memory.

Bong!

The room begins to dissolve and I start to come apart with it. At least the others have now all seen what Blythe did.

Bong!

And even though it hurts, it's a relief to be expelled from this room and launched into nothingness for one brief moment.

Bong!

Drew

WHAT HAPPENED TO LILLIAN? AND what happened to her story? It wasn't that she was forgotten. People remembered her name, but it seems like that was maybe all that they remembered. And is it enough to just remember someone's name?

At Dundalk High, we had an assembly every year on the Trans Day of Remembrance. All of us in the Prism Gender and Sexuality Alliance would line up on the floor of the gymnasium and hold little battery-powered candles in paper cups. Someone would go up to the mic and read off all the names of the people who were murdered that year for being themselves. Some of them were like me. Some of them weren't. It didn't matter either way. They shouldn't have died. Someone should have protected them.

Out of the memory and back in the closet, I stare at Lillian's blood-stained gown and I wonder if the same thing happened to her. Did someone try to hurt her because of who she was? Is that why her story was erased? It's not enough to remember her name if we don't also remember her story. The whole story.

The wildest thing about all of this is that Lillian's story would've stayed under wraps if Charlotte had not also vanished on the same day nearly seventy years later.

People still don't know Charlotte's whole story either . . . It's one that I wish I had nothing to do with. But there's no denying that I am linked to it. I suppose, in a way, I'm tied to Lillian's story too . . .

Both of these girls disappeared without a trace.

Both of these girls haunt me in a way that the others will never understand.

Mom says there are no coincidences, only synchronicities.

Something tells me that this particular tie—the one between Charlotte and Lillian—might be the key to our escape. But that's not what these girls want to talk about right now, not with me anyway. They're too angry to do anything but point fingers at each other.

"So, what caused the reset this time?" Veró demands. "Blythe, did you do something again?"

"No! That wasn't a reset!" Blythe insists. "That was the end of the night. The last thing I remember was watching them take Charlotte away."

"But we don't know necessarily if this was *your* memory," Rory cuts in. "I was there too. I saw what you did. We all did."

"But . . . but I did what you wanted me to, I let the memory play through all the way. That was the end of my loop."

"How are we supposed to trust you after we saw you do something like *that*?" Veró's voice has gained a new edge.

She didn't like what she saw in the loop, any more than the rest of us, and she's not letting Blythe off the hook. "What did y'all do to Charlotte? Where did you take her?"

"I don't know where they took her," Blythe insists. "Rory was the one who told them to get her out of the circle."

Veró's fury kicks back from Blythe and over to Rory. "Of course! You were the one leading this whole thing."

Rory holds up her hands, innocent. "I may have led the Lilies Society this year. But Blythe was Charlotte's big. She's the one who gave her the sand."

"You gonna throw me under the bus now? That is low, Rory, even for you." Blythe's ire is quiet and venomous. "Don't try to pretend you weren't involved. Not after all this shit you've put me through."

"Where did the Lilies take Charlotte?" Veró insists. She's in full-on interrogation mode, face flushed in anger. A lump rises in my throat. We're veering too close to the truth of what happened. Too close to my worst moment, my biggest regret.

Veró hammers on at Rory and Blythe. "Did y'all let her OD? Did you let her die?"

"No!" Rory shouts. "The Lilies are a sisterhood. We would never do something like that."

"A sisterhood that makes girls disappear," Veró snarls.

It's almost like I'm not here. Like I've finally dissolved and have achieved invisibility. Good. I don't want any part of this. I don't want these girls knowing what I know.

I turn toward Lillian's white gown, still hanging off the side of the shelf, and run my finger along the lacy fringe. Rory's not looking, she's too wrapped up in the argument to yell at me for touching it again. Plus, it may be a family heirloom, but it's something else too: proof. Proof that queer people have existed and survived in oppressive places for a long time. I look at the bloodstain and consider how that may be proof of something else as well. Something wrong that can never be made right again.

I feel Death's hot breath close to my ear. *They're going to find out, Drew*, it says. *They're going to see exactly what you did.*

My shoulders meet my ears, my hands clench. I hate that this feeling keeps dogging me.

But I don't have to listen to Death. Not yet. Not as long as we stay in this closet and out of my memory.

The others continue their bickering, focusing on the more obvious villains.

"Do not lump me in with Rory," Blythe cries. "I don't know what happened to Charlotte after initiation. I don't know why she disappeared. And neither of us knows why Lillian Archwell disappeared. That's not Lilies Society shit. That's Rory Archwell shit."

"Right. So you're implying that I coordinated my great-aunt's disappearance, *before my birth*," Rory blurts. She's got a point there. It's not the fairest accusation ever made. But then Rory shoots herself in the foot. "It's not like I'm some kind of mastermind!"

A telling silence follows her outburst. None of us would put it past Rory to orchestrate all the terrible things we've seen. I'm pretty sure if I looked up mastermind in the dictionary I'd find a picture of her. Still, she continues to protest. "I've told you everything I know. I'm not hiding anything. Not anymore. I don't know what happened to Lillian and I don't know what happened to Charlotte. Now can we please move on? We don't have much time. You saw how corroded things are getting out there. What if the loop turns to dust?"

"Have you lost your damn mind?" Blythe's words are a spray of bullets. "I already told you. The memory played out just as I remembered it. It's over. I didn't see what happened to Charlotte. And you know what? I don't want to see."

"Forget y'all," Veró sneers. She turns to me for a brief moment, but it feels like she's looking right through me.

Maybe it's because I'm not here. Brain separated from body—dissociated.

I can't hold all of this. I cannot hold back the void that is Lillian's story. It's a black hole that is swallowing me.

Meanwhile, Veró takes flight. She launches herself at the gowns, yanking them from their hangers. She pulls back the curtain of robes, diving deeper into the back of the closet.

"What the hell are you doing?" Rory rushes to right Veró's path of destruction, but the girl is a tornado.

"We keep ending up back in this damned closet. There's gotta be something in here that explains all this!" she cries, flinging cabinet drawers open and shut. Alarm clocks clank to the floor. A velvety tray of diamond rings is knocked to the ground. The little infinity symbols go flying everywhere, rolling across the floor, knocking into the foot of the silent grandfather clock.

"Stop!" Blythe shouts. "Something's gonna get lost."

"Something like what? Like a whole person . . . completely vanished?" Veró retorts. She pulls a stack of little leather-bound notebooks out of one of the drawers. Then she lets them fall to the floor and covers her face in her hands. Blythe is stooped, trying to collect the diamonds from the floor. She's crying by now. Rory is on her knees in front of me, frozen over a pile of rumpled gowns. Her expression is corkscrewed. She's stuffing something down. She's always pushing something away.

My face is cold. No, it's wet. *Oh.* I realize now that I am also crying. Maybe it's time to stop dissociating.

"I want out of all this," I mutter.

"Me too," Veró says.

"Yep," Blythe adds.

"Definitely," Rory croaks, barely audible.

Slowly, Veró stoops and picks up one of the notebooks. "I'm sorry," she says. "I just . . . want something to make sense again."

"We're on the same page. We all get it," I say.

There's a sense of relief in the closet. Veró's outburst was a pressure valve, bleeding some of the tension out of everyone.

We're all barely making it in here. We don't know how to stop what's happening. Not one of us is sure we'll survive this.

Veró opens the notebook slowly and leafs through the first few pages. "Looks like someone's journal."

"Might be," Rory says. "Lilies don't keep any official records."

"Whose journal is it?" I ask.

"I don't see a name on the inside cover," she says. "There's no year in the dates either. I'm looking for names in the entries but . . ." She flips through a few more pages. "They write about a new Ray Charles record here," she says, flipping forward a few more pages. "There's a reference to President Eisenhower?"

"When was Eisenhower president?" I ask, peering over Veró's shoulder.

She frowns. "Where's Google when you need it?"

Grandma Simmons—Meredith—was involved in all this. I'm half hoping it's her journal. I want to know what she was thinking when she wrote to the Archwells about Adeline and Lillian. I want to understand how my blood got mixed up in all this. But the handwriting is irregular and jagged, nothing like my grandmother's. Still, something tells me she's in these pages somewhere.

Veró keeps thumbing through the journal as the others gather with us. Maybe it's just another distraction. Or maybe Veró's instincts will lead us to . . .

"Look," Rory says, pointing at one of the pages. "The name is right there."

Veró narrows her eyes and reads aloud. "'Evelyn is probably the only other sophomore with comparable grades. She's my only competition, so I'll keep my enemies close.'" Veró holds the journal away from her slightly as if it's dirty somehow. "Ugh. Sounds like something an Archwell girl would write . . . no matter what time they live in." She points to a scribbly *L*-word on the page, one I can't quite make out. "Does that say 'Lillian'?"

We all squint at the lettering. "What's the rest of the sentence say?" I ask. "I can't really read the handwriting but maybe the context will . . . you know . . ."

Blythe begins to read. "'Mother and Father have always favored Lillian . . . They don't know about her and Evelyn . . .' Something, something . . . 'I can use it to my advantage . . .'" She looks up at Rory. "Remind me. Evelyn was friends with your great-aunt Lillian?"

Rory nods. "But the way that's written makes it seem like there was more to it," she admits. "Grandmother Adeline never mentioned anything romantic there. She knew I like girls. I feel like she would've told me if I had a relative who was also queer."

Blythe shrugs. "Could be a generational thing. My grandma gave a lot of advice, but she was never really specific about stories from when she was growing up."

Veró's eyebrow arches. "The person wrote, 'Mother and Father have always favored Lillian.' Does that mean—"

"The journal was Adeline's," Rory confirms.

Call it a coincidence but I choose synchronicity. There's something to this. The closet keeps giving us things, clues like little gifts. It's too peculiar to ignore.

I focus my eyes on the bottom of the page and point to

the one paragraph I can decipher. I read, "'I got Evelyn a bag last time I went to G-town . . . Told her I would lend her my piece . . . When I tell Mother and Father . . . They find her and Lil . . .' Something . . . God this handwriting is bad."

Veró frowns. "From what we can make out, it sounds like some kind of—"

"—setup," Blythe finishes. "She's talking about giving her something, and then telling her parents?"

"Drugs," Rory corrects. "She's talking about drugs. She was an addict when she was young . . . into opium and some other stuff . . . I'm not really supposed to talk about it but—" Out of nowhere, she laughs. It's more than a little unsettling. Rory sounds manic. Out of control. Especially for her. "Another family secret! We are bringing out *all* the skeletons tonight."

Rory's hollow laughter continues. But a question drifts between us like sage smoke.

Veró is the only one with the guts to ask. "Did Adeline try to drug her sister and Evelyn?"

No one answers. None of us knows for sure.

All of a sudden, the air in the closet is thick with dust. It's hard to breathe, but Veró pushes further. "Did someone OD like Charlotte did?"

The gravity in the closet shifts slightly. An alarm clock begins to trill, then another, then another. There's something here with us. Something trying to push its way out of the closet. I listen for Death's rattle but I hear nothing but the sound of alarms. Veró drops the journal.

Bong . . . Bong . . . Bong . . . Bong . . .

The grandfather clock is wailing again. We all plug our ears.

The closet door flies open. I pivot, nearly dislocating my neck in the process. I don't know what I'm expecting to see, but I'm surprised when there's only darkness on the other side of the door.

This feels like it might be the end. Like the loop is collapsing in on itself with us trapped inside.

We didn't escape. We didn't save Charlotte. And we never found out what happened to Lillian.

What a waste.

You know what happens next, right? Death whispers to me. I don't answer. I can't.

Grief and guilt rattle against my ribs. They threaten to break me from the inside.

When I look into that darkness, all I see is a void. One that maybe Meredith, Adeline, and the rest of their so-called friends created.

I won't enter it.

I won't be another name spoken in grief and remembrance.

But something in the closet lurches us forward. And we fall into the dark.

FALLING IN LOVE EVERY DAY. Have you tried it? I would recommend it. It's the best part of reliving a moment.

Her smile brings the morning, and even in a twisted memory, it is glorious.

There has never been anyone like Evelyn. There will never be anyone else like Evelyn ever again.

We began trading notes years ago. We'd meet in the library but we never studied.

Eventually, she gave me a pin to wear on my favorite gray cardi. I was saving up to buy her a ring.

In the loop, I get to kiss Evelyn every day. Here, we don't age and we don't die. But my memory does fail me. Time finds a way.

Sometimes the kiss is bitter. I pull away to find my love's lips rotting away. Her eyes sink until all I can see are empty sockets.

It's a cruel joke that the loop plays on me. Memory erodes. Nothing is forever.

Nothing except the infinite march of time.

20

Veró

I'M GOING STOP BELIEVING IN time after all of this is over . . . if I make it through. It's not that I'm starting to believe that time isn't real. It's just that I'm learning how violent and malevolent it can be. It pulls me out of the closet and through the darkness, and before I know it, it's slamming me onto the stone floor of the library basement. My shoulder pops, nearly dislocating. The sensation brings me right back to the time when Papi yanked me away from *La Revolucionaria* at the Getty Museum. I push away the memory, rolling my shoulder around in its socket a few times, as I try to get my bearings.

The basement is dim and quiet, candlelight flickering against the walls. When I finally catch my breath, I realize that there's barely any smell of decay.

I'm surprised that the odor is gone. I'm not sure what it means yet.

We're in the loop again but the initiation has ended and the crowd has thinned out. Smoke hangs in the air. Half of the candles in the room have already been snuffed. Only a few of the Lilies remain, silently ascending the stairway on the other side of the room.

I glance around and find myself wishing that I had my camera. Not the one on my phone. The fancy one that Mami got me for Christmas with the wide-angle lens. Malcriada would have been able to do some fire installations with images from the Archwell basement. A long exposure photograph in this low candlelight would be perfection, especially with the creepy girls in robes milling around.

"Psst, over here." Rory motions to the rest of us. She's crouched behind a long drop-leaf table, doing her best to stay hidden. I realize that we don't have our robes this time. I feel exposed without the green velvety shroud. I duck behind the table with Rory and Blythe.

"What's happening?" I ask. "I didn't expect the closet to force us out like that . . . I thought that maybe the loop was collapsing."

"No," Rory says. "I think we're in a new memory all together."

"Whose memory?" I ask.

Rory and Blythe share a look, each waiting for the other to volunteer an answer.

"At least we're at a new starting point," Blythe whispers. "If we get this one right the first time, maybe it'll buy us some more time."

"But we're back in the same spot," Rory says. "How are we supposed to—" She cuts herself off just as two figures sweep past our table. They are moving slowly, stooping every few feet to blow out the candles. The smoke in the room thickens. I try not to cough.

"You did good," one of them says to the other. "That went as smoothly as it could have."

"Did you see where Rory went?" This voice is strained and raw. The girl's tone is familiar, nearly identical to the voice of the girl at my right. Blythe shudders against me.

"She left already I think," the first figure says. She blows out the next candle and coughs several times after it goes out. Again, I wish for a camera. The glow of the remaining flames battles against the gathering smoke—it feels symbolic.

"I have to talk to her," the second girl says in Blythe's voice. She pauses close to our table and holds the edges of her hood back, protecting her hair, as she blows out a nearby flame. The candlelight illuminates her face momentarily: rich brown skin, luxurious long eyelashes, glossed lips.

Blythe's double.

I think back to the memory of the party when I ran into myself. The loop creates echoes. Some girls disappear and some girls multiply. If there are two Blythes, that means this can't be part of *her* memory. If that were the case, there would be only one Blythe, so she could reenact it.

The nearby Lilies carry on their conversation.

"Have you tried texting her?" The first girl moves away from us. She's by the candles next to the stairwell.

"Not yet," the other Blythe says. "I'd rather just find her if she's around. It's important." We all freeze for a second as Other Blythe hovers nearby, mere inches from our hiding place in the dark. If she sees us then . . . Well, we've all been through it before, but none of us wants to go through a reset again if we don't have to.

Instinctually, I hold my breath like I used to do when I played hide-and-seek at Tía Yasmine's house. Back then, I liked to hide in the closet across from Yasmine's Diego Rivera poster: a reproduced image of a woman with a bundle of calla lilies. Through the slats of the closet door, I could make out the curvature of her hands. I liked the way her braids gathered behind her back. She was always facing away from me, perhaps playing her own game. But one day, she turned and looked at me over her left shoulder. I was surprised to see that her face was identical to mine. At first, I didn't like it.

It's always been hard to look at myself in the mirror and meet my own eye. When I look at myself I see a girl who can't be trusted . . . someone who hurts people. After what happened with Charlotte, Gabe, and the chancellor, that feeling nearly consumed me. Even now, it won't leave me alone.

But now that I'm remembering how the girl with the calla lilies looked at me, I'm starting to reconsider if I've really earned all this self-hate. She looked at me like a friend, a sister. Thinking about it now feels . . . oddly reassuring.

Here in the basement, I try not to move a muscle. I don't want to catch Other Blythe's eye. Still, I can't look away from her. I stay motionless until she falls back, thankfully moving away from our hiding place. With most of the candles in the room out now, we're shrouded in darkness.

I peek around the edge of the table and check to make sure no one is nearby before I whisper to the others. "Did y'all see who that was?" I ask.

The others nod.

"We just saw Blythe's double, right? That means this isn't a replay of *her* worst memory anymore, otherwise *she* would be out there, reliving the worst parts."

"If it isn't hers, whose is it?" Rory breathes. "I wasn't in the basement after initiation."

"Hold up," Blythe says. "Where is Drew?"

I suppress a cough. The basement is filling with smoke. I look behind me, noticing for the first time that Drew isn't right there.

I scan the open room, now empty except for one shadowy figure bending over the massive infinity symbol of lilies arranged in the center of the floor.

"They were right behind me before," Rory says. "There's no place to really hide without getting caught."

Beep . . . Beep . . . Beep . . . Beep . . . Beep . . .

The fire alarm blares at us, thundering off the brick arches.

I glance at Blythe. "Don't look at me," she says. "I didn't pull the alarm. I've been here with you the whole time."

248

A loud crackling draws my gaze. A flaming infinity symbol is consuming the basement. The flowers are all on fire. And standing over it, candle in hand, is none other than Drew Simmons.

"This didn't happen before," Rory chokes.

"No, it didn't," Blythe breathes.

Without their hooded robe, I can see all of Drew in the firelight. Their hands are curled into fists. Their head is bowed, welcoming the flames. Their eyes, glassy and green, reflect the growing destruction in a low glow.

They know what they are doing. They know what the loop will do now.

This is their memory. It has to be. And they chose to burn it down. Burn it to the ground.

It's at this moment that I know without a doubt they have something to hide.

Betrayal runs in Drew Simmons's blood.

Blythe

MY CUTICLES ARE BLOODY. MY gel polish is long gone. It's a funny thing to notice in the midst of all this. There was no fire that night. So, of course, the memory has reset and we're back in the closet, and yet here I am, picking at myself without realizing it again. It's not surprising. I'd like to rip myself away from this place, to pull myself out of this stupor of memories.

The blood first collects in my nail beds, then drips onto the mess of papers strewn across the closet floor. Veró really ransacked the place when she had her fit. It's utter chaos in here—the closet doesn't reorganize itself like the loop does.

I grab a piece of scrap paper and tear off a bit, wrapping the strip around my index finger to stop the bleeding. Loose-leaf isn't great for blotting up liquid, but at least the pressure of my makeshift bandage will help. I glance back at the scrap paper, assessing whether there's enough of a margin for me to make another bandage for my pinky finger. My eyes fall over the scribbled notes on the page.

"What did you do?" Veró's voice is muffled. I'm not sure who she's talking to. I study the scrap paper more closely.

125–165 lbs—10 mgs
165–200 lbs—15 mgs
Over 200 lbs—18 mgs
Under 125 lbs—8 mgs
... for blood toxicity 50 mgs

I blink. Then I focus in on the last line.

. . . for blood toxicity 50 . . .

How much sand did Rory pour into my hand that night? How much sand did I give to Charlotte?

No. How much of it did *Rory give me* to give to Charlotte?

"You like to play. But I'm not playing right now. What did you do?" Veró's on her feet, towering over the three of us still sprawled across the closet floor.

I hold the paper close to my face.

How much did Charlotte weigh? How much did Rory give me? How much of this was planned?

"What's that, Blythe?" Drew murmurs. "Did you say something?"

I look up. Their face is lined with worry. Veró is back in her warrior stance. And Rory, oh Rory, she has that look of painted-on innocence. She had us all fooled for so long.

"Did you *murder* Charlotte, Rory?" I interrupt Veró, holding the scrap paper out for all to see. "Did you try to make it seem like I overdosed her when it was really *you* doling out the sand? *You* who knew exactly how much would kill her."

"What are you talking about?" Rory's voice is wounded but I can hear a twinge of panic underneath.

"Look," I say to the others. "These are notes on sand dosage by weight. Rory is the one who brings sand to initiations. She's the one who keeps the stuff in her dorm room year-round. She knows *all* about it. So what the hell? How much sand did you give me the night that Charlotte ODed?"

Rory screws up her face, leaning in to study the scrap paper. "That isn't even in my handwriting. And you're the one who was dosing girls at initiation."

"You told me to do it. So you could make what happened to Charlotte seem like it was my fault!"

Drew takes a peek at the note and manages to squeak out an observation. "Rory is right though, Blythe. That scrawl—it looks like the handwriting from Adeline's journal."

"It doesn't fucking matter," I spit. "Charlotte's gone. And Rory covered it up." I turn to her now. "Exactly like your grandmother did when Lillian disappeared."

Rory is as cold as ever. "You're not making sense, Blythe. Do you hear yourself? You sound hysterical." She climbs to her feet, choosing to tower over me and Drew beside Veró. "Don't you dare talk about my family like you know anything about us. You're way out of line."

252

"Why did you do it?" I demand. "Why did you do this to her? To me?"

"Wait a second," Veró barks. "We don't know for sure who's responsible for what happened to Charlotte. We might know more . . . if Drew hadn't reset the loop on their memory."

All eyes shoot over to Drew, sitting cross-legged in their white undershirt and loose brown corduroys. Their gaze is glued to the closet floor. From where I'm sitting, I can see that their mouth is twisted into a grimace. They look like they're in physical pain. I recognize that feeling: that mixture of shame and regret. It rises to the surface when the memory loop has trapped you, the moment you realize that you can't ever escape the past.

I didn't see it with my own eyes, but now I understand where the flames came from. Who set everything ablaze and landed us back in the closet.

"Exactly what were you doing the night that Charlotte disappeared, Drew?" Rory asks. "How and why were you in the basement?"

Drew's body has grown rigid. Their eyes have darkened: no longer the color of fir trees, now nearly black. They keep staring at the floor as if they're being scolded, flinching away from something . . . a sound that the rest of us can't hear.

They know something that we don't. But they remain as silent as a corpse. As stern and final as death itself.

253

IT ALWAYS STARTS AND ENDS with the sound of the alarm. *Not the one for fires. The one for bombs.*

Duck-and-cover drills, we called them. They happened all the time. It was a ritual reminder that we were never really safe.

The drills never happened late at night. Mother and Father didn't want to stir hundreds of young ladies from their beds. They didn't want angry calls from pearl-clutching parents. They had other things, bigger things, to worry about. They knew the danger was closer and more present than a missile from the other side of the world.

The first time the alarm sounded at midnight, I should have known. It was a clue about what would happen next. What would keep happening over and over. A clue that time could tear open and swallow me whole. It could do that to anyone . . . if the conditions were right.

The alarm used to inspire only dread, but now it makes me hopeful. Maybe this time they'll have found a way to understand. Maybe this time they'll have pieced it all together. Maybe this time we will move past survival and on to something else.

Drew

WHEN I WOKE UP ON Saturday morning, the day after it happened, I shuffled my deck and pulled a card. Death.

I spent the day alone in our dorm room, half expecting Charlotte to rematerialize between her green polka-dot sheets. The bedside clock ticked away the hours. I didn't reach for my phone. My computer stayed in my bag. Instead, I watched the sunlight shift on the windowsill.

By afternoon, I had eaten a whole bag of Cheetos, washed my hands, and shuffled the deck again. I pulled another card. Death.

That night I tried to sleep but I couldn't.

Sunday came and I was still alone. It was gray outside. I avoided homework. I pulled another card. Death. This time it spoke to me.

I know what you did.

It has come to me again and again with the same message. But I never quite knew what it meant. I wasn't sure if my memory could be trusted, so I held it far away from me. I turned my back on Death. But now . . . I can't any longer.

In the closet, Rory, Veró, and Blythe are all glaring at me. They are waiting for me to say something. The walls tremble around us and I worry that the closet will expel us out into the darkness like it did before. It wasn't oblivion after all. It was *my* darkness, *my* secret.

It's all on the other side of that door. And I know beyond a doubt that there's no avoiding it, no matter how many libraries I burn down.

"Okay." I hold up my hands, cornered. "Okay, yes, it's my memory. I didn't want to relive it so . . . I just . . . I wanted to get out."

"You'd rather let the loop turn to dust *with us trapped in it* than face what happened?" Veró accuses. The words cut deep, especially coming from her. She drives the knife in further. "I thought I knew you, but I guess I was wrong."

"I'm sorry, Veró," I say. "I really, really am. But look what happened in your loop—your worst memory, your biggest regret—it's like peanuts compared to mine. And Blythe, yes, you gave Charlotte the drugs that caused her overdose, but it's pretty clear that there's more to that." I flash a glance at Rory. There's terror behind the anger in her eyes. I can see it now. I see Death there. And I see what I did to Charlotte all over again.

I shut my eyes and press my fists against the sockets. "Ugh!!!" The sound reverberating from my throat surprises everyone, including me. "I just want this all to stop," I roar. "I can't get away from this feeling. I can't get away from the memory. Even when I'm not in the loop, it won't leave me alone. I just want it to stop."

"Then you have to face it," Blythe says coolly. "Otherwise that feeling is gonna follow you around forever. You have to go back out there and face what happened."

"It's true," Veró says. "Nothing can be changed until it is faced. Some author said that."

"Baldwin," Blythe cuts in. "It was James Baldwin. We read him in Speech and Rhetoric last year."

"All right. Credit where credit is due," Veró says.

I look up at her and see that she's holding her hand out to me, offering to help me up. Maybe she doesn't hate me after all of this, at least not as much as *I* hate me right now.

"But I can't change what happened," I confess. "I know that I can't."

"Then just play it through," Blythe says. "And if Rory's right, the loop might finally let us go."

I take Veró's hand and let her help me to my feet. "I'm scared," I tell her, trying to keep my voice even.

"You should be. It's scary." She lets go of my hand and crosses her arms. "Can you promise not to burn the whole place down again?"

I take a deep breath. "Okay," I say.

"We're trusting you," Blythe tells me. "Don't blow it."

Rory exhales an anxious puff of air out of the side of her mouth. "No funny business, Drew."

I nod. Before anyone can say anything else, and before I

have a chance to second-guess myself, I turn to the door and throw it open.

The basement is darker than before. The sounds of Lilies whispering in the stairwell are hollow. The stench is back, the rot that I've come to know well. Death is close by. The four of us huddle in a shadowy corner. Fortunately, the growing darkness works in our favor.

"What were you doing down here on Founder's Night?" Rory asks again.

"I was locked out of my room before everything started," I whisper back. "At first, I hid out in the library stacks. But then the party got going and I just wanted to be alone and get away from all the nonsense. I thought the basement would be . . . out of the way."

"Were you watching the initiation the whole time?" Blythe asks, mildly horrified.

"No," I murmur. "I was in there." I motion to the graywashed door tucked between the basement's shadows.

"What's back there?" Veró asks, clearly a little spooked.

"Used to be servants' quarters," Rory answers. "Now it's storage. Has been for decades."

We fall silent at the sound of something skittering across the cold bricks underfoot. It could be a rat, but I know the sound of Death drawing near. Something creaks and groans behind the walls. The sound makes it feel like we're not actually in the basement, but instead in the hull of a ship during a violent storm—one that is threatening to break the vessel apart. The loop can't hold. Our time is running out.

"C'mon," I breathe, carefully inching toward the door. The others follow. It opens with a wailing *creeeaaakkkk*. We all freeze, expecting someone in a green robe to appear with a pointed finger. We are intruders here. No one belongs in the loop. Not for long, anyway.

The four of us slip behind the door and I seal us in. I let go of the knob and find that my hands are covered in dust and old paint flakes. I try to wipe the filth away, but I can't seem to get it off. The air in here is damp and mildewed. It makes everything feel sticky. Flies buzz in the darkness. The deepening smell of decay catches in my throat.

"Why would anyone hang out in here?" Blythe whispers.

"It wasn't as bad before," I say. "The loop is making the memory worse. C'mere." I lead the others to the spot I remember, the one behind the lab table shrouded in a dusty sheet. Cardboard boxes are piled on top, blocking our view of the rest of the room except for one little slit.

"What happens now?" Veró asks.

"I was back here reading," I say. "Someone came in, so I flipped off the light on my phone and tried to stay real quiet."

My foot brushes against something. It's heavy and rectangular. I stoop down and squint into the black until I can make it out. It's my book. *A Tarot Guide to Self-Awareness*. It was waiting for me, poised to reenact the memory. I open to a random page. Death's illustrated skull grimaces at me.

I flip to another page but Death is there too. Grinning, hollow. The reaper.

I know you, it whispers. *You're back again.*

I shove through some more pages, but Death is plastered across each one.

You are complicit, it rasps again.

I slam the book closed but I can still hear Death's rattly breath.

Then I realize, it isn't Death. It's someone else. Someone hidden from view. Someone who is wheezing and choking.

"Now what?" Blythe's whisper is shaky.

"Now I notice who is here," I answer Blythe.

The wheezing intensifies. I cover my face with my hands and turn toward the noise. Slowly, I peek through my fingers and into the little crack between the boxes. Charlotte is there, lying on the cold damp floor, just like I remember. Except in the loop, her red hair is sticky with sweat and vomited-up blood. Or maybe that happened in real life too. Either way, it's worse than I remember.

"What happens next?" Rory urges.

I blink my eyes shut again and focus on the shapeless light behind my lids.

"What happened, Drew?" Veró breathes. "Do it just like you remember or we'll all be dust."

"I . . . I . . ." I can't get the words out. I can't pull together a complete thought. I'm alone in a room with a dying girl and I don't know what to do.

"Charlotte?" I manage to say, shakier and more afraid than the first time all this happened.

"Help . . . Help me . . ." she croaks. But it isn't her. It's Death's voice, deep and gravely.

"Now what?" Blythe's voice is as small as a spider's nest.

I try to pull myself together and somehow my knees allow me to stand. They carry me away from the others, around the edge of the lab table, out from behind the boxes. And now Charlotte can see me and I can see her. Except it isn't her. It's someone with black eyes, all skin and bones. She's a skeleton. My chest tightens and I drop to my knees.

"Oh, Charlotte," I say. "Oh my god."

Her eyes loll around inside her skull for a minute before they come into sharp focus on me. She speaks again, this time different, harder. Something toxic is coursing through her bloodstream.

"You," she growls. She chokes on the word, blood spewing a little from the edge of her mouth.

"Oh my god," I say again. It's just as it happened. This is exactly what I said. But this is exactly what anyone would say in this situation. "Charlotte, we need to get you help."

I reach into my pocket and pull out my phone. It's as heavy as lead in my hands. Charlotte speaks in another rattle as I try to unlock it, my fingers shaking.

"Get away," she coughs.

I finally get the phone to open. Where the hell is the call app? Panic makes me hesitate. The screen is automatically showing me my texts, the last app I was using before escaping into the library basement.

I'd wanted to get back into our dorm room, but Charlotte wasn't responding to my messages.

Locking me out is an asshole move, I wrote.

I guess you're just gonna have to tell your grandma meredith to pull some strings, she replied. Just like she did to get you into this school.

Joke's on you. She's dead. I had typed the last bit out but never sent it.

I resist the urge to throw the phone across the room. Rage seeps from my chest down into my fingertips. I didn't choose to be here. I didn't backstab or pull any strings. I'm just existing. So why does Charlotte have to be so hateful toward me?

On the floor in front of me, Charlotte turns away and heaves. Blood spills from her mouth onto the ground.

"It's okay." I reach out to touch her shoulder but she pulls away. "It's gonna be okay. I'm calling for help. Are you sick? Did you take something?"

Charlotte coughs up the last of the blood and gasps for air. She doesn't answer my question. I am on the dial pad and begin punching in the number. *9—*

"I'm going to tell everyone," Charlotte sputters. "Traitor. Backstabber. Bitch."

What the hell is Charlotte talking about? She's not making sense. I remind myself that Charlotte is smacked out of her mind. What the fuck is the emergency number? *9-1—*

"You shouldn't be here," she wheezes. "You don't belong here."

I freeze. My whole body goes cold. The nerves along my spine all pinch together, simultaneously. Charlotte's words hurt even more the second time.

You don't belong here.

She could mean anything. She could mean I don't belong here in the basement, at Archwell . . .

Or she could mean on this earth. People like me don't belong on this earth.

Lots of people believe it. They would love to see me and everyone like me gone. Erased. Turned to dust.

I look down at my phone screen, the only source of light in this godforsaken place. The number is dialed, but I haven't hit the call button yet.

I don't hit it.

I will never hit it, no matter how many times the memory plays on a loop in my head. I will not help someone who doesn't respect my humanity. I will also live to regret it.

I silence the phone screen and plunge us back into darkness.

"You don't belong here," she wheezes one last time. But now, I suddenly realize her tone is different than I remember. Desperate and sorrowful.

My throat tightens, my palms are slick with sweat.

Charlotte is pleading with me.

Does that mean that I've misunderstood everything?

Is Charlotte trying to warn me about something? Is she telling me I don't belong around the treachery of the Lilies? The ones who dosed her, who betrayed her . . .

Is she's telling me to get out while I can?

The muscles in my core seize up. This is fucked-up. I fucked up. I misunderstood.

Then Charlotte's choking starts all over again. The paleness of her face comes into focus as my eyes adjust. Here in the black she looks more like herself. Pretty and delicate, just like I remember. But this lasts for only a second.

I didn't believe it the first time I saw it. That's why I didn't tell anyone. But even if I *had* told someone, they wouldn't have believed me. They would not have believed that Charlotte could just . . . dissolve.

But that is exactly what happens.

A wave of darkness swirls around her, smoky and fine. It wraps around her arms and legs, winding its way around her face, clamping her mouth shut. And now, it's happening again. Each part of her is being consumed. Something is devouring her piece by piece. She tries to scream, but she can't. Something has taken her.

The first time I saw it, I didn't know what it was. How could I? But now I see that whatever it is, it's what's corroding the loop. The same thing that binds the Lilies together. The thing that kept me awake in the hours and days after Charlotte disappeared.

It's not really a thing. It's a feeling. It's shame, coming to feed on our memories.

I don't call for help.

Instead, I wind up alone in the dark room.

And then, out of nowhere, comes the sound of the alarm. *BLEEP-BLEEP-BLEEP . . . BLEEP-BLEEP-BLEEP . . . Warning. Warning. Lockdown. Shelter in place. Secure doors. Warning. Warning.*

Veró

THE PAINTING WAS FROM ONE of my dreams. I put Mami and Papi in it first, then my cousins and my tías, then the principals of Easton Academy and Forrest Gable. Troy the assistant made it in there too. So did Papi's campaign manager, Carla. Above them all, I included my own version of *La Revolucionaria*, Yolanda López's *La Virgen de Guadalupe*, and Manuel Caro's *El Alma de la Virgen*. I added some Archwell girls in tweed blazers into the background of the crowd for good measure.

"I like this one of yours," Mami told me over FaceTime. "It reminds me of Judy Baca. Ever think about doing murals?"

"I guess as soon as I have a wall," I said. "I don't really want to get locked into one medium though. Murals are very time intensive."

"But why did you paint the Archwell girls like that?" Mami asked. "And Dean Treadwell from Easton Academy. Do they all really deserve to be portrayed like diablitos?"

I looked at the little horns and spiky tails I added to the prep school characters in the painting. "Yes, they do."

Mami clicked her tongue. "Verónica, you never let go of a grudge, do you?"

"Why should I?" I put my paintbrush in the cup of dirty water on my dresser and sat down on my extra-long dorm bed. "Anyway, none of them will ever see this piece. Who is it hurting?"

"You, querida. It's hurting you." Mami's words surprised me. I held the phone a little farther away from my face to pretend like I wasn't listening too closely. "Resentment doesn't do anything but make a person miserable. You have to learn to accept the past and move on."

"I don't have to accept things that are unfair."

"You can still fight for a better future—but you have to accept that the past is gone," Mami said. "Be angry, paint little devil horns on mean girls, but then let it go and put your energy toward something that'll change things."

"Art can change things," I say.

"Sure," Mami says. "But it doesn't have to be cruel to do that."

The Archwell girls in my painting smiled at me, their devil horns blushing from a flamingo tone into a shade of ruby. Then they hissed at me, uttering words I didn't yet know.

Ut sacram memoriam. Ut sacram memoriam. Ut sacram memoriam.

I think I hear someone whispering these words again as we are sucked out of the basement and expelled back into

267

the closet. I wind up lying face down on the hardwood floor, grateful to be in one piece again and out of the loop. Nothing has ever felt better than this newfound stillness. I force my eyes open and find that the lights are already on. I rest my cheek against the wood and notice that the floor extends farther than I expected. We're not in the closet anymore. I sit up and find that we're finally back in the chancellor's office, awash with crimson and low lamp light.

"Wow," I breathe. "It's finally over." I think about standing up but something in me feels a bit too delicate. Emotions are coursing through me. Anger and sorrow for everything that just happened. Grief and shame are tied to every memory that was played on repeat. And in the end, we couldn't change the past. Charlotte is gone. Gabe is gone. Archwell stays the same. The thought cuts through me like a knife.

"Drew?" I manage to collect my breath into words. "You good?"

"I'm all right," they whisper back. They are sitting up, back leaning against the side of the chancellor's mahogany desk. Rory is beside them, leaning against the tabletop, hands gripping the edge as if she is still bracing herself against the loop's propulsion.

"Are *you* okay?" Blythe asks me from a spot on the nearby flowery rug.

"Yeah," I say.

We just sit in silence like that for a while. Again, savoring the stillness. Eventually, we each get up off the floor and find a seat in the chancellor's leather tufted chairs. No one meets anyone's eyes. Not yet.

There may be truth now, but there still isn't trust.

"We know what happened to Charlotte," I say, realizing I might be opening Pandora's box. The others might not want to talk about what we just saw, but, again, what choice do we have? There are still missing girls here at Archwell.

"Yes, we do," Rory says, resolved.

"A lot happened to Charlotte," Drew admits.

"She wanted to be a Lily," Blythe says, a bit tearful. "Because she wanted to fit in." She looks at Drew now. "And fitting in with the Lilies meant being cruel."

I think about my painting with the Archwell girls as diablitos. Mami called it cruel, but was it? I painted those girls like that because of how they acted: above it all, cliquey, and conniving. They made me feel like I didn't belong. I know they did the same to others. It occurs to me that exclusion is a form of cruelty too. It'll make people do unspeakable things . . . but in the end, even mean girls are trying to find a way to survive it all.

"She wound up at y'all's cursed initiation," I say.

"Where Blythe gave her an overdose of sand," Rory adds.

"An amount that *you* handed to me without saying anything about it," Blythe bites back. "Then you had her taken to another room and left alone."

"I thought she would shake it off," Rory says. "She was supposed to get only a little sick. The dose wasn't supposed to be toxic. I didn't realize how much she'd been drinking at the party. Then Drew found her."

". . . and I didn't help," they say, voice shaking. "I . . . I couldn't but . . . maybe I . . . No. I couldn't help her." Their face is twisted into a scowl. "But now I'm starting to wish I . . . I dunno."

"Can I ask"—Blythe's voice is careful, gentle—"I know Charlotte was never nice to you but it doesn't seem like you *not* to intervene. I mean, you're a good person, Drew."

"No, I'm not," they growl. "Good people don't watch their roommates choke and struggle and then just . . . disappear. Especially since . . . now that I've actually lived through it again, I'm wondering if I really was understanding what she was saying."

"She was angry about something," I say. "But it didn't seem like she was lucid."

Rory nods in agreement, turning to Drew. "She didn't recognize you."

"I see that now." Drew cringes. "I thought she was calling my grandma a backstabber . . . a bitch. She texted me something about it earlier in the evening, so I just assumed . . . I thought she was telling me that I didn't belong at Archwell."

"I think she was trying to warn you," Blythe soothes. "Warn you about us . . . the Lilies, I mean. She was trying to tell you that it was dangerous. That you didn't belong around all of that."

"And then she just . . . disintegrated," Drew groans,

burying their face in their hands. "Y'all saw for yourselves . . . It's like . . . what even *was* that? We need to know what the hell happened!"

"More like we need to know who is to blame," I say. My eyes pass from face to face. Drew wears a hangdog look. They fold their arms in front of their chest. Blythe is gripping the padded arms of her chair, her fingers demanding vengeance but her mind denying the impulse. Rory is cold, chin held high, but she looks a bit like a tree after a hurricane. She's still trying to stand proud even though the elements have battered her down. She catches me staring.

"Don't look at me like that," she says. "You know this isn't just on me."

"Oh yeah?" I say, taking the bait. "None of this would have gone on without the Lilies. If the initiation hadn't happened, Charlotte wouldn't have disappeared. If the Lilies weren't messing around with girls' worst memories, who knows if the time loop would even exist?"

"We never meant for any of this to happen," Rory retorts.

"I'm not blaming the Lilies, Rory. I'm blaming you. You're the ringleader here. All this messed-up stuff is happening on your watch."

Rory launches toward me. "You see what you want to see, Veró. It doesn't matter how many times I explain it or how many times you watch the loop play out. You just have your mind made up about me." With every sentence, her voice climbs another decibel. "And that's just fine. Be like that. It's your opinion. In the end, it doesn't matter what you think."

Rory's words are designed to be a put-down but the sheer volume of her voice shows me something surprising. Somehow it seems like my opinion might actually matter to Rory Archwell. It's not just that she doesn't want to be responsible for everything that happened. It seems like maybe she might want me to just trust her. I consider it for a moment. Rory's been the bad guy in all of this for me, but does that make her the villain?

Before I can answer that question, the office door swings open. In the low lamplight, the chancellor somehow looks more severe than usual. She's wearing her white pantsuit, the one she wore on Founder's Night.

"What did you do, Rory?" she demands. It doesn't sound like a question. It's more of a threat.

She strides into the room, and startles when she notices that her daughter isn't the only one waiting there.

"What are you all—"

Bong!

Oh shit. The sound is back.

Bong!

The grandfather clock signals another shift.

Bong!

The office disappears into a red blur.

Bong!

I don't understand how this could've happened.

Bong!

We found out what happened to Charlotte. I thought we were done.

My body slams hard onto the closet floor again. The scent of mothballs crowds my sinuses.

"Fucking hell," someone groans.

"What just happened?"

Someone yanks the little metal cord and the light comes on again.

Damn it. I can't believe this.

"The loop wasn't done. We got reset," Blythe exclaims.

"Oh god," grunts Drew. "I'm so fucking over this."

"Whose memory didn't play out?" I ask. "We went through everyone's! Drew, we just did yours. Blythe and Rory's, we did it. Y'all know we did mine already. So what the fuck?"

"I don't know, but y'all know that I'm not playing with this loop anymore," Blythe says. "This is not my idea of fun, so one of y'all better come clean."

"There's unfinished business," Drew says, rising to their feet. "Think about what the vow says: *Only when her sisters' wrongs are once again made right will she escape.* I still don't think that's a metaphor. I mean, everything else in the vow is literal."

"But changing the past hasn't worked," I remind Drew. "I wish it all happened differently. Believe me . . . but—"

"Listen," Rory says. She reaches out for the light's little metal cord, grabs it, and holds it still until it stops swaying. "I thought maybe the loop wouldn't take us here. I thought

273

maybe my initiation memories and Blythe's were all mixed up together, but . . ."

"What are you talking about?" Blythe says. "Are you saying we haven't been through *your* loop yet?"

"No, I don't think we have," Rory utters.

"Motherfu . . ." I breathe.

"Oh, come on," Drew groans, putting their face in their hands. "Seriously?!"

"Something else happened that night. I—I didn't think it would take me back here."

"What *did* you think?" Blythe says. "That you were somehow gonna get off the hook? That you were different from the rest of us? I'm pretty sure your family name doesn't get you out of . . . whatever the hell this is." She gestures wildly at the inside of the closet.

Rory shakes her head and pulls the cord. The closet goes dark.

"Let's go back out there and get this over with, I guess. No point in staying here any longer." Her voice is sodden and defeated, but for the first time I can tell Rory is being real with us.

She is not performing anymore. She's not trying to act the part of the caring friend, the queen, or the martyr. She's just someone's kid—someone who really, really messed up.

And it's that look of defeat—that honest look—that makes me follow her out of the closet one more time.

Rory

I WAS RAISED TO PLAY the game. I tried to live up to my family name, to do what I needed to do to get ahead and stay there. Sometimes people got hurt in the process and that was just collateral damage. That's what I was taught, and I learned from the best.

But I didn't know I could cause this kind of pain, and I had no idea how deep the hurt would run inside of me. I tried not to feel it, but time finally caught up with me. The loop wrapped itself around my throat and began to squeeze.

"Where should we hide?" Drew wants to know.

I motion to the heavy drapes, not quite as velvety as the Lilies robes.

"If you stay really still, a couple of you can hide behind there," I say. "Someone else can go over there." I point to a small gap between the credenza and the office's corner. "We'll pull a chair in front so she can't see you."

The others scatter to their hiding places, covering themselves in gray-green curtains and shadows. I listen for their rustling and breathing but after a few seconds everyone is still. It's as if I'm all alone again, nothing to focus on except the feeling of my teeth grinding together and the sensation that my windpipe is narrowing. I sit down in the chair directly across from my mother's desk. I would never dare sit in *her* chair, especially not now.

The clock on her desk reveals that it's after midnight. My phone buzzes in my pocket. The sensation makes me jump, even though I'm half expecting it. I check the screen. It's a push notification. ALL CAMPUS LOCKDOWN DRILL: COMPLETE.

I check my texts: nothing. Then I look at my recent calls: one outgoing call to my mother, fifteen minutes ago. This is not a drill. I'm about to relive this moment all over again. Every muscle in my body clenches in anticipation.

The door squeals open and I shove my phone into my pocket.

"What did you do, Rory?" My mother's voice is rougher than I remember. She says my name with surprising violence, a tone that she's usually careful to keep hidden.

"What you told me to do," I say.

My mother storms to her desk and sits in her tufted leather chair. She's still in her pantsuit from the Founder's Night party, even though it ended a couple of hours ago. Her face is drawn. It's not just disappointment clouding her expression. It's something else this time . . . disdain.

My heart sinks into my knees. I messed up so badly. The lights flicker and dim. It didn't happen this way the first time, but the loop was bound to play tricks on me the way it did with all the others. The room is getting smaller and darker. My mother and I are alone and she's looking at me like she would an insect that is better off squashed under her heel.

"I told you to step up and lead. I told you to keep the underclassmen in line. I told you to keep the Lilies' secrets under wraps. I didn't tell you to dose your initiates with a controlled substance." My mother's eyes narrow and the walls draw closer around us. There's nowhere to hide. She's watching me squirm. The only thing I can do is ignore and deflect.

"Why did you call for a lockdown drill so late at night?" I ask. "When I heard the alarm, I got scared."

"We did a campus sweep," my mother hisses. "You gave me good cause for it."

"You told security about Charlotte?" My voice is smaller than ever. Fear constricts the words.

"No," she answers. "I'm not a fool. We did it as a standard drill procedure. No one knows about what happened."

"Did you find her?" The wall behind me bumps against my chair, rolling me forward slightly. The office isn't much bigger than the closet now. It's only four red walls, my mother, me, and a desk between us. It didn't happen like this, but it felt exactly this way.

"No," she seethes. "We didn't find anything."

"It was so strange," I say. "Blythe gave Charlotte the sand,

and when she started to look like she was going to be sick, I had some of the girls take her to get some air, but then when I went to find her after initiation she was totally gone. Nowhere. It was like she never existed. I'm sorry. I know this is bad. But I had to call you. I had to get help."

"This isn't you asking for help," she says as the paneled walls press farther in. "This is you thinking *you* could play with fire and *I* could just put out the flames. This is you being stupid, Rory. But I guess I shouldn't be surprised. You always put too much stock in those stories of your grandmother's. The ones about the Lilies' 'glory days.' Dosing initiates might have been part of the original tradition, but it was wrong! And *you* shouldn't have been doing it. I told you as much."

"Okay," I say.

"Are you using again?" she presses. The wall behind her closes in and pushes her chair right up to the desk, squeezing her body against the edge, but she doesn't flinch. "I thought your summer at Northbridge would've squashed your little habits."

I don't answer. I try to look at my shoes like I remember doing, but I've been pushed too close to the desk to see my feet. The room is the size of a coffin.

"I thought you would've been smarter about all of this by now. When you were a freshman, I could understand. You were young and impressionable. But you're nearly grown now, Rory. Real Archwell women don't succumb to their weaknesses."

The mahogany desktop between us begins to crack. The wood splinters and buckles. The clock rolls off the edge onto what's left of the floor. The walls are threatening to crush us, but my mother's tongue-lashing continues.

"You have to be tough. Lilies are not weak."

The desk falls away and we're pushed even closer together, my mother's face is just inches from mine. I can feel her breath. A drop of her spittle lands on my cheek as she speaks.

"Blythe gave Charlotte the drugs, but *you* are the one who had them in the first place. *You* are the one who was trying to cut corners to get ahead. If you were really smart, Rory, you would *be* ahead already. You wouldn't need to go to such desperate measures to eliminate your competition."

I cover my face with my hands. Hearing the truth of the matter out loud feels so much more awful than I remember. Even worse, I know Blythe is watching. She can see what's happening. She can hear my mother's words, understand that, yes, *she* was my target. Yes, Blythe, the only other contender for valedictorian. Blythe, who took the sand from me without looking at how much I'd poured into her hand. Blythe, who gave a heavy dose to the Lilies' biggest blabbermouth. The plan was going to fix all my problems.

But Charlotte wasn't supposed to just . . . disappear.

I squirm in my chair as an explanation worms its way out of me. "I was just trying to do what you told me! I was doing whatever it took to be the best. I wasn't trying to hurt anyone. Charlotte was supposed to maybe get a little sick and

279

get Blythe into trouble. That's all. If it had worked out differently, you would've been proud of me!"

"You're a disgrace." My mother's voice strikes me squarely in the face.

A sob escapes my mouth before I can push it down into my belly.

"I'm sorry," I say. "I didn't mean—"

My mother grips my chin. "You need to think about what you've done."

"Please, I—"

The closet's polished wooden door comes into focus, and I know what's coming next.

My mother drags me from my seat. I hear the keys rattle in her hand. I've been at this threshold hundreds of times. Every mistake, every betrayal, every misstep since I was small has landed me here.

"No, please. I don't want to go in there. I promise I'll—"

"Promise you'll what? Fix it? When have you ever had the wherewithal to clean up your own mess?" She rattles the closet open and pushes me toward it.

I grasp the door's walnut frame, resisting my mother's shoves. It's a trick I've pulled since grade school, although it only delays the inevitable.

My fingers stretch beyond their natural length as I hang on to the outside for dear life.

I don't want to be alone in there. Not again. Every time, the darkness swallows me and twists my thoughts into terrors. It gathers my secrets together and flays each of them like a carcass.

My fingers give way and I fall back into the closet onto what feels like a bed of spiders. In the sliver of light from the closet door's opening, I can see the mess of papers, dresses, and jewelry crawling all around me, like snakes in a pit.

My mother's shadow spills through the doorway, dense and threatening. "You need to reflect on your transgressions. And we both know that this is the best place to do it."

I muster what's left of my voice, trying to say what I remember saying before. It's barely there but I manage to force it out. "Please—"

The closet door snaps shut and the walls begin to squeeze around my body from all sides. Memories invade, pushing reality far, far away. I can't move my arms. I can barely breathe, but the closet just keeps caving in.

I'm five and I've been caught stealing gum from the grocery store checkout.

I'm seven and I've pushed Courtney off the monkey bars.

I'm nine and I've cheated on a spelling test.

I'm thirteen and I posted something rude on the internet.

I did something bad. I let someone down. I betrayed someone.

The evidence is all here, and it consumes me.

I relive each memory again and again until I don't recognize myself or the world anymore. The loop has me.

There's barely space to exist here. There was never

enough space for me here, and now I'm going to be crushed. Destroyed, just like my mother wants.

She wants me to be somebody else. She wants me to be her. And I tried. And now the closet is squeezing so tightly around me that there is no more space for my lungs to expand. My ribs crack under the pressure.

I wait for relief. I know it's about to be over. Soon it will all be over.

And then the sound is back. *Bong . . . Bong . . . Bong!*

THE ALARM CLOCK WAKES ME *in the morning, the same as any other. I dress up in white, put on my pearls. It is senior portrait day.*

After the photos, Father calls me into his office and shows me the letter from Meredith. He is concerned. Not so much about Adeline—he'll deal with her later. But about the nature of Evelyn's and my friendship. He's heard things, he's seen the way we act together, the way we look at each other. I try to explain. He was so understanding before. But this time . . . it's different. It's too much for him. He barks something about burdens and selfishness. Something about decency and the law. I leave in tears.

After lights out, I meet Evelyn at our spot in the servant's corridor. She's acting strangely but promises me she has a way to get my mind off our worries.

I breathe the stuff in and let it take me away. And at first, it is glorious. Evelyn and I are stars in a galaxy, able to be exactly ourselves, unique and still beautiful. But soon I remember that there is no oxygen in outer space.

The worst part of reliving the memory is the choking. I hate staining my dress over and over again. I hate coughing up blood. Evelyn is scared, and then, suddenly, she's gone. The last face I remember seeing isn't hers at all.

The girl is familiar, but I don't know her name. By now, I've seen her so many times, I could probably draw you a picture. Rich brown skin, luxurious long eyelashes, glossed lips. Some might say she doesn't belong at Archwell. But if they knew me, those same people might also say that I don't belong here either.

Each time I see her, I hear the alarm blaring: Beep . . . Beep . . . Beep . . . And I know the loop has come to an end and will begin again like a snake eating its own tail. Still, I'm hopeful. Still, I find a way.

Veró

MALCRIADA LIVED FOR THE NAKED truth. Her art was guided by anger and justice, an eye for an eye. But even her best work—even the most thoughtful art in the world—could not achieve what the loop has done to us. It has taken a magnifying glass to each regret and twisted our memories into something unrecognizable. We've been in the loop for so long now that I'm starting to wonder if maybe that's just how memory works: whatever happens in your head is not exactly the same as what really happened.

Your fear, your anger, your shame, all of that distorts your world. It doesn't change just what you remember. It changes how you see everything. It changes the way you act and the way you treat people. And as long as you try to keep that shame hidden, it'll tear you to shreds from the inside.

Now there's nothing more to hide. The naked truth is finally in front of us. Everyone did something they regret.

Everyone had a role to play in Charlotte's disappearance. Everyone is responsible . . .

"Everyone is so fucked-up," Drew says. They lean against

the wall near the closet's door. They don't reach for the knob. We're not ready to go back out there, not yet. We don't know what's on the other side.

"Some worse than others," Blythe says in a tone that could burn the hair on your knuckles.

"I fucked up," Rory says, sniffling. "Because I'm fucked-up."

We're all silent for a moment, none of us quite sure how to respond. No one wants to hold space for Rory Archwell . . . not really. Still, what we saw in her loop—what the chancellor did—seemed just as messed-up as anything Rory did with the Lilies. For the first time, Rory makes sense to me.

"How long has your mom been locking you in here like that, Rory?" Blythe is standing now, facing her "sister" head-on.

Rory crumples a little and starts to cry softly. Now I've seen everything.

"Forever," she says, sinking to the floor. "It's been my punishment for forever. It's what—" She sniffs a little. "What the Archwells do."

"What does that mean?" Drew asks.

Rory shrugs. She folds her body into itself, making herself as small as possible. She's trying to disappear.

Blythe softens a bit and sits down next to her. "Your mom locked you in here as punishment, the way her mom . . . ?"

Tears drown any hope of a decipherable response from Rory. The rest of us take it as proof that Blythe's guess is accurate. It's easy to see now what shame has done to Rory and her family. What it has done to everyone at Archwell Academy.

"I'm sorry," she cries. "I didn't mean to hurt anybody . . . not like that . . . I'm just . . . I'm just a fuckup."

Rory's tears are steady. Blythe's crying ever so slightly now too. "I wish none of this had ever happened. I wish your mom hadn't done all that. And her mom before her . . . And Charlotte and Lillian . . . I just—"

"So many regrets," Drew murmurs.

So many. If I hadn't done the #transinclusion installation, we might not all be right here now. Gabe would still be a student at Archwell. Charlotte wouldn't have been caught alongside me in the bathroom. And maybe if she hadn't been caught, she might have had the guts to step out of line and follow her instincts. She might have left the Lilies before they could destroy her.

My heart sinks. Then Mami's words come back to me, *You have to learn to accept the past and move on.* But it seems like the loop won't let any of us move on. Shame keeps dogging me.

We fall into silence again. Blythe wipes her face, stands, and stretches. She looks tired. We all do. The truth has destroyed us, but it's also given us a rare moment of peace here in the closet.

"I don't want to be like her, you know," Rory says, wiping her nose with the back of her hand. She's obviously referring to her mom. "I just . . . didn't have a choice."

"That much is clear," I say. I may not agree with my papi's

politics. I may get on his and Mami's last nerve, but he would never treat me the way the chancellor treated Rory.

"For what it's worth," Drew says, "I don't think you are like your mom, actually."

"No," I affirm. "You're not."

"Trauma patterns," Blythe whispers.

"Excuse me?" I say.

"Ever hear of generational trauma? Trauma patterns?" Blythe asks. Everyone stares. "I read about it in sociology. Trauma can be passed down from generation to generation, sometimes without even realizing it. People unconsciously repeat abusive patterns and then pass them down. Like traditions, but"—she glances around at all the Lilies ceremonial crap—"messed-up ones."

"Hurt people hurt people," Drew adds.

Rory nods. Her tears have stopped. "Our grandmothers, and Lillian," she says. "Now . . . us."

We slip into silence again, just as a scrap of paper falls from one of the closet's high shelves. It floats down to the floor like snow. It lands squarely among the four of us, face up.

"I would like this closet to leave us alone now," Drew says. "My brain can't take it anymore."

An awkward giggle escapes my mouth as I stoop to pick up the paper. I study it for a moment. The handwriting is unfamiliar, the edges are withered, but the message is timeless. I look up at Drew.

"It's a love letter." I smile. "It's to Lillian."

"Let me see," Rory says, reaching for the page. I hand it over.

"'Dear Lil,'" she reads. "'You bring me light on my darkest days. You are my every hope for what the future may be. You make it safe for me to dream. I love you. XO, Evelyn.'"

"Aww," Drew says. "Cute! We love to see it!"

"So Charlotte's grandmother and Lillian were in love . . . They were together."

"It was 1958," Blythe reminds us. "They might have been . . . stuck in the closet."

"I know the feeling," I say, looking around at *our* closet.

"Time wouldn't let them be together," Rory says. "And also . . . more than likely my great-grandparents. They loved Lillian. This whole place exists because of her. But the fact that she was trans was a secret. One they were trying to bury right here. And if she was queer *and* trans? It might have been too much for them to handle."

"There were also a bunch of laws at the time against things like homosexuality and wearing clothes that didn't line up with a person's assigned gender," Blythe adds.

I can't help but shake my head. "I'm not sure much has changed," I say, making eye contact with Drew. "The laws may be different but . . . there's still the same old gender oppression and the same old homophobia."

We all stare at the letter, eyes following the graceful lines of Evelyn's handwriting. I trace the word *Love* onto my forearm with my index finger over and over again. My eyes flicker over to Drew, who's staring at Lillian's gown.

"Therein lies infinity—the place where she survives—while we protect our sisterhood, our secrets, and our lives," they mutter to themself. *"For only when her sisters' wrongs are once again made right will she escape anew and take her place within the light. And so shall . . . so shall . . .* What's the end of the Lilies vow again?"

"I thought you had it memorized," Blythe says.

"It's been a long day," Drew counters.

Rory speaks now. *"And so shall four return again beneath the waning moon to resurrect the memory, or find our way to ruin. Ut sacram memoriam."*

"The four," Drew says. "The founders, right? Meredith, Adeline, Evelyn . . . and who else?"

"Lillian?" I volunteer.

Drew shakes their head. "Lillian disappeared before they started the Lilies. That's why it was named after her."

"That's true," Rory affirms.

Drew takes a deep breath and runs their hand over their buzzcut. They meet my eyes. "What if it's us?"

"What?" I yelp.

"What if *we* are 'the four.' *And so shall four return again beneath the waning moon to resurrect the memory, or find our way to ruin.* What if we're the ones who might be able to turn the wrong right? Some of us are descendants of the original four. What if all this is happening . . . because we're here?"

"I dunno, Drew," Blythe says. "The vow says *'again.'* All four of us haven't met before today."

"But time, in this place, is warped," Rory says.

"What does 'again' even mean in a place where everything repeats?" Drew adds. "In a place that's *beyond the bounds of time?*"

They're met with silence as everyone works it through.

"But we tried to change things before—and it didn't work," Rory says.

"We tried to save Charlotte," Blythe reminds us. "That's what didn't work."

"We need to go back farther," Drew says. "Like *way* back."

Blythe runs her hands over her face. "Drew. It's been, like, a *day*. Can you explain this like I'm a three-year-old?"

Rory's eyes narrow. "Drew. Are you suggesting . . . ?"

Drew nods. "I think we need to open that door and try to find the whole truth about what happened to *Lillian*."

"Huh?" Blythe squeaks.

"Her story has been buried all this time," Drew tells her. "If we witness it, then . . ."

After a beat Blythe whispers, "Then the *wrongs are once again made right*."

A strange feeling fills my chest. Something that feels like . . . hope.

The four of us stare at each other, then shift each of our gazes to the door. Its polished wood gleams in the low light.

"Why would the loop let us go back that far?" I ask.

291

"Because we've already survived reliving our own memories," Drew says, "and it's clear whatever is with us in this closet wants us to know what happened to Lillian."

"It's true," Blythe says. "All the clues, everything we've found, has been about her."

We're quiet for a moment, each of us still eyeing the door.

"Let us see what happened," Rory calls out to no one in particular. Her voice is louder than before, more willful. I realize she's not speaking to any of us . . . she's speaking to the walls of the closet. "We four are here to right a wrong." As she speaks one of the alarm clocks on the shelf starts to buzz.

Maybe it's an answer. Maybe we're actually on to something.

"Let us see what happened," Drew says now, as more alarms begin to sound. "No more secrets and lies."

"Let us see what happened," Blythe says as the grandfather clock starts to *bong*. She looks at me as she speaks. "Nothing can be changed until it's faced."

"Let us see what happened," I say. Then I smile because I can't really believe what I'm about to say. "Ut sacram memoriam."

"Ew, Veró," Drew mutters, eyes smiling.

The closet door flings open.

26

the Lilies

Veró

THE MOMENT THE CLOSET DOOR opens, my ears pop. The room becomes a wind tunnel, then a jet engine. Sheer air pressure wrestles each of us through the doorway, and then we're streaking through a passageway so bright that I lose all sight of the others. Something is pulling us through, and all I can do is give in to it. My body becomes a silk ribbon in the wind, flowing and snapping as the force that pulls me forward speeds up.

Then my feet hit softly against carpet. The impact forces me to my hands and knees. Rug burn spreads up my forearms. I gasp for air, gripping at the weave of the burgundy rug. I'm not moving anymore. I've landed. The room around me is still and I'm alone. Where are the others?

As soon as I can breathe a bit, I lift my gaze to the window above me, seeing only blue sky and slate-shingle roofs. In front of me, below the window, there's a twin bed with a flouncy skirt. To my left, there's a small desk with a single chair, both in a blond wood. It clashes a little with the room's cherry paneling. This isn't the library. The loop has taken me somewhere else entirely.

Did it work?

I sit up and something scratches against my legs. I glance down.

Somehow, I'm wearing a skirt. Underneath I find an itchy crinoline lining. Okay, now I *know* I'm tripping. My collared shirt's been replaced by a lavender cardigan buttoned all the way up, topped with a string of pearls.

I would never.

My eyes catch on a pennant tacked to the bulletin board next to the bed. It is forest-green with gold lettering that boldly announces *The Archwell Academy for Girls.* It finally dawns on me that I'm in the Archwell dorms. I rise to my feet and peer out the window at the familiar stone buildings of the central courtyard. They are naked and vineless. Their craggy blockwork is barely weathered. The trees in the courtyard are smaller too. It all looks just like Archwell but . . . everything is *newer.*

I turn to the bulletin board and lean across the bed, kneeling on the mattress to get a better look. There are some magazine cutouts from *Vogue,* a handful of drawings and notes, a certificate of achievement, and a calendar. By the time I notice the month, day, and year marked on the page, I'm not even surprised.

Of course. It's October 6, 1958.

But whose dorm room is it? There are only a handful of options.

I turn to the desk and begin rummaging in the drawers and through the stacks of papers. Nothing. I turn back to the bulletin board and find the certificate of achievement.

For Excellence in French IV, Spring Semester '57: Meredith D. Simmons

Por Dios. This is Drew's grandmother's dorm room. A lair for one of the original Lilies. I can't believe this. Before I know it, I'm pacing the room, pinging from wall to wall. Why am I here? Why am I alone? Why isn't Drew here? Shouldn't they be the one transported back to see their grandmother? This has got to be a mistake.

I pause at the windowsill and notice how Meredith has filled an empty glass bottle with water and a single black-eyed Susan. It looks a bit withered, as if it's been sitting on the ledge for a while. Next to the flower, there is a piece of heavy paper and a little plastic box that I recognize as a watercolor kit. The paper has some pencil marks and brush-strokes: the beginnings of some kind of caricature. I don't recognize the figure, as the piece isn't quite fully developed. I can tell it's a girl, though. She looks suspiciously familiar, a lot like the Archwell girls from my painting. Malcriada would approve.

The door on the far side of the room stirs and I freeze. I don't know if the loop will reset if Meredith finds me here and I don't want to find out. I dive into the dorm room closet and pull the door behind me, leaving it open just a crack so I can still see the desk. I hear the room door open all the way and then shut again. Someone heaves a sigh and shuffles around a bit. Then Meredith Simmons rounds the corner into my line of view and drops into her desk chair. She has Drew's mouth. The way her nostrils flare when she sighs is exactly like her future grandchild . . . who isn't born yet? Is that why Drew isn't with me in this memory? They ceased to exist?

Before the questions can spiral too far away from me, I notice that Meredith is wearing the exact same lavender sweater and striped skirt as I am. Creepy. I hate to think what she might say if she were to find me, a brown girl in her closet dressed as her double.

I watch Drew's grandmother as she putters around her desk, placing a record on her little turntable and letting the needle drop. I'm surprised when I recognize the sound of old-school country and western. Mami has this album in her record collection. Patsy Cline begins to sing:

I can't forget you. I've got these memories of you.

Meredith shifts in her chair, opens the top desk drawer, and reaches in for paper and a fountain pen. I watch as she writes. I've come to recognize her bright, bubbly penmanship. Thankfully, her handwriting is a bit larger than average. It's big enough for me to make out the beginning of the letter she's writing.

Dear Chancellor Archwell,

I'm writing to you because I'm worried about your children . . .

Oh my god. It's a letter to Rory's great-grandfather. *The* letter. The one that exposed Adeline's addiction. The one that misgendered Lillian . . . and possibly outed her romance with Evelyn.

I can't see all of Meredith's face, but October sunlight illuminates her honey hair and a sliver of her profile. I can make out the corner of a deep frown. Her shoulders are stooped and tight. She is a knot of worry. She sniffles softly. Is she crying? Why? She's doing something awful. She's knowingly betraying her friends. She doesn't get to cry.

Meredith pauses and leans back in her chair. She runs her hands under her eyelids, then stretches her arms out wide. "Ah!" she says, shaking out her hands as if trying to throw something off her, something that is tearing her up inside. Then she lets her arms drop and is still for a moment.

Suddenly, I feel the sensation of the sturdy desk chair beneath me. I'm gazing at the letter, leaning over it, the pen in my hand. I *am* Meredith.

Fear and worry prickle at my neck. Tension rides my eyebrows. What Adeline is doing isn't right, and Lil and Evelyn are just ignoring it. Well, I can't ignore it any longer. I have to do something, to let someone know, even if it means they'll all hate me for tattling. I put my pen to the page and finish writing.

Please know that I tell you this as a friend with the very best of intentions . . .

And then I'm somehow in both places: watching from the closet and sitting at the desk signing the note.

Sincerely, Meredith Simmons

Watching Meredith fold and seal the note into a cream-colored envelope, I recognize her for who she is: someone who thinks she's doing good but is actually about to wreak so much damage. I've seen it before. I've lived it. Because I was that person.

I know where that letter is going. I know it will wind up on Chancellor Archwell's desk. What happens after that, I'm not totally sure, but I can make a few informed guesses.

Someone will be outed. Someone will be hurt. Someone will wind up disappearing from Archwell Academy.

It's no different from my installation in the bathroom. It's misguided savior bullshit, done out of concern . . . and ignorance.

I watch as Meredith stands, throws on her jacket, and heads for the door. The envelope for Chancellor Archwell is in her left hand. She doesn't understand what she is doing.

She doesn't know that a ripple across the water can turn into a wave. She doesn't know that her actions today will have consequences tomorrow, and the next day, and decades down the line.

I know these things now, but what I don't know is how I can stop her, stop it all from happening.

The dorm room door closes with a heavy *clunk* and I'm alone again in the closet.

The pattern repeats.

Blythe

YOU'RE IN YOUR BODY, BLYTHE, I remind myself as the tunnel of light disintegrates around me, transforming into a dark brick room. *You're still in your body.* I wrap my arms around myself and find that my blouse has been replaced with a green plaid dress that buttons down the middle. It's an A-line cut, cinched at the waist with a thin leather belt. It's a bit small, and my boobs feel like they might pop out of the top. It's not exactly comfortable and I don't understand what happened to *my* clothes. Or, more important, what happened to the others.

I glance around the windowless room with the arched brick ceiling. The air is crisp and cold. The space is crowded with heavy marble-topped tables and cabinets. There are a few large basins with unusual crank-powered contraptions attached to their sides. Old washing machines? But somehow they look new. Brand-new, in fact. The room is lit by a single bare bulb, illuminating a doorway that leads to a stairwell. I know that stairway. I wish I didn't.

A chill passes through me as I fully realize where I am.

I'm in the basement under the library again, the same room where Charlotte's initiation took place. It's where my and Rory's initiation took place before that. But it isn't dank and stale and packed with spiders, nor is it candlelit and jammed with fresh lilies. It's a laundry room, but I don't remember it like this. I've never seen it this way.

Rory's voice floats through my memory. *The basement used to be servants' quarters.*

That would mean that we did it. We got the loop to take us way back, long before any of us could say the word *Archwell*; before any of us were made. When would the basement have been used as a laundry room? It must've been back around the time when the Archwells first built the place. Back when Grandma Rose's mama, Letty, would've walked these halls.

"Ida called out sick." Someone's voice echoes down the stairwell. My body goes rigid. I have to hide. I duck under one of the work tops, praying that the shadows will cover me. I don't know who's coming down those stairs, but I'm sure anyone at Archwell in the 1950s would not take kindly to a stranger in their midst, a stranger who looks like me, even if I am dressed for the part.

"So when will you get off?" A second voice, similar to the first but younger, bounces down the steps. They are closer now. They're coming down to meet me.

"I don't know, Rose. I'm sorry. You can call your brother to come get you if you want. It's gonna be a late night."

My ears prick up at the sound of the oh-so-familiar name.

The younger voice speaks again. "I don't think Sean is gonna make the trip down from Baltimore just to pick me up and drop me off at home. He doesn't get off until ten o'clock anyway."

The voices are in the laundry room now. I flinch as the lights come on. I'm still sort of hidden underneath the table, but the glare makes the green tiled floor gleam beneath me. Hopefully they won't need to stoop down and get anything out of the lower cabinets. We'd all be in for a shock. I hold my breath, trying not to freak out. I don't want to give in to false hope, to be carried away by the idea that these people might be *my* people.

Someone sets something heavy on the table directly above me and I turn to stone. My eyes latch on to the feet at the table's edge. One pair of white pumps, one pair of brown-and-white oxfords. Both feet are stockinged, off-white nylon shrouding brown skin. I know how Archwell used to be. I know that, in the 1950s, there was only one reason someone who looked like me would be on this campus.

"Well, then you're staying here," the first voice says wearily to the second. "Mr. Thomas said he'd be willing to give us a ride home when his shift is done for the night. You got your books?"

"Yes, ma'am," the second voice says. "They still got that cot down here? I'm not gonna study all night."

"It's in the pantry over there," the first voice says, striding away from the table toward one of the old-school washing machines. "If anyone bothers you overnight, just tell them your mother's Mrs. Harris."

Hearing that name finally confirms what I suspected. All the puzzle pieces click together in my mind. I can't believe I didn't recognize their voices, although I guess they wouldn't recognize me either even though I know we all look alike. Rose Harris, my grandma, and her mother, Letty, my great-grandma, are discussing the logistics of how to get home after a double shift. Grandma Rose used to get the bus to meet her mama at Archwell and then they'd get a ride back home together from Ms. Ida's husband after he dropped her off for her night shift. Rose Harris is alive again, leaning against the tabletop that I'm cowering beneath. It takes every ounce of willpower in me to not wrap my arms around her ankles and just hug her legs against me.

But it kills me that she wouldn't know me. It tears me up that I have to stay hidden here. I can't get a good look at the people who made me. I've only seen pictures of Mama Letty, and I'd love to see Grandma Rose at my age. I study the hem of her skirt. It's a black-and-cream plaid, white petticoat underneath, all very stylish. I wish she'd hung on to this dress for me to keep. I know it's not fancy, but holding anything of hers in my hand makes me feel whole.

I dare to reach out and touch the dress's hem, careful to be gentle so she doesn't startle. The fabric is rough against my fingertip. It's been starched and ironed. The skirt could probably stand up on its own. Then Rose pulls away. Quickly

I yank my hand back, worried that I might have stirred the folds of her skirts, alerting her to my presence, but she just walks across the room over to the little gray pantry door.

She turns and looks back at her mama, and for a brief glorious moment I can see her whole face. It's so much like mine: same lips, same forehead. My brother Sean, named for Rose's brother, would have called it a fivehead, but he is sometimes a shithead, so which is worse?

"You ate already?" she asks her mom.

"Haven't had a chance yet." Mama Letty sighs.

"There's half a sandwich in my bag if you want it," Rose says, opening the gray door and retreating into the pantry with her schoolbooks. "Love you, Mama."

"Love you too, Rosie. Thanks for being patient."

I hear a metallic-sounding switch and the grinding of a machine coming to life. The water runs. Mama Letty is doing laundry. Rose is studying in her hiding spot. Suddenly, this place that was filled with such horror is now humming with love, and I feel the muscles in my body unwinding for the first time in what feels like forever. I'm safe here now. Finally safe. And even if they find me, I know I'll be safe because Grandma Rose loved me. She still loves me. And she's with me here, even in my darkest moments—especially in those moments. She's the one who can bring me back to myself.

You're in your body. You're here in this room. She taught me that.

I close my eyes and fall into peaceful nothingness.

It feels like I'm in this pleasant lull forever, but it also lasts only a split second. I open my eyes and the room is dark again, even the light over the stairwell. Maybe the loop has skipped forward? I glance toward the open pantry door and see Rose's feet dangling from the edge of her cot, tucked just out of sight. She's taken off her shoes. The light in the pantry is out. She must be sleeping. I wonder what time it is and whether I also fell asleep. From my spot under the table, I try to stretch my legs, but as soon as I stir, I hear a sound on the stairwell. The light over the steps flicks on.

"Come with me," someone whispers. I hear footsteps and pull my legs close to me so as not to be seen. I think of Grandma Rose on her cot in the pantry and whether she hears the footsteps on the stairs. I imagine what the cot must feel like beneath her, wire mattress springs digging into her pretty dress, legs dangling off the edge. I glance at the pantry door and notice that I can't see her feet anymore. She's awake. She's heard something. She is hiding now too.

The footsteps trail into the room. Thankfully they don't get too close. They're hesitant and careful: two people trying to not make a sound.

"Is it okay to be down here?" a girl's voice whispers.

"Yes. It doesn't get used at night," says another. "No one comes down here after dark. Now hold out your hand."

There's some rustling before anyone says anything. "Adeline," the first voice whispers, "are you sure Lil will want all this?"

305

"Trust me," says Adeline. "She'll think it's very beat of you. And it is. Evelyn Smith is no square."

I hear Evelyn giggle in the dark.

I realize now what is happening. There are more grand-mothers in my midst: Rory's and Charlotte's. I try to get a good look at them, but the room is dark and they're too far away. I can sort of make out the edge of Evelyn's profile. Her hair is red like Charlotte's but curlier. She's wearing a green plaid dress with black buttons, exactly like mine.

"Hold out your hand again," Adeline whispers. "This dose is for you."

As she says the words, I remember the feeling of the sand hitting my cupped hands as Rory poured it from the little crystal bottle. I can see her doing it, except this time, she's not in a robe and a flower crown. Her blond hair is pinned back, cropped and curled into a bob, like her grandmother's. Her eyes are vacant as she gives me the dose. I trust her. She wouldn't do anything to hurt me. Not me or anyone else. But there's something strange in her expression. Something that tells me there's more to this story, more that I haven't yet seen.

Evelyn and I are the same. Too trusting, too naive. We're doing what we can to protect ourselves in a place that isn't made for us. And when someone promises loyalty, when someone gets close to us, we can't help but love them. But we both were duped by different Archwells. Double-crossed.

All that love from before is now dissolving into hot, sticky anger, spreading through my entire body.

I know what happens now. Adeline gives Evelyn the drugs. Evelyn gives them to Lillian. Then her love is stolen from her. Her future, her hope, all destroyed in a single instant. And I know that it was all by design. Fury rises up from my core into the back of my throat.

I look Adeline in the face. She is Rory. We are the same as the ones who came before us. We are all Lilies, whether we want to be or not.

The pattern repeats.

Rory

IT PLAYS AGAIN AND AGAIN in my memory. I reach out and pour the contents of the crystal bottle into her hand. Blythe takes it and hands it off. Evelyn does the same. It's a mirror image, an echo of itself. The Lilies are everywhere, all around me. Lillian is all around me. She's everything: the reason why all of this exists. Jealousy courses through me, taking ahold of my mind, muting the euphoria of my high.

I can see the pattern now. I wish I had a pen and paper to write it all down because I don't know if I will remember it when I'm sober again. Instead, I just repeat what I know in my head, hoping it'll all imprint into my memory in the way the envy and the shame have.

Adeline and I are shadows of one another, moving in tandem, repeating history. Addiction. Jealousy. Striving. Rejection. Pain. Then betrayal. We did it for ourselves. We were only thinking of ourselves. We weren't thinking clearly, but that's not really an excuse. What happened was because of us, and it is happening again.

I watch from the shadows, just like Adeline, as Lillian

joins Evelyn in the basement. She's tall and beautiful with high cheekbones and red lipstick that perfectly complements her white gown. She's been crying. Her father knows about her and Evelyn. He's threatening to tear them apart.

A simmering pain shoots up my left side. My great-grandfather has hurt my great-aunt. He's helped her, yes, but he's hurt her even more. I never knew my own father, but I know what they say about patriarchs. They make the rules. They protect. But now I'm starting to wonder who it is they're really protecting? Archwell Academy was supposed to be safe for Lillian, but it isn't. If it isn't safe for her, who is it safe for? There's so much more that Lillian wants to be, but her father won't let her. Time won't let her.

Evelyn and Lillian escape into another world, each inhaling a dose of fantasy. Evelyn gives Lillian the lion's share, just like she was told. She doesn't know any better. I want to fly away with them. The three of us could be safe together in that other world, but instead I face the horror of Lillian's choking, her blood emerging from the corner of her beautiful mouth, dripping onto the prized white dress. She falls to the floor, her head smacking against the shiny emerald tiles.

I know now that what I'm witnessing is pure malice taking hold. Adeline and I have done evil. We have hurt the ones we love. And we will be punished for it because we will never be able to forget this. We will never be able to let go of the shame. Its grip on us will only tighten, the roots will dig deeper and deeper until we think that's all we are.

We are our shame. We are the horrible things we've done. All we can do is pretend that it isn't all happening again and again in our minds. But the horrors we've done will always haunt us . . . unless we see them for what they really are.

The pattern repeats.

Drew

I'M A DECENT SPY. I'M good at hiding. But hiding in this place—behind a door in the room where everything happened—is difficult. Every fiber of my body is telling me to get out of this basement, get away from this memory. I manage to remind myself that the memory isn't mine, even though it happened in the same exact spot.

The gray pantry door shields me from Rose's view as she perches on the nearby cot, completely motionless. I peer at her from the crack between the door's hinges. She's barely breathing, straining to listen to what's happening outside. So am I.

"Lil," Evelyn whispers in the next room. "Lillian? What's going on?" Her voice is a handful of glass shards. She's shaky and scared. Lillian's breath is ragged. She coughs, chokes. I hear something splatter on the floor.

"Oh god," Evelyn says. "I have to get Adeline, don't move."

I listen for Death's rattle and brace myself for its demands. There's so much about this moment that is known to me. Charlotte was left alone here, in this room, slowly suffocating under the weight of being a Lily. Now, through the slit between the door and the wall, I watch the same thing happen to Lillian as Evelyn staggers to the stairwell and rushes to find her false savior.

Rose and I sit in silence and listen to Lillian's unsteady breath. We're both scared. We're not supposed to be here. If we go out there, maybe the people who run this place will think we did this to their daughter. It's not beyond imagination, but it is agony to sit here and try to keep still. Rose pulls her green velvety blanket closer to her body. In an instant, I can feel the covering around me. I *am* her. I'm waiting motionless on my cot, praying for all of this to be over.

Lillian stirs on the floor.

"Help . . ." she croaks. "Help me."

I can't bear it anymore.

I stand and round the corner of the doorway, my blanket still wrapped tightly around me. I approach the body on the floor, careful not to make a sound. But then a wave of darkness swirls around Lillian, extending its smoky tendrils around her wrists and ankles.

"Oh my god," I mutter.

From behind the gray pantry door, I watch as Rose drops to her knees. The green blanket falls to the floor beside Lillian's face. She gags and then coughs up something black and thick. Then the darkness wraps itself around her face, devouring her.

Rose stays frozen. She doesn't believe her eyes. She doesn't trust herself and she knows that no one will trust her, even if she were to tell the truth. I know because, in this way, we're the same. We are bystanders, paralyzed by fear and resentment for this place and everything it represents. We do nothing. We can only watch in horror as time swallows those who seek our help, and the loop distorts our memories.

But I can't let this happen again. I won't let Death haunt me anymore. I've had enough.

I don't want to keep this secret. I don't want to be a Lily.

I take a deep breath and push the door away from me. Stepping around it, I fly to Rose's side. "We have to do something," I say, reaching out for what's left of Lillian, but she's slipping through my fingers.

Rose looks at me, terrified, but a little relieved. She isn't alone anymore. Someone is here to help. "What do we do?" she says.

I reach for Lillian's hand. Her long, graceful fingers are a little bony at the knuckle, just like mine. The flesh of her palm is still solid. Her hand is still warm. It's not too late. It's not too late to save her and Charlotte. It's not too late to stop this cycle. The pattern can be broken.

I look up at the raw brick wall and my eyes narrow in on it: the red metal box with the heavy handle. The words *Duck & Cover* are painted across the top in a fresh white. I let go of Lillian's hand and run for the alarm. The handle is cold and weighty, but I use all my might and push the thing down. The alarm triggers. It bounds around the building announcing our presence. I turn around and lock eyes with Rose, who is now holding on to Lillian, anchoring her in this world. She will not let her go.

The pattern repeats.

Bong!

Bong!

Bong!

Blythe

I CAN KEEP A SECRET. My grandmother taught me how, and now I know why she was so good at it too.

"Sometimes, you have to let the past be the past," she said. "Sometimes it's better to let sleeping dogs lie." I wonder if she ever took her own advice.

Now that I know what happened, I don't think she ever forgot what she saw in that basement. She certainly never told anybody about it, but she often dropped hints. She was always trying to warn me about what might happen to me at Archwell Academy. She wanted me to be safe, to be careful.

Back in the closet with the others again, I finally feel safe the way Rose wanted me to, the way I felt when I was with her and Mama Letty. I felt their love around me and I knew that nothing could touch me. Here in the closet, I still feel it. I know now that I will always be safe as long as I can remember them and keep them with me.

"Is it over?" Veró asks shakily.

"I dunno," Drew says, clicking on the light.

"Are we starting over?" Rory asks. "I'm not sure I can do that again."

I look up at the hangers on the closet's bar. They're swaying ever so slightly. A few dresses remain hanging, but the rest are in a big heap on the floor. The shelves are still trashed and the ground is still covered in old papers and diamond rings. We've really done a number on this place.

"Who knows," I say, rolling over onto my side to face the door. The polished walnut shines, and underneath the foot of the door there's a beam of light creeping into the closet. There's something out there. It might be something terrible or something great. I do not know, and I finally accept that I cannot know. There's no snooping I can do that will reveal our futures. There's no rerouting whatever happens next. The lump of anxiety is still in my throat, but it's a little smaller now than when we started. I breathe in.

I'm in my body. I'm in this room. I'm gonna be all right.

The knob turns on its own. The door springs open. Daylight enters the closet. Someone is standing there. She's tall with high cheekbones. Her spotless ivory dress is cut in a way that shows off her pretty white shoulders. The look is offset by a bold red lip.

"What are you all doing in my closet?" she asks.

Lillian Archwell is staring at the four of us. Her expression is a mixture of amusement and concern. Her auburn hair falls over her right shoulder as she leans into the doorway and takes a look around.

"It's a damn mess in here," she says.

She's alive. She's alive and she's *talking* to us. Like nothing has happened at all. Shock keeps us all silent.

"Seriously though," Lillian says. She shifts her hair over her shoulder and it catches the light. In an instant, it turns white. Her smile stays put as the muscles of her face shift and sag. The fabric of her dress begins to spread and morph, tailoring itself into a completely new garment: a white cable-knit sweater over a pair of light-gray slacks.

"I understand wanting to come see me for a visit," she says as her skin withers. Sunspots bloom on her forehead and wrinkles run across her eyes. The lines of her smile deepen. She is aging in front of us. "But stowing away in my closet? Are you all playing a trick on me?"

I steal a look at the others. Rory is slack-jawed, eyes wide with disbelief. Veró is completely still, as if she's afraid moving will shatter the moment. Drew is beaming.

"It worked," they say.

"What worked?" Lillian's voice has aged as much as her face. The seventeen-year-old is gone, replaced by a woman well into her eighties. "Is this a joke? For the TicTack?"

I rise to my feet. "For what?" I ask.

"You know. The TicTack? That app on your phones you all use."

"Oh." I try not to laugh. "It's not called that . . . and no, we're not trying to play a trick on you."

"Good," she says. "Because I'm eighty-three years old, I'm about to retire, and I don't have time for this. Come outta there, would ya?" Lillian pulls the door farther ajar. "That closet is embarrassing. I'm such a pack rat. Rory, your mom will tell you, I never throw anything away."

"Umm . . . yeah," Rory says. "Yeah, I guess she has mentioned that." I steal a look at her and she shrugs at me and shakes her head a little.

"Step into my office," Lillian invites us. We exit the closet as if in slow motion, stepping into the chancellor's lair—but it has changed. The red paint is gone, replaced by a deep forest green. The photos on the wall are still there, but they're all arranged slightly differently and there are more of them. Some are black-and-white but many more are in color.

There's a photo of Edgar Archwell and his wife, Anne, next to Lillian's and Adeline's senior portraits. There's a color photo of Eleanor Archwell cuddling a plump baby with Rory's eyes. Then there's a pantheon of group photos of Archwell students throughout the years: celebrating spring on the quad, marching together on the National Mall, standing alongside a slightly younger-looking Lillian with the pride flag. But they aren't just girls, they're all kinds of kids. The photo wall is awash with so much color and life, it's hard to look away.

My eyes land on a photo of Drew and Rory. They can't be more than eight or nine. They're sitting on the stone wall that surrounds Archwell's campus, grinning and pointing to a bronze sign that reads *The Archwell Academy for All*.

I look back at the others, each riding the wave of amazement. More than one thing is different here.

Absolutely everything is different.

"I like what you've done with the place," Drew says.

Lillian gives them a sidelong look as she sits down at the desk.

"Drew Simmons, I know very well that I've barely changed this room since I started the chancellor job in '72. I admit it could use an update, but you don't have to razz me about it." She picks up the desk phone and dials. "You are just like your grandmother." She shakes her head at Drew but still offers them a little smile.

"You have some new photos," Veró points out, barely able to suppress her excitement. Lillian glances at the photo wall and half nods, half shrugs.

Veró leans close to the wall, eyes widening with recognition. "It's Gabe," she whispers, pointing to one of the photos. It's true. In the picture, Gabe Lewis is grinning and holding up some kind of award. Then I notice who he's standing next to, but I can't quite believe my eyes. It's none other than Eleanor Archwell.

"Eleanor, darling?" Lillian speaks into the phone. "Yes. I have your daughter and some other hooligans here . . ." She smiles, listening to whatever Rory's mom is saying on the other end. "Yes, I know." She flashes a warm glance at Rory and mouths, *She says, Love you*. Then she clicks into business mode, turning back to the phone. "Anyway, I wanted to check in about our hand-off meeting with Latrice tomorrow . . . Yes, I'm worried about the weather. I think we should move it inside. It's going to be too cold to meet in the gazebo."

I drop into one of the tufted leather chairs. Suddenly, I'm very tired. Veró slides into the chair next to me. "Is this for real?" she asks. "I'm, like, waiting for all of this to go away."

"Same." I laugh.

"Let's hope that it won't," Drew says. "But I hear you. I still kinda feel uneasy."

"We just went through a lot of bad," I acknowledge.

"It's true," Rory says. "And now it's, like . . . everything is fixed?"

"I mean, not *everything* is fixed, I'm sure," Veró says. "This one thing changed. Lillian didn't disappear. That changed everything about what Archwell is . . . and what it has become. But I'm sure there is still, like, global warming and white supremacy and all that other shit."

"For sure," Drew says. "But this one change—"

"Huge," I say. I turn back to the photographs, scanning over all the faces that look like mine. It occurs to me that making Archwell a safer place for some folks has had ripple effects for all. The air is clearer somehow. The sun is shining brighter through the windows. Is this what it feels like to be safe at school?

I look back at Chancellor Lillian, cradling the phone in the crook of her neck as she types something onto her tablet. If things turned out differently for her, maybe things turned out differently for Grandma Rose too . . . Maybe she lived her life with less regret. Maybe there turned out to be fewer reasons to be wary of Archwell girls. Maybe this small change of fate made a big difference for her. What would that mean for our family? I don't how to parse this yet, but I'm suddenly bursting for answers. I want to talk to Salim.

To Sean. To Mama and Daddy. It's possible that—in this reality—I'll be able to talk to Rose too.

Before I can dig up my phone and blow everyone up with texts, Rory speaks.

"No one's going to know what we all went through to get here," she says. "No one can know."

Oh, man. She's right . . . If I tell Salim and Sean what happened in the closet, they're gonna think I've inhaled a deadly amount of sand. But I don't know if my heart has room for more secrets.

"I hear ya. But do any of y'all feel weird about keeping all of this to ourselves?" I ask. "It feels like . . . I dunno."

"Like you'll always be waiting for the other shoe to drop?" Drew asks, reaching into the candy bowl on the coffee table for a fistful of butterscotches. They offer me one but I wave it away. They unwrap one of the candies and pop it in their mouth. "Trauma's gonna have us looking over our shoulders for a while," they say. "No one else is gonna understand why."

"So what do we do with *that*?" Rory asks. "Now we all just have a *new* secret we need to keep." Her face is surprisingly strained. Even in a world where her life seems to have notably improved, she's still carrying around the past like deadweight.

"Well, it doesn't have to be a secret between *us*," Veró says as she stands, stretches, and leans against the back of her chair. "I'm not about to pretend like all of that was just a bad dream. It wasn't just in our heads."

"For sure not," Drew says. "But I want to make sure that nothing like that can happen again, at least not here at Archwell."

"How do you do that?" Rory asks.

"It's gonna look different for everyone," Veró says.

"How?" Rory is as bewildered as ever. "What does that even mean?"

None of us is quite sure how to answer her. We sit there for a moment. The only sound is Lillian's murmuring into the phone.

"Mmm, yes. Yes, I see what you're saying," she says. Hearing her voice is comforting. Like when you finally get to listen to a song after hours of the melody swirling around your brain.

"You just have to find what that means for yourself," Drew finally says. "It's gonna grow and change . . . like everything else."

"It's true," I say. "All of us will have to show up differently, regardless. No more lying. No more fronting."

"No more backstabbing," Rory says.

"Mmm, mm, mm." Veró grins. "Rory Archwell. I never thought I'd see the day."

Someone knocks on the office door and opens it. I nearly slide out of the chair when Charlotte walks in carrying a stack of papers. She smiles and waves at Drew as she walks to Lillian's desk and drops the pages in a tray labeled *In*.

Lillian covers the mouthpiece of the phone. "Student

assistant extraordinaire," she whispers to Charlotte, and winks before turning back to her conversation with Rory's mom.

Charlotte turns to leave. "See y'all later," she says faintly.

"Hang on just a sec, Charlotte," Rory says. "I just . . . have a quick question."

Drew and Veró both meet my eyes. We brace ourselves, preparing for whatever Rory might have up her sleeve this time.

"I just wanted to know if you've ever heard of . . . the Lilies?"

"Is that like a band or something?" Charlotte asks.

"Um . . ." Rory turns to me, her eyes the size of dinner plates. "No . . . I mean . . . Yes . . . sort of."

"Should I have heard of them?" Charlotte asks.

"No."

"Nah."

"Definitely not."

"I think they kinda suck."

Charlotte replicates Lillian's side-eye, examining each of our grinning faces. "Um, okay, whatever," she says. "See y'all later."

"Yep," Drew says. "Later."

"Like maybe tomorrow," Veró says, locking eyes with them. I can tell what will happen next, even though I haven't seen it play out yet. Veró and Drew are bound to be something more.

"Tomorrow could work." Drew shrugs and smiles. "Or maybe the next day."

"Or after that," Veró offers. "We've got time."

"Yes, we do," Drew answers. "So much time."

Acknowledgments

FOR EVERY THRESHOLD AND EVERY milestone in the writing of this book, there was someone there to support my process and offer encouragement. These people acted from a place of joy and unwavering patience. Their kindness is something I'm endlessly grateful for, especially as a debut author.

My partner, Natan, gave me the love and support that I needed to stay whole throughout this process—my love, you win the award for Most Patient. My parents, Michael and Mel, and my sister, Julia, continuously celebrated this story's progress and stoked my excitement in the face of challenges—thank you for supporting me in all my iterations. As I learned more and more about publishing, Sarah Ropp generously offered her thoughts, opinions, and contagious glee—thank you for being the sort of friend who every writer dreams of. Miriam Cummons, Genna Ayers, and the Ticket-to-Ride group chat fielded my many late-night texts—thank you for being there for me.

If this book were a baby, it would have two editor mommies: Kristen Pettit and Alice Jerman. This story would not exist in its current form without Kristen. She was a believer in *The Lilies* from the beginning and her guidance made it far better than I could have on my own. Her thoughtful input helped me grow as a writer, and her even-handed approach—come hell or high water—helped pilot this project to safe harbor. Picking up where Kristen left off, Alice nurtured this story to maturity, approaching each revision with grace and consideration. She saw *The Lilies* through to fruition and for that I'm forever grateful. Thank you, Kristen and Alice, for your kindness and enthusiasm.

A massive thank-you is due to the amazing people at New Leaf Literary. Thank you to Kate Sullivan for midwifing this story in its early stages. Thank you to Meredith Barnes and Joanna Volpe for your fantastic guidance and insight. Thank you to Kendra Coet and Olivia Coleman for coordinating all the logistics. And a very special thank-you to Sophia Ramos for being an awesome cheerleader and for ushering this project along the publishing path. This brings me to Suzie Townsend, an extraordinary agent and champion for storytellers—I feel so deeply privileged to have worked with you. Thank you for showing me the ropes and for setting the bar.

Thank you to the entire team at HarperTeen—especially to Alexandra Rakaczki and Emily Andrukaitis for such a responsive copyedit. Thank you to Alejandra Torres, Fin Leary, and Natalie Norwood for your readership and expertise. Thank you to Erica Sussman and Clare Vaughn for pinch-hitting at the end of the publication process.

gratitude and credit is due to every single person

ctric Postcard Entertainment: Carlyn Greenwald,

orrell, Shelly Romero, Haneen Oriqat, and Eve Peña.

collaboration has made this story what it is. Thank you

your creative fellowship and your generosity of spirit.

Last but not least, we have Dhonielle Clayton—my teacher, mentor, and YA fairy godmother. Reader, if you didn't already know, Dhonielle is a visionary who is reshaping the landscape of young people's literature. This story was her brainchild and I'm unspeakably grateful that she trusted me to write it. Thank you for believing in me, mentoring me, and making this dream a reality.